Praise for John Baker

'John Baker brings altogether more heart, invention and wit to the business of adapting the tough-guy novel to the realities of contemporary Britain' *Independent on Sunday*

'Engagingly credible, off the wall, romantic without being sentimental, a sharp sense of humour ... a great cast of characters I look forward to meeting again' Val McDermid

'Baker's books just get better and better' *Tangled Web*

'Strong, dark and discursive ... there's no doubt that – with his York setting and up-from-the-gutter hero – Baker has added something new to the crime scene' Philip Oakes, *Literary Review*

'Great characters, idiosyncratic plot – a definite original' Maxim Jakubowski, *Time Out*

'Absorbing and well-written with an exciting finale' T.J. Binyon, *Evening Standard*

'The characters, the setting and particularly the writing, are completely successful' *Birmingham Post*

'Something quite unexpected ... Entrancing and funny' *TLS*

'Neatly plotted and engagingly and wittily written: Sam's next case is something to look forward to' *Daily Mail*

Born in Hull in 1942, and educated at the university there, John Baker has worked as a social worker, shipbroker, truck driver and milkman, and most recently in the computer industry. He has twice received a Yorkshire Arts Association Writers' Bursary. He is the author of five Sam Turner novels; the next title in the series is called *Shooting in the Dark*. John Baker is married with five children and lives in York. If you have enjoyed this book, you can find out more about other books by John Baker at: www.johnbakeronline.co.uk

By John Baker

Poet in the Gutter
Death Minus Zero
King of the Streets
Walking with Ghosts
The Chinese Girl

THE CHINESE GIRL

John Baker

ORION

An Orion Paperback

First published in Great Britain in 2000
by Victor Gollancz
This paperback edition published in 2001
by Orion Books Ltd,
Orion House, 5 Upper St Martin's Lane
London WC2H 9EA

Second impression 2001

A CIP catalogue record for this book
is available from the British Library

ISBN 0 75284 373 7

Typeset by Deltatype Ltd, Birkenhead, Merseyside
Printed and bound in Great Britain by
Clays Ltd, St Ives plc

For Anne

'The best style is the style you don't notice'
Somerset Maugham

'Listen, if anything happens to Yoko and me,
it was not an accident'
John Lennon

The city and places in this novel owe as much to the imagination as to the physical reality. The characters and institutions are all fictitious, and any resemblance to real people, living or dead, is purely coincidental.

I would like to thank Anne Baker, Simon Stevens, Peter Fjågesund and Rob Watkinson for their valuable and helpful criticism. It is also necessary to say that any offended sensibilities are the responsibility of the writer alone.

I
TOO MANY MOVIES

1

A BUNDLE OF OLD CLOTHES

Stone Lewis left the bar of the Minerva three minutes after the landlord called time. The young guys in the lounge were murdering a medley of doo-wop classics, and looked set on more destruction once they'd finished. They were past reason, and Stone knew from experience that his tattooed face and shaven head conjured up the wrong kind of pulling power when young males and a few pints of Pilot's Pride got mixed up to boiling point.

The landlord nodded as Stone went through the door, and Stone tapped the bar with the index finger of his left hand. Neither of them spoke. It was the first time Stone had been acknowledged kindly in the Minerva. His previous visits had been regarded suspiciously, the very earliest ones with hostility, as though he ate children for breakfast.

It was a porcelain-blue evening. The moon was up, casting a pale glow over the Humber estuary, sending a silver arrow along the length of the river. It was warm, and Stone walked with his denim jacket slung over his shoulder, feeling the tingling of the breeze on his bare forearms. On the corner of Freehold Street a fanfare of strumpets, newly evicted from a bar, whistled and shouted at him. He waved and walked on. It was still strange to him, the city of Hull, as any city in the world would be after the cramped and cramping confines of a prison cell. The people here did more or less as they liked. There were rules, but not like the rules he had had to master inside.

The siren of an ambulance sounded a couple of streets away. Stone froze momentarily, then shook his head and walked on. There must be more than a quarter of a million people in the city and he still thought the sirens were for him alone. It was going slowly, the rehab. But he could wait. The prison system had taught him to do that. And it was better waiting on the bricks than it had been while he was on ice.

The flat was in the basement of a decrepit Victorian building off Spring Bank, and before he began the descent to the entrance he knew something was wrong. He stopped at the top of the stone steps and cocked his head to listen.

Nothing. The sounds of the city behind him, but in the darkened entrance to his flat nothing stirred. He gripped his keys in his right hand, let a couple of them slip between his fingers, forming an impromptu knuckle-duster. Just in case.

Might be a cat. Or nothing at all, the moon and the night sending mixed signals. Sometimes people used his front door as a urinal. Nothing personal, they'd had a few jars too many, and needed to leak it out somewhere. 'Oh, look here, a basement flat, the very thing, piss all over the front door.' Little smile on his face while the guy's doing it. See how high he can piss up the door; spray it around a bit. The really intelligent ones, the ones who were capable of having two thoughts at the same time, sometimes hit on the idea of pissing through the letterbox. Real jokers.

When he reached the bottom step someone sprang at him out of the darkened passage. It happened too quickly for Stone to move aside, and he didn't get to use his knucks. Whoever it was came at him low, ramming his head into Stone's midriff and forcing him back on to the steps. Then the guy scrambled over him and was away down the street while Stone was still trying to shake his vision back into place.

When he reached to feel the trickle at the back of his

head, Stone's fingers came away sticky with blood. He wiped it off on the steps, careful not to stain his new chinos. He thought of going after the guy, but the sound of running footsteps had already receded. He was well clear. Another phantom pisser, maybe, or was it an attempt at a break-in?

Stone got to his feet and walked into the alcove that concealed his door. There was a bundle on the ground, which he tried to sweep aside with his foot, but it was too heavy to move. It crossed his mind that the guy might have been sleeping in his doorway, the town centre was littered with homeless people and beggars, many of them young, and all of them at risk of a beating from taxpayers after dark.

He reached for the trickle at the back of his head, make sure it hadn't run down as far as the collar of his Roebucks shirt. Bloodstains weren't cool on the out, made you look like a prat.

He got the key in the lock and opened the door, stepped over the bundle and switched on the light. When he turned again to inspect what had been left in his doorway, it seemed to consist of old clothes. There was a long green skirt, a silk scarf, and what appeared to be a purple or mauve boot. It was only when Stone Lewis knelt down to take a closer look that he noticed the face.

Pale and round, with a trace of yellow. Long, jet-black hair parted in the middle and spread out like a dark halo around head and shoulders. The eyes were closed, and there was no movement. Stone leaned forward and placed his cheek near the slightly flattened nose. He felt the stream of breath, and reached for the carotid pulse on the side of the neck to double-check that life was still present.

When he was sure, he checked the limbs for breaks or wounds, finding only bruises. There was a swelling on the left side of her head, and dark striations around her neck that had not been inflicted by a friendly hand.

Stone gathered the Chinese girl into his arms and took her inside the flat, shutting the outer door with his heel as he turned towards the bedroom.

2

TWIST AND TWIRL

The quilt was on the floor, where it had fallen when he got out of bed that morning. Stone stepped over it and eased the girl on to the narrow bed. He brushed her hair away from her face, pulled several strands from between her lips, then backed away to the wall to get a different perspective.

She smelt of booze and spew, and despite being manhandled she showed no signs of waking up.

Looked like being a long night. Stone reflected that nobody else would've brought her into the flat, they'd've left her where she was and rung an ambulance. But Stone Lewis couldn't afford to do that, if he'd rung an ambulance tonight, it would've arrived with a cop in tow. Next thing they'd've read his jacket, found he was out under licence, and bounced him straight back into the joint.

And another thing, if she died in his bed tonight, he'd never explain it to the bottles and stoppers. 'You found her on your fuckin' doorstep? Come on, Lewis, we heard better porkies in kindergarten. You sure she wasn't delivered by Group Four?'

He went to the kitchen and filled a plastic bowl with water from the immersion heater. The thing worked fine for about half a bowl, then it hissed and cracked, dripped and spurted the last couple of pints. Stone was used to washing his socks and underpants with half a bowl of water, but for a whole girl with vomit in her hair, he reckoned he'd need the bowl filling twice over.

He cleaned her up as best he could, got the spew out of her hair, left her with her underclothes, changed the sheet on the bed and wrapped her in the quilt. She was wearing more make-up than she needed, a white base like cold semolina, painted eyes and lips. He washed it all away. He put her blouse in a bucket to soak, and the rest of her clothes he hung over the chair by the bed.

She was still out of it. Her breathing was rhythmic but shallow, her pulse rapid and weak. Stone thought she looked a little healthier than when he'd found her, but he sat and watched her all the same. If anything changed, he might *have* to get her to a hospital.

He couldn't guess her age from her face. It was unlined, smooth and soft to the touch, but the oriental features were impenetrable to him. He would have believed anything between twelve and twenty-five. Her body was a better indicator, she was way past puberty, and his best guess was somewhere in the early twenties. Maybe a little older than he had been when they'd banged him away.

He liked her face. It was a face to bring hermits down out of the hills. He watched her closed eyelids, wondering what they hid. He liked her hair as well; he'd even liked it before he'd cleaned the vomit out of it. And he liked the line of her neck, the way it moved down to her shoulder, tucked away beneath the quilt. He couldn't think what colour her skin was, olive, green, yellow, none of them really described the way the colour held depth. There was a copper sheen to it, and silver as well. She was all the colours of the rainbow. She wasn't a woman, just a multicoloured twist-and-twirl, and she was there, alive, breathing, in his bed.

She had a bag, a large leather thing that was more like a pannier than a handbag. Stone had left it at the end of the bed while he got the girl settled. Now he reached for it and undid the brass clasp. Most of the space inside was taken up with bundles of letters; all of them addressed to Ginny

Bradshaw in Los Angeles, California. He glanced at the twist-and-twirl, she was still breathing regularly, and she didn't look as though she was called Ginny Bradshaw. He'd expected her to be called something like Suzie Wong. He scrutinized several of the envelopes, they were written in the same hand, and were postmarked from Hull. They'd all started off in this town, gone over to America, and had now been brought back again. Stone Lewis stacked them on the floor at his feet and turned his attention to the remaining contents of the bag.

He took out a lipstick and a make-up bag with foundation, blusher and eyeshadow, a hairbrush, a small wad of traveller's cheques and a torch key-ring with two keys on it. There was a sketchpad and an assortment of coloured pens. He found a passport in the name of Virginia Rebecca Bradshaw, and inside the covers a small photograph of her with her eyes open. So that's how they looked, black eyes, like elongated almonds. Eyes that subtly changed the proportions of her face, adding perhaps two or three years to her age, and bestowing on her a degree of experience and intelligence that the inert body on the bed did not seem to possess. There was the hint of a smile, too, in the photograph, betraying the presence of an ironic humour; a wry smile that accepted the convention and the necessity, but also found something irrepressibly funny in posing for a camera.

Her purse contained 180 pounds in twenties, and another tenner in small change. There were three credit cards and a couple of loose photographs. One of a young oriental man dressed in a T-shirt and a white wide-brimmed hat, the other of a girl about the same age as Virginia Rebecca Bradshaw but with Western features. The unknown girl was posing like a model, wearing a mini-skirt and a tight sweater that looked like it was packed way beyond its natural capacity. The kind of photograph cons would fight for.

In a side pocket of the bag was an opened pack of Silk Cut, some Rizlas, and a tiny piece of Rocky wrapped in silver foil, enough for a couple of joints.

Her breathing faltered momentarily and Stone tensed himself, the muscles in his forearms twitched as he readied himself to move to her aid. But she took a deep breath and the quilt above her chest re-established the rhythmic rise and fall.

He pushed himself back in the chair and wondered how she had got there. The prison dream had been that something like this would fall out of heaven, because when you're banged up inside those walls the only possibility of this happening would be if one of the gods decided to throw a party and invite you along. She hadn't fallen out of heaven, though, because she wouldn't have got the bruises. You fall out of heaven, must be odds-on you land on your feet.

There was a school of thought, and among prison populations it was fairly popular, that the gods were incompetent, that they juggled people's destinies like a cack-handed circus clown. Stone didn't go along with that all the time. Life was hard without miracles.

Was it domestic, then? Was it her boyfriend or husband who beat her up and then butted him on the steps? Was he the Chinese-looking guy in the photograph? And if that was what happened, if it was a domestic dispute that had been acted out on his doorstep, would the guy come back?

Maybe she was being raped or robbed? Although it didn't look as though she had been interfered with. Her clothes weren't torn or disarranged, and her handbag was still here with plenty of cash in it.

A straightforward physical assault, then? The kind of thing that happens every day in prison. Suddenly a guy needs to hit out, to smash someone, anyone. Maybe kill someone. He doesn't know why, it feels like he's defending himself, or he's making a statement. Could be that. Some fucking nutter in the night, his brain burned out with PCP and petrol or crack and benzocaine, and all his life he's thought women were punch-bags.

Or was it a gang thing? Some Triad cell meting out punishment? Because she wasn't obeying orders, or hadn't paid the vig on her debts?

Like everybody in the world, Stone had seen too many movies. Flickering images came at him faster than he could digest them, damsels in distress and the guys that were supposed to give them a helping hand. At this stage there was a big problem, you just didn't know if it was gonna be a comedy or a tragedy. Whether it was gonna be a romp with a few laughs thrown in along the way, or if somebody with rabies and a bazooka was already standing outside the door.

Could be any of those things. Stone didn't know where she'd come from. He'd have to wait until she woke to get his answers. One thing he knew, she looked good there in his bed. He'd have to make himself as comfortable as he could in the chair, but he didn't care. Even if he had to sleep on the floor and spend a restless night getting stiff bones, he'd rather have her there in his bed, and look forward to her opening those eyes in the morning.

The worst thing he could think of was that he'd wake up in the morning and find it was all a dream. That he was there laid out in the chair, and his bed was empty and cold. Could be that it wasn't a dream at all, but that she'd woken up in the night, taken all her things and vanished. Crept out of the room while he slept. Then he'd never know if tonight had happened or not. He'd never see her again, or hear the sound of her voice. It would be another dimension in his life over which he had no control, the time the Chinese twist-and-twirl fell out of the sky and landed at his feet, only to disappear again before they could be introduced. He took her purple DMs and put them in a Tesco carrier bag on the top shelf of the wardrobe, covered the bag with a cushion. She wouldn't go far without hooves.

His head lolling and nodding with fatigue, Stone wondered about AIDS. He had been careful when washing away her blood, but in the prison they'd said there were always minor abrasions and cuts on the surface of the skin, and the AIDS virus was carried by blood. But if he was going to get AIDS, he'd already have it by now. There were times he'd used other people's needles in the joint, not to mention the tattoos, and the four times he'd been unable to fight off a gang rape.

There was never a day went by when you couldn't score on the inside. Angel dust, Devil's dandruff, Hessle or Herb, everyone used it whenever they could. It was the only way to forget about the bars and the locks and hallucinate freedom. The names themselves began to make you free. Paradise white, Quicksilver, Rainbows, Satan's secret, Blowcaine.

And on the inside they'd told him he'd never adjust to the world outside the walls. Not after an eleven stretch. On the out he'd go looking for blow or happy pills of one description or another, next thing he'd be up to his neck in the drug wars, get himself killed or end up back in the slammer. Cons laughed when they told you stuff like that. Prison was full of comedians. Stone hadn't said anything. He'd listened, though, and when he got out he'd had a couple of pints and caught the train back to Hull. Gone to see Sally, his mother, who'd cried for most of the visit. Spent a couple of hours with her and Aunt Nell. The next week he found work at System.ini, an Internet café on the dockside, two days a week, but it was a start. The same day he moved into his flat. It was two streets away from Sally and Aunt Nell, so he could keep an eye on them, drop off bread and cakes on his way home, whatever was leftover from the day's trading. That was six weeks ago. He hadn't touched any drugs apart from the beer and a couple of spliffs at the weekend. He'd kept away from trouble. And he still had the flat and the job.

Stone moved his leg to get more comfortable in the chair and knocked over the stack of letters. He picked up a bundle and fingered them. Why do people keep letters? Stone didn't have any at all of his own. He knew he could look through his possessions and not find one old letter. Every day of his life he made a point of throwing something away. If you didn't do that, you collected so much stuff you couldn't move. The stuff became like prison bars, it hemmed you in, confined you to the past and to memories, some of which you could only half-remember. Things, material trivia, were all that stood between Stone and freedom. The state had let him go; OK, only on licence, but these days he decided when he went to bed and what time he got up in the morning. He chose and bought his own clothes and food. He didn't have anyone breathing down his neck.

The girl spoke. She was still out of it, but she said something in a language that could have been German. A short sentence, maybe eight or ten words. Stone tried to hang on to them, but they evaporated as she lapsed back into silence. German? Stone didn't have any language but English. Could be she had spoken in Swedish or Danish. There was no way he could be sure. But he knew it didn't sound Chinese.

What makes you open someone else's mail? You look at the envelope and maybe there's a sound somewhere, a long way off, like the whistle of a train, and the two things together form a kind of trigger? Could be something like that, the butterfly effect. Or, if not a sound, maybe an odour? More likely is a relationship to the handwriting on the envelope. But connections fall into place which make you believe there's something important in that envelope, and even though it's not addressed to you, your hand snakes towards it, and something you aren't conscious of draws the letter out. You take a breath, glance quickly at the vision in the bed, and begin to read.

II
LETTERS FROM JULIET

3

RAPIST IN A LEATHER HOOD

Dear Ginny,

Thanks for your letter. LA sounds really wild. Sorry I haven't replied for a while, but things have been happening to me here in Hull. Not everything happens in America. I woke up with a man in my bed.

I was at one of Jean Hellier's parties, bored out of my skull. It's been like that since my affair with Edward. (Tragic! Oh, so tragic.) And since you deserted the flat to go to the Wild West.

Bored. So I drank. You know how it is. Then nothing, complete blackness until I woke up in the morning. I thought I'd got Edward back at first, but it wasn't him. A sleeping man, naked. He was lying on his side, facing me, with one hand over my stomach. He stirred at the same time and tightened his grip on me, still half-asleep, and began mumbling nonsense, calling me Margot, until he opened his eyes.

'God,' says he, as surprised as I had been a minute before.

'No,' I said, ready for him. 'My name's Juliet. God lives in the flat downstairs. Who are you?'

He's called Vince Gurney. Crap name, isn't it? We stayed put all morning and most of the afternoon, getting to know each other. You know how it is. Maybe you don't. I thought I knew before that day. I thought I knew everything after Edward. But this was different.

He'd been at Jean's party, of course, and he didn't remember anything either. When we got dressed I remembered that I'd seen him there, and he said he remembered me as well, but I think he was lying. I'd seen him a few times before, with Edward, but we'd never actually met. It was strange to see him with clothes on. He looks much better without them. Doesn't seem to have any style at all. That was disappointing, which is strange, because it's usually the other way round. I mean, they usually look better with their clothes on. That's what I think.

Anyway, he thought it was phenomenal. He was full of the usual shit about my name, saying how much it suited me. Why do they all come out with that stuff? But I think he really likes me, which is doing wonders for my ego. And I like him (apart from his clothes and his hairstyle – my God, Ginny, his hairstyle is appalling, like something out of the sixties).

We were both wondering if it was a one-night stand (one night-and-day stand, more like) or whether we were on the verge of something bigger. I played it casually right through, not wanting him to get the feeling that I was tying him up in chains, so he'd run down the street with his tail between his legs.

God forbid, it's quite a nice tail. We're going to the movies on Wednesday. What happens after that is anyone's guess.

That all happened today. He left at 9 p.m., which is when I started writing this letter. God knows how I'll live till Wednesday. We clung to each other like clams before he went, and I thought we might get back into bed. I was dribbling at both ends. But he went. He lives with his grandmother, and she gets worried. He's old-fashioned.

I cursed myself after he'd gone for not asking him who Margot was. An old girlfriend probably. I hope so, anyway, the older the better. I wouldn't mind if she was eighty. But I'll ask him on Wednesday.

Lots and lots and lots of love
Juliet

Dear Ginny,

I'll try to bring you up to date, but life has been such a whirl I'll probably get everything out of sequence. Never mind. I'm in love, that's all this letter can possibly say.

I wish you'd met Vince, that you knew him as I do (well, not quite). He's different to usual blokes. He reads poetry, like you. And he likes to get me cornered and read to me. Not that the poetry is bad, it's just that I can't seem to take it in. Vince says that isn't the point, that you take poetry in whether you know it or not, that true poetry is like a rapist in a leather hood. If you resist or not, it makes no difference. He talks like that. In pictures.

We see each other every night except Thursday when he goes to a Labour Party meeting. That gives me a chance to wash my hair and write to you. Clean the flat. Which means I look at the mess, and then forget it. When Vince's here he falls over things all the time, and he tends to tidy up as he's moving about the room. He even washes the dishes. I felt guilty the first time, because there was so much. But it's a thing with him. I can't see the point in washing pots for the sake of doing it. I would feel like my mother if I did that. And when he's done it there's this clean space, the draining board and the sink all shining and bright and completely incongruous with the rest of the room. It's like a wound. You can't do anything but look at it, like modern art. But after a cup of tea and a bowl of cornflakes it's back to its real self again.

I couldn't get anything out of him about Margot. He said it wasn't important and I believed him. I wanted to believe him, so I believed him. But when he's off-guard, late at night or early in the morning he calls me Margot. I've decided to leave it for the time being, because he obviously can't talk about it. But I'll get to the bottom of it eventually. Whoever she is I hate her.

Next thing is he wants me to meet his grandmother. Which is the beginning of the wedding ceremony, isn't it? That's a joke, Ginny.

What will I wear? What will I say to her? What will she say to me? I can't bear to think about it. I'm terrified.

Lots of love
Juliet

Dear Ginny,

She made me feel like shit. I'm not good enough for her darling Vince.

Ginny, was I pissed off? I had my hair done, bought new tights, borrowed a handbag the same colour as my red shoes. I was fucking perfect. And she saw right through me. And she's almost blind . . . and deaf. I walked into the room and she took one look at me, and guess what she saw?

Juliet.

Me.

As I am.

I might as well have been naked.

I smiled all the way through it, screaming inside (and she knew I was screaming inside), hoping Vince wouldn't notice. And he didn't, bless him.

What the old crone saw in me was horrible. I can't really believe it's there. I felt she saw something in me that was evil. Not that she imagined it, but that she actually perceived evil in me. I could have killed her. Vince introduced me, and she sort of gasped and shrivelled away behind her arthritis and her museum teapot.

There was a stain on the wallpaper that looked like dried

blood. Probably the spot where the old witch sacrificed one of Vince's previous girlfriends.

I really felt like shit. I wish I could explain that to you, because I felt good before I met her. I'd really tried. I was looking and feeling good. And she destroyed me.

So when she'd gone to bed I sat on this lumpy chair feeling like the end of the world and Vince stood by the mantelpiece, holding it, gripping it; and neither of us had anything to say. Vince was weird. I'd never seen him like that before.

He's a strange guy.

But they all are. I could do worse than Vince. I've done worse before. Edward was into buying old nightdresses from jumble sales so he could rip them off me. Simulated rape, he used to call it. Bloody perv. At least Vince's not a perv.

Love for now
Juliet

Dear Ginny,

You know my mother still hasn't accepted that I live by myself, that I've left their cosy nest and struck out into the world. I told them about Vince and my mother went into her old wheezing act. 'Not another new boyfriend, Juliet; you'll get a bad name for yourself.' I feel sorry for my dad when I see them together like that.

They're decorating the sitting room again. Every bloody year they decorate that room. The old paper comes off, and new paper goes on. Even as a child I knew they were kidding themselves about that. It doesn't change anything, Ginny; nothing at all. It's only paper. Paper and paste.

But that's enough about them. I'll tell you about my old-fashioned boyfriend. Yes, we're still together. I've had enough of running around. I'm going to stick to Vince with inflexible tenacity. Edward told me that's what I've got: inflexible tenacity. It's on account of me being a Crab. Mind you, Edward told me lots of things.

I keep changing my mind about Vince. I like him. And then ... I look at him and wonder what I'm doing with such an old-fashioned boy, and then I think I can change him. And then I wonder if it's worth the effort.

I don't know if I could live with anyone else, anyway. I'm not used to sleeping with other people. Know what I mean? Really sleeping. I'd much rather have the bed to myself.

My room was perfect. No chairs. A bed, and a big cupboard for my clothes. Then Vince started grumbling about there being no chairs, and so as not to be unreasonable I let him bring a chair. When he comes he sits in it, and I sit on the bed. That's OK. But when he's not here the chair is always in the way. I shift it around the room. Once I put it on the landing, but it was still in the way. I hate chairs.

Ginny, why do I hate chairs?

Am I crazy?

Joke. Ha ha.

But furniture, and especially chairs, have always got me down. Probably because they mean so much to my parents. I'll get over everything eventually, when I stop fluctuating.

Love

Juliet

Dear Ginny,

I was depressed when I last wrote to you. I suppose it was because a kind of reality had crept into Vince's and my relationship. Before the episode with 'granny' it had been a fairy story, and that night the magic stopped working, and I couldn't accept it for a while. I was sorry I'd sent that letter to you, because I was hanging my sorrow and disappointment on you, and I didn't want to do that, but I had to do something with it.

Things are better now. Not like before, because before there was illusion, and, well, I suppose the word is ecstasy. I'm not ecstatic any more. But I'm happy with Vince. He's a good man.

With most men I have the feeling they are laughing at me, or patronizing, or simply lying all the time. But not with Vince. He listens and sometimes we talk right through the night.

Sex is good as well.

We spent an evening with Edward and his girlfriend, which was OK. Edward's girlfriend is called Beige; she's very giggly. In the pub Vince and Edward talked about politics, and I was left to squeeze some mileage out of Beige. It was hard going. She looks like Scary Spice, you know, the one with the frizzy corkscrews. God knows what Edward sees in her, apart from sex. Though that's probably enough for him. She talked about menstruation for ninety minutes.

Bleedin' boring.

I miss you, Ginny, and the times we used to have. Sometimes I think about all that and wish you'd come back home.

Sometimes I think I'll never meet anyone like you again, and you'll stay in America for ever, and all we'll have together are these letters.

Love
Juliet

Dear Ginny,

Thanks for all the postcards, I got one every day for a week. But you shouldn't worry about me; I've got lots of news for you.

Edward and Beige have got married. You can't see

anything yet, but there are a million eyes on her stomach. Registry Office job, no friends invited. The only people there were Edward's mother and Beige's parents.

They're living in Greek Street. I'll let you know as soon as the baby shows.

Vince bought me a dress for Christmas. He came with me to Hammonds and stood about wonderfully patient while I spent hours trying on everything they had. It's a super dress, a kind of mossy green colour. Vince says I look like Kate Moss in it.

I bought him an umbrella, which is what he wanted, and it's amazing what it does for his image.

Keep sending the letters.

Love

Juliet

4

ONLY A BABY

Dear Ginny,

Beige had her baby on 30 July. Looks like Edward, and he'll be called Darren.

We see more of them these days, because they've got a house, and all we've got is my filthy flat (it hasn't had a good clean since you deserted). Vince and Edward are close, but I find Beige more difficult now she's had the baby. Not that I'm jealous. Well, I am, but when I find myself thinking like that, I remember that if I had her baby, I'd have to have her husband. And I'd rather have Vince. Life isn't easy, is it?

    Lots of love
    Juliet

Dear Ginny,

I've had my hair cut very short. It's amazing; I don't need a comb or a mirror any more. I'm getting free, except I'm short of money. Short hair, short skirt, and short of money.

Now I have a secret plan. Don't tell anyone. Vince is like something out of the Middle Ages. Edward is the same; they haven't realized that the twentieth century is finished. So Beige and I are putting on the pressure to get them to cut their hair, and start wearing designer trousers. Vince is going to be difficult, especially about the trousers – he really hates designer clothes. I might get him to cut his hair, but he regards the trousers as exploitation. I also want him to buy a tailored coat. I'm keeping my fingers crossed about that.

Vince bought the Stone Roses CD, and he sings the songs all the time. I still like Oasis, especially Liam.

Write again soon.

Lots of love

Juliet

Dear Ginny,

I got carried away by a bloke from the hairdressers. We talked, and he seemed good fun, and, well . . . I didn't think about the consequences.

I met him for a drink when Vince was at his meeting, and then he brought me home. It was a relief to laugh and be irresponsible.

He had me stripped down to nothing before I started to feel guilty. I still don't know why I stopped him. I *did* want him. Only, at the last minute I started thinking about Vince, and then it didn't seem right.

He was really good about it, as well. Shrugged his shoulders. Said he didn't want to do it if I wasn't ready. The trouble was, I *was* ready. I'd never been more ready in my life, except for the thought of Vince. I made myself cry, and he fussed about, made me a cup of tea. If he'd been just the tiniest bit pushy, I'd have done it.

I'm seeing him again this Thursday. I've been thinking about him all week. We're sure to do it this time. I've played it over in my mind a million times.

Am I heading for a mess? I don't know. Vince has been much cooler lately. Is he going off me, anyway? I don't know.

Oh, hell.

Love

Juliet

Dear Ginny,

I'm writing this letter in the middle of the night.

The truth is, Ginny, I'm all at sixes-and-sevens. When I first met Vince I was madly in love with him, and I think he was with me. I know that feeling doesn't last for ever, but now I think sometimes that he doesn't like me at all. It was too much before, when he was the only thing in my mind. It was glorious, but it was too much, like living on the edge of a precipice. But it seems to have gone the other way now. I think he's bored with me.

He says he'll come at seven, and I'm still waiting for him at half-past-eight. Then when he arrives he's tired.

I don't understand it. I can't understand why he keeps coming if he doesn't like me. If I say anything, he makes some excuse about his granny.

Oh, hell, Ginny, I don't know why I'm telling you all this. It's not so bad as I make it sound. It's just . . . disappointing.

Then there's my hairdresser, who is exciting.

Send me a sleeping pill. Make my period start.

Love

Juliet

Dear Ginny,

I haven't told Vince yet. God knows what he'll say. God knows what he'll *do*. I didn't think it would happen to me. Who'd be a woman?

It's due on the first of May, so there's still plenty of time. Vince might want me to get rid of it. I don't know if he could afford it, or if I want to have it cut out of me.

I've been thinking of going on the pill. But it's too late now. I've caught it. God knows what my mother will say. It'll be the loony bin for her. It'll be worse than when John Lennon got shot. She'll never get over it. She's been expecting this since I was ten.

What gets me is that I never expected it. I never even worried about it. We took precautions (is that the word?), or at least Vince did. I can't understand what went wrong. It must have been a dud. I've heard that people in the rubber factory stick pins in them for a laugh. They should come here and laugh.

Oh, Ginny, what am I going to do? Why aren't you here with me now, when I need you? It's all my responsibility, my body, my baby, my fault, and I can't stand it. How could I think it would never happen? It happens all the time.

Help.

Juliet

Dear Ginny,

Vince went white when I told him.

My mother ran upstairs screaming three days ago and she's not come down yet. Dad says she's had a brainstorm. The only one who was any use at all was Beige. She puts things in perspective for me. 'They'll all forget about it,' she says. 'You have to be miserable and humble for a few months, and then they forget about it and let you live your life.'

It's only a baby. *My* baby. I'm going to have a baby. If Vince comes round, I'll be happy. I'll be sick in the morning and happy in the afternoon. In the evening Vince will read his poems to me. We'll be a family.

Love

Juliet

PS. It's going to be a boy. How do I know? I just do.

5

AN EIGHTEENTH-CENTURY HAG-MASS

Dear Ginny,

Here are a couple of photographs of the wedding. The first one shows the happy (and beautiful) couple (you should note that the girl is not normally as fat as she seems in this photograph); and the other one shows the couple and their guests. Vince is the one next to me in the designer trousers with short hair. Next to him is his grandmother, and behind them are his friends from the Labour Party and assorted cronies (Edward was the best man but he doesn't seem to be in this group). Next to me is my dad, then Mother wheezing and looking worried; then comes Beige with her baby Darren, and behind them my aunts and uncles and cousins and their neighbours and lodgers.

We went to Paris for a week and I'm sorry to say it wasn't the most wonderful holiday of my life. Vince enjoyed it, but he was worrying about his grandmother most of the time. She's never had to manage on her own before. I enjoyed the first couple of days, but dragging round Paris looking at pictures isn't really my idea of a good time.

Our house is nice, near the shops. And the park will be useful once the baby is born. We haven't got a cooker yet. We ordered it before we went to Paris, and expected it to be fitted and working when we got back. But it's still not come. I telephone the electricity people every day.

While Vince's at work I spend my time with Beige. We listen to Viking FM and talk all day. I don't know what I'd do without her. She takes the pill. She says that women who have side effects imagine it.

My tummy is bigger every day, and I don't feel the right shape for sex. Sometimes Vince is too serious about sex. We never get down to a good slap-and-tickle. Sex is the highest aspiration of human love to him, which robs it of something.

He's visiting his grandmother tonight. I was going to get bathed and watch TV, but I fancied a chat with you.

Love
Juliet Gurney (Mrs)

Dear Ginny,

I've gone blonde. I had to do something; I can't sit here watching myself getting more balloon-like every day. I think I got pregnant as a punishment from God. My mini-skirt hangs in the cupboard, and I walk around in sacks.

Beige called round to see if I'd go for a walk in the park with her and Darren, but I'm fed up of being a walking lump. I feel like a carthorse when I'm with her.

I'd give anything for a flat tummy. After this is over I'm going on the pill, and I'll never get pregnant again. Women who like being pregnant are crazy.

So I'm fat and blonde now, waiting for the waters to break.

Love
Juliet

Dear Ginny,

I never see Vince these days. I was thinking about the week, and apart from his being at work all day, Sunday he goes to see Granny, Tuesday he's out drinking with Edward, Wednesday he's with Granny again, Thursday the Labour

Party, and Saturday he babysits for Beige and Edward. Which leaves Monday and Friday when he's at home having a bath or reading his poetry books. Before we got married I saw him every day.

He comes home from work and eats his dinner, then he goes out again. He never complains about the food, even though sometimes it's burnt cinders. He doesn't notice. He shovels it into his mouth. I sometimes ask him:

'What shall we have for dinner tomorrow?'

'I don't mind,' he says. 'Whatever's easy.'

Nothing's easy. He doesn't realize that. Whatever I cook he shovels it in. He never says he likes it, and he never says it's horrible. Just shovels away, like a worm eating soil.

It's the same with the washing: I tell him I haven't washed his shirts. My tummy's got so big I can't struggle to the launderette with the washing.

'Don't worry,' he says. 'I'll do it.'

And that's the end of it. He does it as well, and I sit at home and wait for him. I don't think he likes me any more. His grandmother sees more of him than I do.

I suppose it's because I'm fat and horrible, and after the baby's born it'll be different.

Love

Juliet

Dear Ginny,

The horror stories are true. The curse of Eve is an understatement. I never want to go through it again.

When I was a week overdue they decided to induce it, and I went into a ten-hour labour before they cut me open. I screamed myself hoarse. They stuck needles in me and gave me laughing gas, and I gave birth to a cathedral.

It's changed me.

I've been at home for a week, and John (my son – I feel

31

really strange calling him that) is asleep for the first time. Between feeds he screams and I carry him round the room . . . all day and all night.

Vince takes him sometimes, but he has to work during the day. It's hell. I hope he doesn't wake up for a week.

But the birth!

Vince was with his granny who, as far as I can make out, died at about the same time John was born. Vince didn't know the exact time she went, somewhere between one and two in the morning. John was born at 1.43 a.m. He doesn't respond to me; neither did she. I'm not a good mother. It's true. I don't feel like mothers feel. I don't want to hold him. I just want him to shut up. I want to sleep.

Beige's been round a couple of times. When she picks him up he stops crying, then she gives him back to me and he howls. It's the same with Vince. He's quiet for Vince. But for me he screams. I think he hates me (can babies hate?), and granny hated me as well. I bet she died at 1.43 a.m.

(next day)

I gave him an aspirin. I know you're not supposed to, but it's him or me . . .

Vince was useless when I came home. My husband was crying for his dead granny. Am I mad, Ginny; have I got it all wrong? When I came home with that baby, after going through hell, still bleeding, feeling hopeless and inadequate, do you know what I had to do? I had to *comfort* Vince. The baby was crying, Vince was crying, the house was upside down, and I was supposed to be the strong one. I was supposed to be the one who could cope with them both, make them both feel better. Me? And I did it. I took a deep breath and did it. Hoping that it was a temporary emergency.

It's been a temporary emergency for the last eight days.

Vince hasn't noticed the baby yet. He doesn't see any point in living now his granny's dead.

Ginny, I feel like one of those eighteenth-century hag-masses.

Jesus, he's awake again.

No, false alarm. He shouted out in his sleep. I felt like throwing him at the wall. I'm frightened, Ginny. I'm really frightened, because I might do it. I have a fantasy that I'll find blood on my hands, and John will have his brains battered out, and I'll have done it. It frightens me because it could happen. Sometimes I'm so close to doing it I just throw him in his crib and walk out of the house. That's sanity; that's the nearest I get to sanity, to throw my baby in his crib and leave him screaming while I walk round the park. It's sanity, Ginny; do you realize that? Because if I didn't do that sane thing, I might easily do the other. Oh, Jesus, he *is* awake.

(two days later – or is it longer than that?)
And nothing's changed. Ha ha. Except change.

I've explained to John that I'm going to finish this letter and post it. He ignores me. Vince ignores me. They are both too involved in themselves to notice me, but I'm working on them.

Vince came home from work yesterday and I put a piece of cheese on the table. No plate, no knife, just a piece of cheese. It was about two inches square; yellow Cheddar, dry, with cracks in it. *I* wouldn't have eaten it. He sat looking at it with the silence he brings into the house. I could feel him glancing at me out of the corner of his eye. I started humming *Candle in the Wind*: I'd been humming it all day. It seems to be in my head.

I couldn't look back at him, but he was looking at me all the time while I pottered about the kitchen singing my song. He was noticing me all right. He noticed me more in that couple of minutes than he has done for months.

Then he ate the cheese.

Tonight I'm going to give him a piece of wood.

But first I'll find an envelope and take this to the post office. You love me.

Juliet

Dear Ginny,

Nothing works. My tits are enormous and painful. I take tablets to scale the milk away, but it dribbles out all the time.

I live with the smell of spew and shit. More comes out of this baby than I put into it. I make a bottle and he drinks it and five minutes later he brings it all up.

His cot is wet and stinking. Our bed is the same; well, *my* side of it is.

What am I supposed to do with all these nappies? They're supposed to be disposable. The lavatory has been blocked for two days now. Vince says a plumber's going to come, but where is he?

How can I go out? All my clothes stink. I've smashed the mirror. Seven years bad luck. Who's going to sweep the glass up?

Everyone tells lies. The radio tells lies. It pretends everything is wonderful. Vince tells lies, he pretends to eat pieces of wood, and stones, and tins of cat food. But he doesn't eat them. He puts them in his pocket. I've seen him doing it. Beige tells lies. She says she's busy all the time. Even the milkman tells lies. They think I'm stupid.

And this house is too big. What do I want with all these rooms? I only ever needed one room. I could manage that easily.

Everything's my fault. Vince blames me for the smell. But babies *do* smell. He blames me for the mess. Why do I move the furniture about so much? That's what he asked me yesterday. I don't want all this furniture. I never use it. It's in the way. I'm forever having to shift it. Bloody tables everywhere. Chairs. What do I want with thirteen chairs? There's only me. Babies don't use chairs. I put twelve of them in the spare room. Nearly broke my back. And when Vince came home he put them all back in the kitchen and the sitting room and the hall and the bedrooms. Why do I waste my time? I try to make space.

Can you come home now, Ginny?

You've been away long enough.

Juliet

6

THE BEDROOM THREW ME

Dear Ginny,

I can't go on with people shouting at me all the bloody time and having no one to turn to. I've asked you nicely to help me and you don't even reply and the sodding cooker blew up this morning. That health visitor was mad screaming at me about the smell as though it was all my fault she couldn't get through the front door. There isn't room for that sofa in the living room. Furniture takes up space and it stinks and it's ugly and I'm not fit to be a mother and the law of the land provides for behaviour like this and she gets paid to go barging into peoples houses and snarling at them and saying everything's filthy and other peoples kids are undernourished and never in her entire experience has she witnessed such appalling conditions and its no good me just sitting there crying and feeling sorry for myself and where's my husband and how does he put up with it and how long's the baby been losing weight and don't I think he ought to see a doctor and its absolutely crazy to have furniture piled up at the door and what would i do if the house caught fire and Mrs Gurney there's absolutely no excuse for this kind of behaviour just look at the condition of your child have you no heart?

She's gone now but she's coming back with an order and a doctor and the police and Vince will come home from work and there's no one else but you Ginny and you're not here and how can I have it all explained to me with all this fucking furniture everywhere and I've locked the doors and I haven't got a stamp for this letter and its raining and the man from the salvation army reported me for offering to give him all the furniture and that's what you get trying to be kind to people I could have sold this furniture for money but I didn't want to do that and i thought the salvation army like to have things given so they can give it away to other people who like bloody furniture which i don't and never have done and he told her and she came round like a ton of bricks hammering on the front door and refusing to go round the back so I had to shift the sodding sofa out of the way out of the kindness of my heart and now she doesn't even think I've got one.

and this baby is in distress and women like me should be compulsorily sterilized and do I realize that there are lots of women who can't conceive and how blessed i am to have a baby at all and a house and to treat it like a dog and why don't I pull myself together and see what a wonderful opportunity I've thrown away and bawling at me with her huge red mouth and fat stomach and varicose veined legs and real leather handbag

and making more noise than the kid and the radio together and screaming like a fishwife.

i told her I can't bear to touch it and she mouths why at me why why why why why why and doesn't seem to understand its not a baby but a reincarnation and that old cow never liked me and thought I was evil and even Vince understands that and her big red mouth and long teeth keep telling me she doesn't even know who Vince is and am I out of my mind. Did I tell you about the dream i had in Paris with Diana, Princess of Wales and Naomi Campbell buying clothes by the armful all made out of never-die fabrics and everything was fresh and new and you were there with Michael Chang and Versace was still alive and it had all been a mistake him being shot and somebody stole the world cup and it was wonderful and we were all so happy.

There's a hell of a row going on outside police and ambulances and crowds of people something must be wrong it's not a nice neighbourhood . . .

Dear Ginny,

i don't know how to write this letter.

I wanted to put one of your cards on the wall above my bed, but that's not allowed.

The nurse i asked, she didn't like the card.

i think that was the reason.

But i liked it . . . the one of the woman in the blue dress with the long neck.

i liked her green eyeshadow and tiny mouth, and the way she wears her hair like a helmet.

There are lots of women in here who look like her.

They sit just as quietly, smooth as eggs.

Love

Juliet

Dear Ginny,

Yes, i'll tell you all about it.

i've finished the ECT treatment, and hope it has done some good.

Afterwards i didn't know who i was, which was the best part about it.

Now i take the syrup three times a day, but they say i'm getting better, and i feel they're right most of the time.

The nurses are not kind.

They have too much to think about.

So many crazy women.

But they like it if you obey their orders quickly.

They like it if you can make yourself invisible.

Love

Juliet

Dear Ginny,

He comes every Sunday, but not the other days.

He babysits for Beige, as Edward's away in Kosovo.

I think it's because of Vince that I'm getting better.

He has stood by me.

I think I like it here.

Not the nights, because there's so much noise, and the women don't go to the lavatory, so it stinks by morning.

I work in the garden, weeding.

I can't think of anything else to say.

Love

Juliet

Dear Ginny,

It turned out right in the end. Vince couldn't manage with the baby and his job, so they have given it to foster parents. They are experienced people. They will look after it. Which is the best thing. It doesn't get sick any more, or scream, and it will be potty-trained soon. They have given me a photograph.

It didn't want me to touch it.

Vince goes to see it, and he tells me about it. But I don't want to see it again, not until I'm strong, or until it has the sense not to upset me. If I went to see it and it began to scream I don't . . .

I do remember everything. I went mad on purpose. I thought I was acting it out, but the character took over. The doctor says it doesn't help to think of it as madness, that it was a breakdown. A breakdown is something you can get over, he says. Madness is incurable.

They look after me.

There are trees outside the window. Some of them are over a hundred years old. When my dad comes we go outside and sit under them and I feel like a little girl again; but when he comes with Mother we go in the canteen and eat chocolates and I feel much older.

But I don't mind.

I can't complain.

Love

Juliet

Dear Ginny,

Yes, I'd love to come to America and stay with you in LA. It makes me happy to think about it.

So happy.

I don't think I was meant to live with other people. I told the doctor that, but he didn't believe me.

Maybe he's right. I am unreasonable sometimes. Only, I have been happiest when I've been living alone.

If I wasn't married already, I'd remain single. I'd run my own boutique with inflexible tenacity.

Love

Juliet

Dear Ginny,

I'm going home soon. At first it will be for weekends, and if that works OK, I'll go home altogether.

To Vince.

It's frightening. It's safe here. I know what to expect. I've learned.

Vince is looking forward to it.

It will be nice if it's like it was before the baby.

I heard Mary Black sing *The Holy Ground* on the radio.

The nurses say it's good to see me laughing again. I'm frightened of manipulating myself again. Because I know that it's possible to point myself in one direction and then difficult to deflect myself away from it. The drugs keep me calm.

But this whole experience has made me different to other people. I know too much. I see too far. I seem to hear what people mean rather than what they say, and you're not supposed to do that.

I do it, and I'm not strong enough to do it. To do that you have to be stronger than everybody else.

I have a dream in which my breasts fill up with milk and start leaking, but the nurse says that is not a real nightmare. I think she doesn't want to talk about it. It *is* a nightmare to me.

Love
Juliet

Dear Ginny,

I'm back in the hospital after a weekend with Vince.

It wasn't impossible, but it nearly was. The nurses say it will get better.

He came to collect me on Saturday morning and we drove straight home. I didn't want to go in the house. There was a new front door. When they came for me they smashed the door down with axes. I don't know why they did that. It seemed unnecessary. If they'd knocked I would have opened it. That health visitor must have put them up to it.

When I saw the new front door I didn't want to go inside. Vince took me to a café, and he held my hand and reasoned with me until I agreed to go back to the house. We went in the back way.

Then everything was all right until we went upstairs. I hardly recognized the downstairs room. It was neat and tidy, and it had been cleaned. I could smell it in the air. It was never like that before, except the day we moved in. There was a new cooker in the kitchen.

I'd feared that the house would drive me mad again, but

it didn't. It seemed anonymous. As though I'd never been there before. And Vince was somehow the same. I kept looking at him during the day and wondering where he had come from. I couldn't remember anything about him. I couldn't think why we had got married.

We went into town, and down to the pier. We sat and watched the ships until we were cold, and then a hot drink. My nose was red and the steam from the cup made it run, and Vince gave me his handkerchief.

Then we went home again and the bedroom threw me.

There was a space on the wall where the cot had been. I closed my eyes and took a deep breath. I'd taken my tablets, and knew everything should be all right.

It wasn't until I'd got undressed that I noticed the photographs. Vince had put them both in the same frame and stood it on his bedside cupboard. Gran and John. The two of them. I should have said something about it then, but I didn't. What I wanted to say would have sounded unreasonable.

Vince wanted sex and I told him the hospital had said I wasn't ready for it. I hadn't thought about sex. I was shocked that he wanted sex. We hardly knew each other.

When Vince was asleep I took the photographs in the frame and threw them out the window.

And that wasn't right. I shouldn't have done that. Vince was upset the next morning. He found the frame in the garden, with the glass broken. It had rained in the night and the photographs were wet and muddy. I couldn't explain to him why I had done it. He couldn't understand my reasons. We didn't argue, but he was quiet with me, and I remembered what it was about him that was important.

He makes me feel guilty.

So I was glad to come back to the hospital.

Love

Juliet

Dear Ginny,

My third weekend with Vince. I should be home permanently by Christmas. I've moved the bed to cover the space on the wall. Vince thought I was going mad again when I started moving it, but I explained to him about where the cot had been, and he understood.

The tablets keep me straight. I'm much stronger. We had sex this time, which made me feel normal. I let it happen. I'm on the pill and I'd just finished a period so it should be safe. I hope so. I had to pretend. Vince was so heavy. I thought he would crush me.

The thing that got me, before I had the breakdown, was Vince's granny. I got confused about her and the baby. They both treated me the same. I can see now that that was crazy, and I think I'd like the baby back. Not now. It wouldn't work yet. But I'm working towards it. I haven't seen him since he went to the foster parents, but I think about him more than I used to.

I think about loving him. Trying to.

After the breakdown I was in a Mother and Baby Unit at the hospital, and they kept bringing him to me and trying to make me hold him. But I didn't want to. I hadn't touched him for weeks. Even changing his nappy and feeding him I made sure we didn't come into contact. If we did, accidentally, I'd have to wash my hands. Can you imagine that, Ginny? I couldn't bear to touch my own baby. I was pretty far gone.

Now I'm coming back. Pulling myself into life.

Love
Juliet

7

IS ANYONE EVER THE FIRST?

Dear Ginny,

The house makes me nervous. I walk through the rooms and search through the drawers and cupboards, turning everything out and putting it back again. I suppose I'm trying to penetrate the house, but there is a large chunk of me that would rather not be here.

The hospital will never see me again. I'll have to take the drugs for a long time, but I don't mind that. They work for me. The worst thing to live with is that no one trusts me. They're frightened of me. Everyone tries to act normal. But I can see through them. They think I could go mad any time. And they're wrong. It's more likely to happen to them than it is to me.

He keeps a diary. He's never said anything about it, and I haven't seen him writing it. But I found it the other day with his birth certificate and his grandmother's photographs. I didn't read it. At one time I wouldn't have hesitated, but nowadays I'm more careful.

What about you, Ginny? Are you frightened of me? Do you think I'm crazy, or likely to end up in the hospital again? I don't think so. I think I can trust you. Tell me if my letters are the ramblings of an idiot. I won't mind. I'm strong, and I'm only twenty-three. There's still a lot of living in me.

Love
Juliet

Dear Ginny,

It looks as if Beige and Edward are breaking up. Edward went on a lecture tour with Zuzy Tindal, and now he seems to be living with her in London.

Beige's being brave. She smiles all the time. Darren, her little boy, is beautiful. How Edward can leave him is beyond my comprehension.

And yet I gave up my own child.

I'm going to see him. The social worker tried to talk me out of it, but I've been quietly persistent, and now they've agreed. It will be for half an hour on Tuesday. I'm terrified at the thought of it, but nothing *will* go wrong. I'm so set on it, so sure of myself, of my need to start again with him. I'm going by myself. I want to experience my own feelings, and if Vince was there it would be impossible.

Wish me luck, Ginny.

Love

Juliet

Dear Ginny,

Harry Hellier has come to live with us. I don't know if you remember him? Jean's son? He's going on seventeen now, but must have been about twelve when you last saw him. We weren't looking for a lodger, but he fits in OK. He's New Age. Quite funny. It's good to have someone else in the house.

I'm seeing John regularly now, once a fortnight. He walks and tries to talk, and he looks like my dad. The first time we didn't touch; it was horrifying because I couldn't manage to touch him, and when the time was up I suddenly reached out for him, and he backed away. I rushed all the way home to get my tablets. I'd lost my rhythm, and everything came towards me in huge waves. I thought I was going again, but

I managed to contain it. I know it'll take a long time before I become a proper mother. Too many things have come between John and me for it to be easy.

Now when we meet he recognizes me, and holds my hand, and he calls me Woogie, or something like that. In those moments I feel like I'm bursting. But with joy.

You'd better send me a photograph of this fiancé of yours. I'm dying to see what he looks like.

Love
Woogiet

Dear Ginny,

Thanks for the photograph. Wow! He's a beautiful man, isn't he? And so tanned. Are you that colour?

You'd better not bring him to England. You might lose him.

My news is good and bad.

Vince went down to London for a weekend to see Edward, and left me here with Harry. The lodger? Harry had some dope, and got stoned. He wanted me to smoke as well, but I don't think it's a good idea with these drugs I take. I don't want to slip back.

Harry tried to chat me up, but I put him down. He's still only a kid to me.

It was flattering, though. Know what I mean?

That was the good news.

The bad news is that I read Vince's diaries. It's not a good thing to know how other people really see you. Especially when you're married to them.

From the moment I first told him I was pregnant he's felt trapped. He felt trapped when he married me. And he feels trapped now.

Ginny, I never wanted to do that to him.

And he's been seeing Margot regularly. Remember

Margot? He sees her every Thursday at the Labour Party. He's been seeing her for years and never breathed a word.

I'm still digesting all this.

When I read it I wished I'd had some of Harry's dope.

Love

Juliet

Dear Ginny,

I've been weeping a lot, depressed.

Vince has been using me. It's as though he's punishing me because of something Margot did to him. Without my fortnightly visits to John I could easily go over the top again.

It doesn't seem that Vince has ever loved me. I caught him on the rebound from Margot.

I don't want a big scene until I'm sure I can cope with it.

And something else nags all the time.

If I confront Vince with the diary, he might leave me. And if he leaves me, what chance will I have to get John back?

Oh, Ginny, I wish we lived on a desert island.

Love

Juliet

Dear Ginny,

I'm having an affair. I don't care. There has to be some excitement in life, some release from the pressure.

I know he's a lot younger than me. But at least he's kind. He cares about me. I had an attack of conscience.

Guilt.

It was dreadful.

I thought, this is wrong, I can't go on like this. I'm being unfaithful to my husband, putting my marriage in jeopardy. I swore to myself that I wouldn't sleep with Harry again.

And then it was over ... the guilt, I mean.

And it hasn't come back.

I needed to do that, the self-searching bit.

We play Russian roulette, snatching a kiss when Vince goes to the lavatory and another when he's in the kitchen. Any one of those kisses could be a loaded gun.

This is a very explosive affair.

I don't even have time to write to you. I hope you understand.

Love

Juliet

8

RUTTING AWAY IN FRONT OF HIS NOSE

Dear Ginny,

I'm seeing John every week now, and the social worker says we can try to have him overnight. Imagine that, he'll be back with me. I'm getting a second chance.

And I want it so much, Ginny. To have him back, to be able to give him everything that I couldn't manage before. With Harry here as well, it makes such a difference. Before, I was isolated with John, but now with Harry and Vince to help, it will be much easier.

I think Vince must know about me and Harry. Everyone must know. But it's never mentioned. A taboo.

A baby in the house.

There were times when that thought would have filled me with dread. But now it seems as though it will make my happiness complete.

Does Vince know about me and Harry, or am I kidding myself? I think he must know, and yet he's never mentioned it.

And another nag: Harry and I dream of being together, just the two of us (though now we include John in it). But is it just a dream? Will Vince let me go? And the big one, will Harry still want me when I finally become available?

I've got *almost* everything I want. Vince is going away next week and Harry and I will stay in bed together for forty-eight hours.

Love
Juliet

Dear Ginny,

My mother died last Tuesday. She had a heart attack in the doctor's surgery.

I haven't taken it in yet. There doesn't seem to be room in my life for something as big as this. I feel as though I should sit down in a darkened room and meditate on it, on her and on our relationship. But I don't do anything.

My dad is devastated. I've tried to comfort him, but he says the world has turned to stone.

The funeral is the day after tomorrow, and I expect I'll be able to cry then. I hope so. Sometimes over the last couple of days I've thought that my mother might've been the only real friend I have in the world. Not counting you, of course.

Love

Juliet

Dear Ginny,

There was a time not so very long ago when I was mad and the rest of the world was sane. Now it seems the other way round. The world is spinning crazy.

It was a complete surprise to him. Harry and I have been rutting away in front of his nose for a year, and he didn't have the faintest idea what was happening.

Now he will do anything if I'll give Harry up. He'll change his brain cells. He'll be my slave, sleeping like a dog at the foot of my bed. He's dropped every vestige of dignity. He whines at me all the time.

Harry has gone to stay with his mother. He's looking for somewhere we can live together.

Vince talks about it to everyone. I can't blame him for putting it around, because everyone knew what was happening anyway. Everyone except Vince.

Harry thinks we should blow. Go away as far as possible. He says they'll never give us a chance. And he says that Vince will only pull himself together if I'm no longer there.

But I can't go away. I'm waiting for John. When I see John, I look at him and I think I'll hate him when he's grown up. Because of him I might have to give Harry up, and Harry is my only chance of real happiness.

Especially now that my mother has gone.

Love

Juliet

Dear Ginny,

Harry went to London three days ago, and he's staying with Edward and Zuzy.

I'm hanging on here until they give me back my son, and then I'll go to Harry.

He said he'll wait for me.

I hope so.

I miss him dreadfully. I live for the postman. I sit and look at the telephone.

Love

Juliet

Dear Ginny,

Vince has come to his senses. He was obsessed about Harry, and about me meeting him, and now he knows that Harry isn't here any more he's able to relax.

There have been a couple of evenings lately when we have had a good time together. You know, laughed about it.

It's not normal. I don't suppose it ever could be now, but it's better than it was. Vince wants to make love every night, and he wants me to compare his lovemaking with Harry's. What he actually wants is for me to say that he's better than

Harry. And I can't say that, because it isn't true. Harry could turn me on with a glance. Harry can turn me on with his handwriting on an envelope. Vince has to work hard.

But you can't compare. Know what I mean?

I wish Vince didn't love me. It's no fun being loved by someone you don't want.

Love
Juliet

9

A COUPLE OF DRINKS

Dear Ginny,

I went to London for a weekend. It took a long time to get Vince to agree, but he could see in the end that I would go whether he wanted me to or not.

Harry has this bedsitter in Camden Town and I went on the train on Saturday morning. He met me at King's Cross and we went straight to his place and made love. It was wonderful. The last weeks ground themselves free of me.

I'd forgotten how young he is. Vince is like an old man, and living with him you come to believe that all men are old. But Harry isn't. He's young. He'd cut his hair.

He told me he'd been seeing someone else. He was apologetic about it, saying he was sorry and that it wouldn't happen again. But I didn't mind. Somehow I'd been expecting it. If you knew Harry, you'd know what I mean. He couldn't be faithful. When he told me, a great gong sounded in my chest, and I was sad about it, but I couldn't cry.

Vince had been saying for weeks that Harry used me, and it was true, and I knew it was true, but it didn't matter because I was using him as well. We were using each other, and somehow we had agreed to do that, and to enjoy it. For as long as it lasted.

Harry and I left it in the air. He was still saying he was sorry about this other girl, Josephine something or other, and that he'd never see her again. And I'm sure he believed it. But I didn't. The dreams have faded for me.

Vince cheered up when I told him. I won't be going to London. I don't know where I'll be going. But I won't stay in this house. And I won't stay with Vince. We have hurt each other too much.

Love
Juliet

Dear Ginny,

I'm getting John back.

Tomorrow.

Dear God, I've cleaned his room four times today.

I cleaned it six times yesterday.

My teeth ache with smiling.

Harry's moved in with his Josephine. She's seventeen. I hope they're happy.

I feel more excited than I did on my first date.

I can't write this letter.

Love
Juliet

Dear Ginny,

I'll never forget when John was born, and those first weeks I spent with him on my own. It was hell. And this house and Vince are still here as they were then, and they're constant reminders. I can't begin life again while they're here.

Having John back makes a difference, of course. He's no trouble at all. Even when he's ill, or when he doesn't sleep through the night, I never experience him as a pressure. I experience the house and Vince as constant pressures. I want to start life again with my son. Just me and him.

Vince doesn't understand. Since Harry's been gone Vince

thinks we can pick up the pieces and go on as before. He says it doesn't matter that I don't love him, that I'll learn to love him in time. He can wait.

I can't.

He doesn't understand but he realizes that he has to go.

If he went tomorrow, I'd move in with Beige. That would be ideal because we could babysit for each other. Our children play together like brothers.

I'm not mad, Ginny. For the first time in my life I feel that I want to be responsible for myself. I'm strong these days and I can manage whatever life has to offer.

Love

Juliet

Dear Ginny,

Things are looking up.

Vince has decided to go to India. He's finally realized that we can't stay together. Life for him would be hopeless with me. He can't make me happy.

I won't let him.

We'll sell this house and use the money to buy another one in Greek Street, just a few doors away from Beige. That's better than moving in with her, because living with someone else might not be my scene. The difference in the house prices will leave enough for Vince to go to India.

I honestly think it's for the best. Vince has been repressed all the time we've been together. I told you what he wrote in his diary about seeing Margot, etc. You know it was all a dream. He's never been with anyone else since we got married. Can you believe it? I can, and you would too if you'd met him.

I wasn't going to tell you how I finally got Vince to change his mind and leave. But I know you'll ask, so you might as well have it straight. There was this guy, you see

. . . I didn't even fancy him very much. I was buying a pair of boots and a jacket in Next and he was fluttering about supervising the girls who were serving. I don't like fluttering men, but, somehow it was not only possible, it was also expedient. I didn't mean to sleep with him, I thought it would be enough to let him flutter for a while where Vince could see him. But you know what it's like after a couple of drinks?

Love from your (slightly) ashamed friend
Juliet

Dear Ginny,

Thanks for the brooch. It's the reddest ladybird I've ever seen in my life, and the most beautiful. I'm lucky to have such a talented friend. I wear it all the time, and everyone asks me where I got it. It's so nice to say, Oh, my friend Ginny made it for me. I love it. I wish I could make something only half as nice for you.

I moved house last week. There are two bedrooms, one for me and one for John. We had to get rid of a lot of the furniture from the other place. I telephoned a second-hand shop and they came round and took everything I didn't want for £95.00.

I feel a lot younger for the move. Harry brought his Josephine two days after I moved in. He brought her primarily to show to Jean, but they came to me for a cup of tea. She's such a little thing, pretty as the day, all willowy and blonde. I felt quite maternal towards her. I hope Harry's good to her. He can be rough sometimes.

Oh, God, and Ginny, I almost forgot to tell you; I've got a job. In Next. It's only part time, three days a week, but I can buy clothes at a discount. And Beige will look after John while I'm working.

I'm going to be the best-dressed girl in town. But even if

I can't afford all the clothes I want, at least I'll be working amongst them. I've wanted to do this for so long.

I took John to see Vince off at the station. My heart was stuck in my throat. He was brave about it, though; he kissed us both and went through the barrier. I waited there in case he turned to wave, but when he got to the train he just climbed aboard and disappeared.

I don't think I'll ever get married again. I've had a husband now. He was filling without being satisfying.

Love
Juliet

Dear Ginny,

I dreamed my parents came round to inspect the house, and my mother was disappointed that I hadn't papered the walls. She sniffed a lot while she was here. She thinks paint is cheap. What could I say: Mother, I *like* it like this.

John is very well. He's past the toddling stage now, and has become a little boy. He looks more like my dad every day. I think in some ways he had a memory of his first weeks at the other house, and he never really blossomed while we were there.

It's much better for him here, as I don't have as much furniture, and there's room for him to run around. I borrowed a couple of chairs from Beige when my father came. He said I shouldn't worry about not having much furniture. 'You can buy it as you go along,' he said. He'll never understand that I don't like the stuff. He's deteriorating rapidly. Definitely losing his marbles.

I've started saving for my trip to LA. I'm determined to come as soon as possible. I'll have to bring John as well, you do realize that? I couldn't possibly be without him for a whole month.

There's something else happening here that makes me want to get away as soon as possible.

In your next letter you must tell me when would be the best time to come (soon). And in *my* next letter I'll tell you about my new boyfriend.

Love
Juliet

III
THE CHINESE GIRL

10

VERMIN

Shooter got his nickname at school because he was always ready to tell the other kids how great he was. He'd tell the teachers, anybody who would listen, that his old man was a war hero who'd been offed by the Nazis on a beach at Dunkirk.

But most people in Hull, around that area of Hedon Road, knew that Shooter's old man had deserted shortly after he was called up and spent the rest of the war hiding in a cellar in Wincolmlee.

Shooter couldn't remember where the nickname originated. But, as nicknames go, it seemed to fit, so he didn't fight it.

No one expected Shooter to make a mark on the world. He had an over-active imagination, but he would never succeed with anything. His mother and his two aunts thought he was like his father. They listened to his stories and said private prayers for the girl, whoever she would turn out to be, who would be his wife.

After school he didn't manage to get an apprenticeship at Blackburn's, working on the Buccaneer, like most of the other lads in his year. But he did break into a house on Holderness Road and the authorities sorted out a place for him at the North Sea Camp, a remand centre for young offenders.

When he returned to Hull a year later, he'd added four

inches to his height, and if he'd been good at shooting shit at school, now he was full of it.

There was a small café in Posterngate at the time, and Shooter could be found in there most days of the week. His nights were spent in the Star of Bethlehem. Both places were hang-outs for local scumbags who would plan break-ins together or waylay the occasional customer and relieve them of their worldly goods. Punters, they called them, or vermin. The favourite trick of the group was rolling drunks, and Shooter was better at it than the others. He could make a drunk roll further than anyone else.

Against all the odds, Shooter eventually surfaced as the leader of the pack. It wasn't a meteoric rise to stardom like some of the rock'n'rollin' teenagers of the day, but it was enough to put a swagger in his step. It allowed him to wear a purple shirt open to the waist, and sport a gold bar on a thick chain around his neck.

Shooter picked up a gun from a police superintendent's house on Beverley Road and shot a drunk who refused to hand over his wallet. He shot the drunk in the stomach, and the man lingered for a week before he eventually died in the infirmary without identifying his assailant.

What Shooter discovered about himself during that time was that he enjoyed shooting the man. He loved it that the guy didn't die instantly, but that the moment was pro-longed over nights and days. Shooter considered he had moved up in the world, that he had progressed from childhood and become a man. He would kill again. For the feelings it gave him, for the excitement and the exhilaration.

Soon after he'd shot the drunk, the very next day, Shooter noticed that the hungry pigeons on Queen Victoria's Square wanted nothing to do with him. When he walked on to the square the birds flapped away to higher perches under the eaves of the city hall. But that was all right. They were only vermin.

11

A JANUS HEAD

Ginny felt as if her period was about to start. She didn't want to open her eyes. She didn't want to move at all, or make any effort apart from breathing. In her imagination she was back in LA, although she knew the reality, that she was in Hull, in her hotel room at the Willows on Chanterlands Avenue. Her landlady's chin puckered into wrinkles when she dealt with Asian or coloured folk. For her white guests she was all smiles.

The quilt had slipped from her shoulder and she sighed and pulled it up to her chin, and as she did so she heard a movement close to her bed. What Ginny would've liked was the sound to be something falling off her bed when she tugged at the quilt, her skirt, say, or her bag. But she knew that wasn't what made the sound, because, ever so faintly, she could hear breathing.

Someone was in the room with her.

She opened her eyes and tried to focus on the scene. But there was nothing she recognized. This was not her hotel room, not the bed she had slept in since her arrival from LA. The room wavered as her vision tried to pin it down. There was a sharp pain in her head, and aches all over her body.

What she had first identified as PMT suddenly meta-morphosed into a liquid stomach which winged its way upward against the laws of gravity. She threw herself to the edge of the bed and watched a large white plastic bowl come towards her face. Then she retched and saw the yellow bile spill from her throat, felt the spray as it hit the bottom of the bowl and bounced back at her face.

'Just let it come,' a voice said. A masculine voice. 'Try to hit the bowl. Let it come.' An English accent with a rough edge, not a voice that had an echo in her memory.

Ginny had time to wonder if she was in hospital before she retched again, and another mouthful of the disgusting brew spewed out of her. Her hair fell forward into the bowl, and she whipped it away, but not before it was coated with vomit. A tattooed hand offered her a tissue, and she accepted it and wiped her chin and lips. She glanced upwards to see his face, but her stomach sent another load of toxic waste up through her oesophagus, and she had to dive into the bowl again.

There were three hands holding the bowl. Two of them were hers, and they grasped the rim so tightly the fingers had turned the white of aspirin. The other hand did not belong to her, and was half as big again as her own. Dark hairs sprouted from the upper phalanxes of each finger, and the back of the hand had an image of a Gurkha sword tattooed in black ink. Ginny couldn't believe this hand belonged to a nurse. If she was in hospital, it seemed the ancillary staff was caring for her.

But Ginny couldn't deal with that; she was too busy doing reality. The contents of her stomach sailed up and out of her with such velocity that she couldn't devote an ounce of strength to the wider environment of bed and room. Her whole world was focused on the twenty square centimetres of space occupied by her face and the white plastic bowl, and it seemed as though, at least for the span of this lifetime, the future did not hold a wider perspective. The surface of the bowl was pitted with use, and fine striations embedded in the plastic formed intricate patterns which could have been blueprints for spider webs. The former contents of Ginny's stomach, which slopped about only three or four inches away from her face, were an eloquent comment on the condition of the human race.

Through a stupor Ginny realized that long swathes of time passed during which she was not conscious. Her head was still in the bowl, but she couldn't remember when she last vomited. She thought it might have been several minutes ago. The man with the tattooed hand had spoken to her, and she had tried to formulate a reply, say something back to him, but now she had forgotten what he said, and wasn't sure if he had spoken at all. A line from Keats filled her head and the bowl that held it: *Philosophy will clip an Angel's wings.*

She watched the man's fingers prise her hands from the lip of the bowl. Then he placed the palm of his hand on her forehead and lifted her head back to the pillow. Her teeth chattered briefly, and she felt as though her brain shook. The man pulled the quilt up to her chin and looked down at her. She breathed the air that was free of her own vomit. Air that had a peculiar chemical tang to it, something unnaturally clean.

He wore a grey T-shirt with a Janus head. His biceps stretched the fabric of the sleeves, and his forearms were each tattooed with a symbol that looked like the cross of the St. John Ambulance Association. His head was shaved and in his right ear he wore what looked like a wedding ring. His face was tattooed with a teardrop under his left eye and what were supposed to be bullet holes, an entry and exit wound, on each side of his forehead.

'Did you say something?' she asked. The sound of her voice seemed to come from somewhere else in the room. Usually, when she spoke, she could locate the sound somewhere in her head, in the region just below her ears. But when she spoke just then, when she asked that question, it seemed as though her voice had come from a metre away, somewhere to the right of her. She involuntarily looked to the side, and immediately felt bilious again, grabbed for the bowl.

'You're concussed,' he said. 'It'll pass, but you need to rest.' He took the bowl away from her and pushed her back on to the pillow. He ran his hand over her head, smoothed back her hair. His hand was dry, with a slightly dangerous scent.

Ginny closed her eyes. If you didn't look at him, if you listened to his voice and felt the touch of his hand on your head, warm on the side of your face, he was a great comfort. She had concussion and a great comfort. She didn't mind the shaven head, but the tattoos were over the top. Tattooing was still forbidden in some of the states. If she'd met him in a dark lane at night, she'd have run a mile. Odd, then, that she meets him in a strange bed in a room that could never be a hospital, and she feels no fear at all. Well, maybe a little.

She couldn't remember how she'd got there, what had happened to her. But she felt no sense of urgency. She was sure everything would become clear. She opened her eyes and looked back at him, tried to get behind the tattoos. She was looking for vulnerability, because if someone can be vulnerable, they can be compassionate, and they also have the capacity for change. His eyes were dark and unfathomable, and Ginny's own vision was not reliable. The perimeter of the man's face was unstable, the more she looked at him the more he merged with the background.

'Try to rest,' he said. She closed her eyes and played his voice back in her head. She felt herself slip into sleep with the sound of his voice, the memory of his touch, and that dangerous scent jingling away in her brain. There was compassion there. The tattoos were a mask, she thought, something to hide behind. The tattoos were a pity, but they wouldn't keep her awake. He wasn't pretty, but he wasn't a monster.

Janus was a Roman god who had no direct counterpart in Greece. He had given his name to January, the first month of the year, because from there he could look forward to the coming year, and he could look back to the year that had passed. Nothing is simply one thing to Janus. He is always aware of the thing itself, but at the same time he looks behind it, sees the other side.

She drifted in and out of consciousness. When she half-opened her eyes she was aware of him sitting by the bed, the two faces of Janus on the front of his T-shirt. Her mind played tricks, so that occasionally she would see Janus himself sitting there, wearing a T-shirt with the shaven head of a tattooed man on the front.

When she surfaced again she asked for the bowl. He reached under the bed and gave it to her. He'd washed it with pine disinfectant. She didn't vomit again, there was nothing left in her stomach. She belched long and loud, set up an amplified echo in the bowl, and felt she had to apologize. He shrugged his shoulders.

He told her he was called Stone Lewis and she wondered if she would remember it, manage to hold the two names in her head. Or would she always call him Janus?

'I'm Ginny,' she said. 'I must look a sight.' No make-up. She was out in the world without make-up of any kind, no barrier between world and self.

'Yes, Ginny. Virginia Rebecca Bradshaw. I went through your bag. You don't look as bad as you feel.'

He knew everything about her. He'd undressed her. He was a stranger; all she knew about him was his name. His name and his tattoos. Ginny was angry, suddenly aware that her fists were balled up tight. Her temper was not always controllable, even when it would've been to her advantage.

69

But she let it go this time, surrendered to the greater power of lassitude. She saw the bundles of letters from Juliet at his feet.

'Did you read them?' she asked.

He nodded. 'Couldn't resist.' There was playfulness around his eyes. 'Thought I might learn something about the girl in my bed. You weren't talking at the time.'

Ginny chose her words carefully. There was a hint of lasciviousness when he mentioned the bed. She didn't want him to get the wrong idea. The words came out clipped, even harsh. 'And did you? Learn anything?'

'Not a lot,' he said. 'Name and address. I learned that you don't carry a diabetic or steroid card. No medic-alert bracelet. I thought you might sleep it off, but I wanted to make sure there wouldn't be any complications.'

All that was straightforward. She couldn't think why she'd thought he was lascivious a moment ago. She wanted to sleep again.

'I feel like shit,' she said. He thought he knew everything, but he didn't know she was pregnant. Everything seemed to be all right down there, despite the beating and the concussion. There had been moments when she was vomiting, Ginny had been certain she was aborting. But the foetus was still there, developing and growing. 'Is there some make-up in my bag?'

'You don't need it. You need to rest. I'm going out to work in a while. You can stay here and sleep.'

'That won't be necessary.' Blood ran every which way in her head. No one was going to tell her what to do. 'I can get a taxi.'

Stone shook his head. 'You won't make it.' He looked different, quieter. He had sharp, light-blue, Nordic eyes.

Her spirit wanted to prove him wrong, but she knew her legs wouldn't hold her. 'I'll have to let the hotel know,' she said. 'They'll wonder what's happened.'

It was like he didn't hear her. He stared at her, watched her face, her eyes, as though he'd never seen anything living and breathing before.

Ginny wanted her make-up bag. She raised her eyebrows. 'Hello, in there.'

'What?'

'The hotel. They'll wonder what's happened. I should telephone them.'

'There's no phone here. I'll ring them from work.'

She looked up into his face. She phased out the tattoos, kept his eyes in focus. 'Juliet,' she said. 'My friend, who wrote the letters. She's disappeared. I couldn't find what happened to her in the States, so I came over to look for her. No one seems to know where she is.'

Stone shrugged. 'People move on.'

'I know that,' she told him. 'But Juliet would've told me if she was moving. She told me everything. I think something's happened to her.'

'Maybe,' he said, but with no conviction in his voice. 'You won't be able to do anything for a couple of days. After that you can go look for her.'

'I don't know what happened last night,' Ginny said. 'I'm affected by the moon.'

'You were pissed and somebody slugged you with a straight right. No moon involved.' He hit her with a smile, which managed to push its way past the tattoos. 'You're cream crackered,' he said. 'Try to rest.'

12

THE INNER FLASH

Stone passed the diamond-black Scorpio Granada parked outside the flat and walked off along the street towards System.ini. Peripheral consciousness told him the guy sitting in the car might be watching the flat, but it didn't seem likely. Don't be paranoid, but don't be stupid either.

Spring Bank was lined with shoestring businesses. There was a Pizza Joint, a couple of Indian takeaways, two bargain centres, a house-clearance specialist, and several loan sharks. For the most part it was abandoned shops. The only established businesses on the strip, which was lined with shop-fronts, were Cliff Pratt's bicycle shop and the Spring Bank Tavern. Outside the basement flats and between the iron railings that surrounded them, litter bloomed like tropical vegetation. Apple Cars, the taxi office, was luminous with orange, green and blue paint. Spring Bank might've been something once, long time ago, a wide boulevard with grand houses, but now it was a wasteland.

Stone wore a pair of green trousers he'd got from Aunt Nell's catalogue. Big mistake. They'd been too long when they arrived, but he'd taken them up and now the cuffs fell just right on his DMs. Still didn't feel comfortable, though, because the waistband was too high. When they fitted his crotch the waistband was up around his lower chest, and when he pulled them down to where his waist was, the crotch of the trousers got dangerously near his knees. If he ever went in for a career as a circus clown, they'd come in useful, but for now they just ruined his day. Couldn't bring himself to throw them away, though, not before he'd finished the payments.

He'd thought about clothes since getting out of the joint, at first as a disguise. He suspected everyone knew he was an ex-con because of what he wore. After spending years in prison clobber and seeing everyone around you dressed the same, you get to associate the clothes with the lifestyle. The first threads he put on when he got home were the ones his mother had kept for him in the wardrobe. Old clothes from another time and place, made him look like Robert Mitchum, Burt Lancaster, one of those guys. It took a while before he realized that it wasn't the threads that made him look like an ex-con, it was something way deeper than that, something embedded in his movements, his general demeanour. It was the years and years of being banged away which had lodged itself in his thoughts, in his attitude, in his mind-set, and which informed on him whenever he was out mixing it with the world.

Stone had the style of an ex-con, and if he wore a space suit, there'd be people who'd see right through it and know where he'd been. He watched other people, and tried to work out how they did it, where it was they kept their style, so they looked easy with it.

He knew it wasn't about clothes, but he used clothes, experimented with clothes, tried to make himself conscious of cut and colour, because that was all part of the learning experience. Style wasn't about looking, it was about *being*. And *being* was about getting to the core of yourself, a long and a dangerous journey. But, as a starter, he needed threads that felt comfortable.

Maybe he should try America, like the Chinese girl? Perhaps there was room there for someone like him. Forget about England and its badly fitting trousers from catalogue stores, strike out for the land that spawned Dashiell

Hammett and Robert Johnson. A place where he had no past, no heritage to cart around.

But America wasn't really what he wanted. It wouldn't help to swap one country for another. If there was such a thing as freedom, it lay in the possibility of becoming a citizen of the world.

Los Angeles, maybe, but New York as well, and Berlin and Paris and Barcelona.

Stone felt he should go everywhere, visit all those cities in the world. Live amongst the urban populations and see how they coped with personal freedom and imprisonment and style and somehow put it all together.

Because one thing was certain, freedom didn't lie in uniformity; it only blossomed in diversity.

Sounded nice. Forget the past and go away. Except you can't forget the past, not when you've spent a large part of it planning the future. And when the future involves killing someone. All the cities of the world might have been possible if he didn't have a score to settle, another life to take.

He took out his keys and let himself into System.ini. He switched on the water boiler. He got a clean apron from the laundry cupboard and tied it around his waist. It covered the green trousers and significantly brightened up the day. He retrieved the float from a saucepan in the kitchen and counted it into the till. Then he turned on the terminals, made coffee, and sat behind the counter to drink it while he waited for Eve to arrive. After a couple of sips he reached for the phone and rang Aunt Nell, told her there was a woman at home in his bed. Told her she was injured, been beaten up.

'Who beat her?'

'Dunno. Some guy.'

'It wasn't you, Stone?'

'I told you. She was on my doorstep.'

'OK, I'll take a look. See if she needs anything.'

There was a woman at home in his bed. Stone shook his head, shook it really hard, but when he'd finished shaking it, the truth hadn't shifted. Ginny Bradshaw was still there, he hadn't dreamed it, she'd been there all night, and he hadn't touched her, and she was still there this morning. He was going to ring her hotel and tell them she wouldn't be there today. So she'd still be in his room when he got home tonight. He didn't believe for a minute that the moon affected her. What was all that shit about? She'd been drinking. She'd got pissed and someone had tried to take advantage of her. Nothing to do with the moon, unless she meant moonshine.

But people make excuses; unless you know them well, they don't tell you how it really is. Stone Lewis didn't. They'd run a mile if he came out and told them. 'Oh, yeah, I was in prison for killing someone.'

Stone didn't speak about it. What was there to say? 'I lost my rag.' He hadn't known he was going to kill the guy before it happened. He hadn't intended to use that much force. But he had. And now he knew something that most people didn't know. It was possible. A possibility for everyone.

Still, there was zilch to say about it. 'I want to put it all behind me, but it seems to've kept abreast of me.' At school he'd been a marathon runner, learned that if you wanted to be among the leaders at the end of a long race, you had to wait, bide your time. There was a moment, in a long race, when a light flashed inside your head. It might happen so quickly you didn't notice it, and then you were lost. But if you kept awake and concentrated, you'd see the flash, and you'd know to lengthen your stride, to start going away from the field, and you'd know that nobody would be able to go with you. Because you took it on when it was right for you and wrong for the others, they'd lose heart, and you'd know the race was in your pocket.

That's what Stone had been doing since they let him out of stir, and he was doing it now.

He was nurturing a tiny fire inside himself, making sure that it never died. A flame of revenge on Shooter for what Shooter had done to Stone's mother, and for the humiliation that Shooter had continued to heap on Stone himself.

There would come a time when Shooter and Stone would stand and face each other and only one of them would walk away from the confrontation. Stone knew this to be true. He wasn't a fortune teller and he couldn't see into the future, but he would use his will, and for almost as long as he could remember, that was the way it had been directed.

He would bide his time, wait for that inner flash to happen, then he'd kill Shooter Wilde and be away, leaving the past behind. It would swirl out behind him like the exhaust fumes of an old bus.

He was emptying the dishwasher when Eve arrived. They acknowledged each other but didn't talk. Eve was his employer. Eve Caldwell. Thirty-nine-year-old divorcee, bisexual, a life-long member of the Labour Party until Tony Blair was elected leader. Then she resigned and opened System.ini. Eve was a freedom fighter who saw prisons as a political tool, a necessary part of a repressive system that would be dismantled in the future dawn of a humanitarian socialism. That's how Stone had got the job. Positive discrimination. Wasn't always easy working for someone who was wacky, but a job was a job.

When everything was ready, Stone put on the Robert Johnson CD and opened the door. 'You want coffee?' he asked.

'Yeah.' She stood next to him while he poured the coffee

into two mugs. She looked at his forehead. 'Is that where they've been working?' she asked. She reached up and touched his forehead.

Stone flinched at the touch. 'Yeah. Can you see anything?'

'Not much.' She put her head closer to get a really good look at him. 'If I didn't know there'd been something there, I wouldn't've noticed. Slight discoloration of the skin.'

Before he'd left the joint, some of Shooter's cronies had held him down and tattooed the word SCUM on his forehead. The teardrop and the bullet wounds had been added as an after-thought. 'Could've disfigured you with a razor,' Shooter had told him. 'But I don't hold a grudge.'

'It'll fade in time,' he said to Eve. 'It's called paradoxical darkening. They used two lasers, and one of them interacted with the ink.'

Eve smiled. 'Won't be long, then, before you stop frightening the customers.'

'A while, yet. I can only afford one treatment a week.'

Eve took her coffee and sat at a table. 'I could help with the expense.'

'It's not your problem,' he said.

But she wouldn't drop it. 'While you've got tattoos on your face, you're not ideally suited to work in a café. It's in my interests to get you cleaned up as soon as possible.'

'Mine, too,' he said. 'It's not gonna take long.'

'If I needed a driver, I'd expect to pay for driving lessons. Don't be proud, Stone. It's old-fashioned.'

'They don't like to give more than two treatments a week,' he said. 'It's bad for the system, can make you sick.'

'OK,' she said.

'OK, what?'

'You pay for one and I'll pay for the other. You get to be beautiful, and I get more customers.'

Robert Johnson went into *Kind Hearted Woman Blues*.

13

MR BIG

Aunt Nell left the Shōgun where it was and got her bike out of the shed. She put her handbag in the basket and kicked off along the street. The sun was pale, being filtered through a low cloud, but it warmed her face as she rode along Spring Bank towards Stone's flat.

He'd been a vulnerable child, always falling over. Sally, his mother, Nell's sister, insisted that he'd inherited weak ankles from their maternal grandmother, but Nell didn't believe it. The little Stone fell over all the time because he didn't look where he was going. He tried to walk through walls.

Towards the end of adolescence he'd hung around with Shooter Wilde's crowd, slipped into criminal company as easily as a silver spoon into cream. Nell blamed Sally, his mother, for that development. Sally was her sister, and Nell loved her dearly, but Sally had always been a floozy, almost from the day she was born. And it had been Sally's dalliance with Shooter that had led to Stone's first introduction to criminal company.

And there was a time, though it was short-lived, when the older Shooter had become a paternal symbol for young Stone, and in a way both of them had benefited from it. Shooter adopted Stone as a personal responsibility, saw the boy's strengths and did what he could to develop them. Stone, on the other hand, rose to the challenge of pleasing Shooter. Where in the past he would have given up the fight, he now strove to maintain the older man's faith in him.

Shooter was Mister Big in the neighbourhood. Drove an American car, white and red Pontiac, and always had a wad of notes in his pocket. He was a god to the young Stone.

But the relationship between Shooter and Sally was founded on a series of weak and corrupted links. Shooter could never keep his zip up, and it wasn't long before he was cheating on Sally with a string of younger women. Sally could have accepted her humiliation gracefully and faded into the background, but she had to go and screw a couple of Shooter's closest mates, and then blag it around the town. Sally and Shooter went at it hammer and tongs, and the one caught in the middle was Stone.

Nell locked her bike to the railings and fished in her bag for the key to Stone's door. She knocked and let herself in. 'Hello-o,' she called, dropped the last 'o' a full tone, and liked the sound of it so much she did it again as she made for the bedroom. 'Hello-o.'

The girl in Stone's bed had been sleeping, but she was awake now. Japanese? Why hadn't he mentioned that? But on second thoughts, not Japanese. Malayan? Her hair was a luxuriant black, tumbling over and round her bruised face.

'Don't try to get up, love,' Nell told her. 'Stone asked me to call in, see if you needed anything.' Nell sat on the edge of the bed and placed her hand on the girl's forehead. 'Something to eat? A drink? How d'you feel?'

'I don't know if I can keep anything down. Maybe a drink.' No Asian accent, maybe a touch of American in there, but the bulk of it was north-east England, Hull, west side of the river.

'I'll put the kettle on.' Nell walked through to the kitchen. Beautiful eyes. Deep and black. And the tone of her voice, the way she shaped her words. There was education there. Stone must've thought it was his birthday when he found her on the doorstep. Nell had nursed a secret dream that Stone would find a girl who wasn't a topless dancer, or someone who was temporarily on the game, or whose husband had scored a five stretch for GBH. Someone who wasn't a slag or a tart and who had more than a couple of brain cells. It didn't seem like a lot to hope for, but lately she'd wondered if she wasn't over-ambitious.

Stone should've stayed away from criminal company when he came out of prison, but Nell knew he was working for Shooter again. He'd got the flat and the work at System.ini, but he was doing odd jobs for Shooter as well, collecting bad debts and rents from the girls, sometimes driving when one of Shooter's regulars was away. He seemed to manage, but she hadn't seen a lot of life or hope or interest in his eyes. He had few friends or commitments, and Nell had lain awake nights fretting that he would slip back into the stream that he knew.

This morning, when he had rung her from work, told her about the girl in his flat, there had been something of the old Stone in his voice. Only a hint of it, but nevertheless it had been there, a bubbling, playful tone which recognized no gathering clouds and saw a clear blue sky stretching towards the horizon.

The girl, Ginny, was weary. She smiled, but said little, listened politely as Nell rambled on about Stone and his mother, about his job at System.ini. She drank the tea that Nell made, then settled back down into the bed and closed her eyes. Nell left her, promising to return the next day.

She wouldn't be able to tell Sally about her visit, because Sally would never understand why Stone had asked Nell to go see the girl instead of his mother. She sighed. Families were the most complicated things in the universe. Scientists had dug deeper and deeper into the nature of different molecules, atoms, genes, chromosomes, all the tiny stuff that were the building blocks of different organisms. But the most complicated of them all, and the most inaccessible, was the little unit they were born into and that they would spend the rest of their days trying to fathom.

If and when Stone decided to introduce Ginny to his mother, Nell would have to play dumb, pretend that she'd never met the girl before, never even heard of her.

When she got home she rang Stone at System.ini. 'Beautiful girl,' she said. 'Gorgeous.'

'How was she?'

'OK. Tired. I've never seen anything as beautiful.'

Stone laughed. 'Yeah,' he said. Just that one word, but caught up in it was all the excitement she hadn't really heard from him since he was a boy. When she put the phone down she dug out an old Beatles album and played *Love Me Do*. First time she'd done that in maybe fifteen years.

They were like Beauty and the Beast. Ginny was a beauty, and Stone the beast. Except he wasn't a beast, he was a real dazzler behind the tattoos.

That was all down to Shooter Wilde. He'd had Stone disfigured when they were in prison. The perverted bastard had slashed Sally's face with a razor, and then got his minions to work on Stone's face. And all because Sally had played around with a couple of his soldiers.

Nell thought about that for the rest of the afternoon. Long after the Beatles had stopped singing their songs, she got out of her chair and switched off the low drone from the stereo system. If she was a man, she'd take Shooter on. Make him think twice about messing with her family. But she wasn't a man; she was well on the way to being an old woman.

14

A SWALLOW ON THE WING

The Scorpio was still there, parked on the other side of the road now, but there was no one in it. It was a small piece of the day that didn't fit. He went over and had a look through the windows. There was a pair of leather driving gloves on the passenger seat and an AA map-book thrown in the back. Nothing to indicate who the driver might be, or what his business was.

Ginny was sitting up in bed when he got inside. She'd brushed her hair, and it lay like a sleek black pelt on her shoulders.

'How're you feeling?' he asked.

'Few aches and pains. I got up to use the bathroom. My legs're like jelly; I'm as lame as a husband's excuse. Oh, and your aunt came, made me some tea.'

He sat on the side of the bed and looked into her eyes, make sure she could focus. 'Hungry?' he asked.

'I haven't eaten all day. Suppose I should try something. Did you ring the hotel?'

'Yeah. They'll hold your room a couple of days. If it's gonna be longer than that, you'll have to collect your bags.'

He went through to the kitchen and warmed the creamed celery soup he'd brought from work. He cut a couple of slices of granary bread and brought it through to her. He used the breadboard as a tray. 'See if you can keep this down,' he said.

She sipped from the spoon. She tore a piece of bread and

dipped it into the soup. Stone watched her lips, saw how the soup coated them until she licked them clean.

'Did you grow up here?' he asked.

She swallowed. 'No, but I used to think so. Had to go away to do it.'

'Yeah,' he said absently. 'So did I.'

'How do you know about concussion?' she asked. 'You some kind of medic?'

Stone shook his head. 'I did a course. I watched somebody have a heart attack, and I didn't know what to do. So I took a first-aid course.'

They fell silent. Ginny ate her soup and Stone watched.

'Where was that?' she asked.

He knew she meant was it in Hull. She was making conversation, asking him where he did his first-aid course. So he told her.

'I was in prison for eleven years,' he said. 'The guy I shared a cell with had a heart attack one night. He died. The doctor told me if I'd known what to do, he wouldn't've died. So I applied to take a course. I learned about heart attacks, scalding, poisoning, broken bones, shock, all the things that can happen to people. One of them was concussion.'

'Was that where you got the tattoos?'

Stone smiled. He hadn't told too many people about being in prison. But of the ones he'd told, she was the first not to ask, straight off, what he'd done to get himself such a long sentence. She'd ask soon enough, maybe that'd be her next question. But she hadn't asked yet.

His hand went up to his face and he fingered the image of the teardrop under his left eye. 'Guys get bored inside,' he said. 'Out of their minds. They look around for something to destroy. They wanna hurt someone, maim someone. They feel bad inside, and they wanna make everyone else feel bad.'

He watched her eyes flicker from the teardrop to the blue bullet holes at his temples. Then down to his hands. 'I didn't think they were professional,' she said, engaging his eyes.

He didn't want her to be frightened of him. He didn't think she was frightened, but he didn't want to take the chance. Anyway, he was talking now, the words tumbling out of him, like they'd been banged away inside of him, and someone had just blown away the door.

'I'm thirty-three years old,' he said. 'And I haven't had a life. You don't live in prison; you stagger from one day to the next. You dream time away; you take drugs, fight, sleep. And the people you're with, other cons, they don't have time for you, there's a million other people they'd rather be with.

'How does someone get to be as old as me and still not have a life? It's incredible. It's like I've been in pause mode. I got switched off back then, and nothing's happened since. I haven't been anywhere. Like you, you live in LA. Christ, I haven't lived in England. The places I've been, I never even saw them, apart from the occasional glimpse through prison bars. But LA, Jesus. Somewhere as big as that, or Prague, say, Oslo, New York, that's where I should be. One of those places.

'Since I got out I've been looking for people who know how to live. Been trying to meet people with some style, some idea about life. I want to be different to all the people I know, all the people I've ever met, d'you know what I mean? I want to get away from Hull and England and everything that's grey.'

'There's plenty of grey in LA,' Ginny said. 'When I'm over there I sometimes long to get back to England.'

Stone laughed. 'I know that. I'd probably be the same after a while. Longing to get back to the grey. But at least I'd've been and done it.'

He looked down to see her stroking the back of his hand. She was tracing the outline of the Gurkha sword with her ring finger. Her nails were manicured; the cuticles pulled down to reveal tiny half-moons. He wanted to lift her hand to his lips.

'You've been kind to me,' she said.

Stone didn't reply. When he'd undressed her last night, he'd pushed the sexual tension aside, but he couldn't do that for ever. He wanted to tell her that, that he hadn't been kind. That as soon as she was feeling better he'd be trying to get into her pants. That's how it was. Eleven years was a long time. The girl said nothing, and Stone listened to her breathing. When he looked up at her face, her eyes were closed. She opened them and returned his stare. There was no invitation in her eyes, no question. Way back there was weariness, the lingering effects of the concussion.

'I killed a man,' he said quietly. 'Long time ago.'

She breathed deeply, took in more oxygen than he thought she could hold. She looked as secure as a turkey when the wassailers are out. He could smell her fear. It was too early to tell her. If she'd been fit, she'd be halfway along the street by now. He watched her absorb the fact that he'd killed someone, and he saw her file it away in memory. She closed the filing cabinet and turned to meet his gaze. Her fingers touched the sketchpad on the bed and flicked it open. When she spoke, she'd lost the fear of a moment before. 'I've been working today,' she said. The pages were covered with miniatures of butterflies and moths, fantastic insects, frogs and lizards. The last page had a life-size drawing of a swallow on the wing, forked tail, red throat, with a deep blue back. There was a quality of feathers about it, the warmth of down. You looked at it and expected it to leave the page, to soar away out of the window and up into the heavens.

'That's beautiful,' he said.

'Thank you, sir.' There was a weary laughter in her voice.

'No, I really like it. Prisoners like birds, they're free, they can move around.' He picked up the sketchpad to get a better look. 'D'you do this for a living?'

'They're just ideas,' she said. 'I work with ceramics, brooches, jewellery.' She took the sketchpad from him and flicked to the front. 'I made a brooch like this,' she said, 'and sent it to Juliet last Christmas.' She showed him a drawing of a ladybird, six spots on its back, only one centimetre long, but the parts perfectly proportioned.

'Juliet. That the girl you're looking for?'

Ginny nodded. 'My friend.'

'It's a very red ladybird,' he said.

'Yes. Juliet likes red.'

He looked at it for a moment, then turned back to the life-size swallow.

'You can have it if you like,' she said.

'Hell, no, it's your work.'

She tore the drawing from the sketchpad and handed it to him. 'Put it on the wall. Every time you see it, you'll think of me.'

'Jesus,' he said. 'I'll get it framed.'

She sank back on the pillow and closed her eyes.

Stone got a plastic carrier out of the cupboard under the sink and put a couple of paperback books in it, a novel called *A City on a Hill*, and some short stories by Erskine Caldwell, *Men and Women*. Something inside him wanted to hold on to *Men and Women*, but he put it in the bag anyway. The things you liked pinned you down harder than the things that didn't touch you. He picked up a key-ring and a pair of acupuncture balls from the shelf and put them in the bag. There was a green sweater in his wardrobe, an imitation snake-skin belt and a multi-coloured silk tie. He put them in the bag, too, and placed the bag next to the door so he would remember to drop it off at a charity shop in the morning.

Ginny woke two hours later and Stone fixed her some cocoa. He sat in the chair and watched her sip from the mug. There was duck meat in the corners of her eyes and she looked like she'd been beaten up. She was the best thing he'd seen in a long time. Couldn't remember seeing anything better. Untouchable, though. You couldn't just take the things you wanted. There were laws. You had to wait and plan and get everyone's consent.

'On Juliet's birthday I rang her to say, "Have a good day," but all I could get was the disconnected signal. I tried again the next day and the day after that, but it was the same. I rang a friend of hers called Beige, she lives here in Hull. Beige told me she was worried, too, because she hadn't seen Juliet for over a week. No one knew where she was.

'I just dropped everything. I threw some things into a case and caught the next flight to England. I didn't know what else to do.'

Stone watched a lone teardrop run down her cheek.

'And it's true,' Ginny said. 'She's disappeared. Vanished. I can't find a trace of her.'

'I might be able to help,' he told her.

'How?'

'I don't know, but I'm not doing anything else. If two of us're looking, it must be better than one. People don't just vanish, I'm sure we'll find her.'

'I want to get up,' she said. 'Just for a while. And tomorrow I'm going outside.'

She eased herself to the side of the bed and slid her legs out. The old letch in him reared its head. She reached for her skirt and sniffed at it, then dropped it on the floor. 'D'you have anything I can wear?' she asked. 'I'll do some washing tomorrow.'

He went to the cupboard and looked at his clothes. He

couldn't imagine her wearing any of them. Maybe he should just tell her: *I'd like to fuck you.* Put all his cards on the table. 'You spoke in a foreign language,' he said. 'When you were unconscious. Sounded like German.'

'That's strange,' she said. 'I don't know a lot of German. You sure it wasn't French?'

'Could've been. I didn't really catch it.'

'Spanish?'

He turned to look at her. 'How many languages d'you speak?'

'Four or five,' she said. 'I've got a Russian friend in LA. But I'm not fluent.'

Stone thought if he had only one word with which to describe her, that was the one he'd choose. Fluent. Ginny Fluent.

He found her a pair of jeans and a checked shirt, both of them four sizes too big. 'I don't mind,' she said, tucking the shirt inside the waistband of the jeans and rolling up the bottoms of the legs. 'You have to think positively about yourself, otherwise you look like a sack whatever you're wearing. Just tell yourself you can carry it, and you'll get away with it.'

She twirled around, but reached for the bed to steady herself. 'Uh, oh, maybe not ready for that yet. I feel dizzy.'

She had it packed into every move she made, it was there when she was quiet, and when she was giving it mouth. He'd thought she had it when he first saw her in a bundle on his doorstep, and now she was dizzy, almost ready to fall down, but she was dizzy with style.

15

HEARTBREAK

Danny Boy, one of Shooter's inner circle, crept up on Heartbreak that morning. Usually Heartbreak would have been off the estate and back home in his house on Newland Avenue by ten o'clock, but a cat had got in with Shooter's chickens in the night, and he'd had to stay behind to clear up, get the birds settled down.

'If they stop laying,' Danny Boy said, 'Shooter's gonna be pissed off.' He was leaning against a corner of the shed, paring his finger nails with a curved-blade hunting knife, his face looking as though it had been sprayed with blackheads. 'And if Shooter's pissed off, he takes it out on whoever's closest. Might be Cuddles, in which case I don't care. But it might be me, in which case I'll turn up here one night and skin you alive.' He sent a poisoned smile across the gap which separated him from Heartbreak, and Heartbreak swallowed it. If he played this right, he could be back home in half an hour without any bruises, but if he made a wrong move, Danny Boy would nail him to the door. Violence was one of Danny Boy's skills, second only to his persistent brown-nosing of the boss.

'They won't stop laying,' he said. 'It'll be all right.'

Danny Boy concentrated on his nails. He held the smile on his face, but he didn't reply or look at Heartbreak. When he heard Shooter approaching, he ducked inside the shed.

Shooter came up to the chicken run with a tall redheaded man. They both ignored Heartbreak. Shooter's hair was cropped close to his head. He was scowling, looking like he wanted to hurt someone. 'She's a Chink,' said the redhead. 'Maybe half-caste. Dunno. But she must be holed up in the flat.'

'Where?'

'On Spring Bank.'

'Could be dead?' said Shooter. He cleared his throat and gobbed through the chicken wire.

'No, it wasn't that bad. I reckon she's inside the flat, and the guy's looking after her.'

Shooter kicked out at a small blackcurrant bush. 'Sort it,' he said. His lips were a thin line. 'I want her out of my hair.'

'OK,' said the redhead.

'Piss off,' Shooter told him.

When the redhead had gone Shooter stood by the wire for a couple of minutes watching a bantam hen scratching in the dirt. Eventually he focused on Heartbreak. 'I heard something about a cat,' he said.

'Yeah, got in in the night,' Heartbreak told him. 'Took two birds.'

Shooter thought about it for a couple of shakes, then he turned towards the house. Without looking back he said, 'If I don't get me eggs, I'll throw you to the fucking dogs.'

Danny Boy's chuckle came from the interior of the shed. He reappeared, still paring his finger nails. 'See what I mean?' he said. 'The boss's keen on his eggs.' He looked back towards the house. 'The redhead is called Harvey,' he said. 'He's a cop.'

Heartbreak stuffed a few loose feathers into a sack. He affected not to have registered the information. Knowing too much always led to trouble. He walked into a fence post, gave himself a black eye. Couldn't understand why it was he felt as though he'd been pushed.

When he'd finished with the chickens, Heartbreak got his coat from the shed and walked through the garden towards the house. Shooter was with Cuddles in the old-fashioned terrace.

Heartbreak slowed down and stood under a maple for a few minutes. Shooter was sitting on a wrought-iron chair with his legs spread wide, and he held out his arms towards the girl. Cuddles smiled. She looked as though she was twenty, but some of the guys reckoned she was no more than sixteen.

She went over to Shooter and sat on his knee, and Shooter enfolded her in his arms and buried his face in her neck. He was tender with her, as though he was afraid she'd break.

Shooter groaned and said she felt good, and Cuddles sighed, and then the two of them started sucking face like a couple of teenagers.

Heartbreak moved away, started for home.

Later in the day Heartbreak scored a bunch of cut flowers and took them round to Nell's house. He held them behind his back until she opened the door, then thrust them towards her and watched the look of amazement on her face.

'For me?' she said. 'I haven't had flowers since . . . I don't know . . . since I was a girl.'

He pushed them into her arms. Watched as she leaned forward and planted a big wet one on his cheek.

'Come in,' she said. 'I'll find a vase. Oh, Heartbreak, they're lovely.'

He followed her into the house, feeling a warm smile spreading itself over his face. Once or twice lately he'd called round and offered to clean her car, or weed the garden, and usually she'd looked disappointed when she opened the door and saw it was him. But the flowers seemed to have made him more attractive.

Heartbreak had been grieving the loss of the love of his

life for forty years, and had not had time for another serious affair. Whenever he'd felt the urge he'd gone to see a tart and got rid of it as quick as possible. But in the last weeks Nell had seemed to look better every time he'd seen her.

She found a vase and put the flowers in it, placed it in the centre of the table. 'Brightened up the day,' she said. 'I can't think of anything nicer.' She looked at him with her head cocked to one side. 'What happened to your eye?'

'Walked into somefing,' he said. 'Down at Shooter's.'

She shook her head. 'Shooter Wilde. Why d'you work for him?'

'It's a living,' he said.

'You don't have to get yourself cut up to make a living these days. There're laws.'

'Aw, I can manage Shooter,' Heartbreak said. 'Been keeping my end up with guys like him since Eve went into the fruit and vegetable business.'

'A knee-slapper, that, Heartbreak. You're making my eyes water.' She leaned over the table and moved the vase of flowers fractionally to one side. 'D'you come across Stone?'

Heartbreak shook his head. 'Shooter won't have him on the estate. Just does odd jobs on the outside. Can't be earning much. How's he doing?'

'OK,' she said. 'He's not dependent on Shooter. Got a part time job on the Internet. Got himself a flat down Spring Bank, and now there's a girlfriend.'

'I'll keep me fingers crossed for him.'

'Lovely girl,' said Nell. 'Chinese. Somebody beat her up and left her on his doorstep.'

Heartbreak did a double-take. He didn't say anything. He leaned forward and took a good whiff of the flowers on the table. 'I've got to go,' he said. 'Just wanted to drop these off on you.' He made for the door.

'One thing,' he said, as he stood on the path. 'What's

Stone's address? I could call round and see him sometime. Talk about old times.'

16

AN OVERGROWN, QUIVERING COP NOSE

Ginny opened her eyes and for the first time she wasn't disoriented in that room. The clock on the chair said it was 13.30. Outside in the street a dog barked and a cyclist rang his bell. Someone swore. Inside the flat there was only silence. She sat up and found a note on the bed. His handwriting was careful, studied, as though he didn't believe anyone would understand it.

> Dear Ginny,
>   Gone to work. Use anything you find in the flat, food, etc.
> I'll bring something to eat when I come home.
>   Stone

She found muesli and milk. Must eat now she was feeding two. As she moved around the flat she went warily, fearing the dizziness might return, but her head was clear. Her neck was stiff, but otherwise she felt like her old self.

Odd, though, how life leads you along by the nose, and then one morning you wake up in a strange flat with a convicted murderer. Ginny wasn't afraid of him; the thought that he might harm her in some way had presented itself fleetingly. But whatever had led him to kill in the past was not a factor in their relationship.

After breakfast she washed her clothes and hung them to dry. She sat at the table and tried to gather her thoughts.

How did she come to be here? Was she any closer to finding Juliet now than she had been before she left LA?

She'd spoken to Beige, and she'd telephoned Juliet's old boyfriend, Harry, who was living in London. But neither of them had been able to help. Then she'd gone to the police, who already had Juliet registered as a missing person. Juliet and her son. She'd been felt up in the police station by the eyes of a racist cop. Eyes that masked hatred with pity. Eyes that reached through her clothes to the flesh beneath. An overgrown, quivering cop nose that imagined it had captured her scent.

'I know what you're doing,' she'd told him. 'I'm not stupid.'

'Miss?' The wreckage of his smile still smouldered.

Ginny wanted to hit out at him. Wipe the smugness from his face. 'You're disgusting,' she said. She'd spoken loudly, the WPC at the next desk looked up from her papers.

The cop flushed. His eyes now as cold as a banker's heart. 'Trying to make me look foolish?' he said.

Ginny turned for the door. 'God's already beaten us both to it.'

After that she'd gone to see her mother and got into drinking, not knowing what else to do. Then she was beaten up.

Why?

Was the beating a warning? Had she inadvertently come close to the truth about Juliet's disappearance? Had someone been worried by her, and decided to stop her looking for Juliet?

Surely not. And yet, what other explanation could there be?

Beige was a young woman with a small son. Harry, Juliet's old boyfriend, was two hundred miles away. And anyway, they'd both been open and friendly, worried too. Ginny could think of no reason why either of them would have anything to hide, nor how either of them could be behind Juliet's disappearance or her own beating. Beige had been friendly, even laid off a little ganja on her.

Around four o'clock she decided to go for a walk outside, test her legs a little more. She made herself up, using the large mirror in the bathroom. Foundation applied with fingers, then a strong pink blusher from cheekbone to temple. She brushed her eyebrows into shape and darkened them with a black pencil, adding white eyeshadow within the lower lashes. She finished with a bright pink lipstick, blotted it with toilet tissue and applied the lipstick again. She dressed in the clothes she had borrowed from Stone, but couldn't find anything to wear on her feet. Another mystery. Her bag and its contents were intact. Although her clothes had been stained with blood and vomit, they were all there. So where were her DMs?

What kind of naff mugger was it that unlaced her boots and ran off with them into the night, leaving behind all her cash? OK, they were nice boots, the leather was soft and they fitted well, but she'd never thought of getting them insured.

When Stone returned with a large quiche, that was the first thing she said to him. 'He stole my boots. The guy who mugged me, he stole my boots. Can you believe that?'

'Ah,' Stone said, looking like he'd been caught shaking someone's piggy bank.

'Ah, what?' Ginny felt the tension in her throat, a swelling in her abdomen. Her fists clenched and unclenched at the sides of her thighs

'I hid them,' he said. He went to the wardrobe and retrieved the boots from the top shelf. He held them out to her. 'Sorry,' he said.

Ginny blew up. She didn't have a choice. Suddenly she was a mistral, laying waste to everything around her. 'You *hid* my boots? You hid my fucking boots in the wardrobe.

Who the hell are you?' She took the boots from his outstretched hand and flung them across the room. 'I don't believe this,' she shouted. She flung herself at Stone, and he held both of her arms. She kicked at his shins, and he deposited her on the bed and sat on her.

'Let me go, you bastard.'

'You won't throw anything?'

'Just let me go.'

'You gonna calm down?'

'I'll fucking scream.'

'No change there, then.'

He released her and cast his eyes about the floor, glanced towards the door as if he might make a run for it. 'I didn't want you to leave.'

Ginny stood, then sat on the bed again. 'Jesus,' she said, trying to calm herself. 'Hid them! I can't believe it. I wanted to go for a walk this afternoon, out in the world, like other people. But I couldn't, because I didn't have any boots. How can you hide someone's boots? What is it with you?' She closed her eyes and counted to ten. When she opened them he was still there; he'd collected her boots from the other side of the room and held one in each hand. He was smiling, like it was a joke. She took the boots from him. When she spoke again her tone was more restrained. 'I don't think there's anything funny about it.'

He shook his head, still smiling. 'About as funny as the clap.'

'D'you wanna tell me why you hid my boots?'

'It was an impulse. After I found you, I thought you might disappear in the night. So I hid them. I meant to get them out again yesterday, leave them under the bed, but I forgot.'

'I've spent half the day wondering why a mugger ran off with my boots.'

'Foot-fetishist?'

The smile flitted over his face. Ginny could see there was a funny side to it, but she wasn't ready to laugh yet. It would take another five minutes at least.

He put the quiche in the oven and set the table. 'Hell of a temper,' he said. 'Could get you into trouble.' He put water in the kettle and set it to boil. Ginny sat on the bed with the boots in her lap, hugging them as though they were long-lost relations. In her mind she told him to go fuck himself. Her womb contracted and she sucked in a lungful of air. She dropped the boots and her hands went involuntarily towards her lower stomach. The contraction came again, sharper this time, then everything was still.

'Something wrong?' he asked.

Ginny shook her head. 'I must be hungry,' she lied.

'This is ready now,' he said eventually, putting the quiche on the table. 'D'you wanna eat over here?'

Ginny pushed her boots under the bed and walked to the table. She let him off the hook, gave him a smile because it felt right, and because she wanted to believe that he would be unable to function without one.

'You look better,' he said. 'You're made up.'

'Thanks.'

He continued to stare at her face.

'Something wrong?' she asked.

'I thought you looked good without the make-up.'

She flushed and said thanks again, but he kept on staring.

'Honk if you see something you like,' she said after he'd been staring at her for fifteen seconds.

'You don't need that much make-up.'

'My face,' she told him. 'My life. I'll wear as much make-up as I want. Are we going to eat?'

He cut the quiche exactly in two and transferred it to plates. 'I bought a frame,' he said. 'For the swallow.'

'Really?' she said, trying to sound normal and relaxed, as though she was sharing a meal with someone who hadn't hidden her boots and criticized her make-up. 'I'll mount it for you, see if we can brighten up this room.'

She watched him eat, the movement of his lean jaws, the dark hollows under his eyes. A question was begging at the periphery of her consciousness. How could she be sure that it wasn't Stone Lewis who had beaten her up? And if it had been him, was there a possibility that he'd do it again?

Ginny watched him chewing his food. The shaven head, the tattoos. What did she really know about him? Could she trust the guy?

17

THE NIGHT WE CALLED IT A DAY

'I started reading this today,' Ginny said. 'Found it by your bed.' She was flicking through an old Penguin paperback of *The Thin Man.*

It was half an hour before midnight. They'd finished framing her picture of the swallow and had hung it on the wall opposite the door, so it was the first thing that hit you when you walked into the flat.

Earlier, the old guy called Heartbreak had come to the door and taken Stone for a walk down the street. Private business. Ginny had only glimpsed Heartbreak for a moment, not long enough to form an impression, except that he had an impediment in his speech. That, and a bald spot – actually most of his head. Stone had come back alone and thoughtful, he had lit his small wood-burning stove, and the room was now muggy and warm, felt comfortable and intimate.

'Hammett,' he said. 'We couldn't get his books inside. There was a guy I shared with for a while; he was always talking Hammett novels, but I've had to wait years before I could read them.'

'It's an allegory, isn't it? Freudian. The detective is the super-ego and the criminal the id.'

'Pass,' said Stone.

'What does that mean?'

'You've lost me.'

'I mean, generally, detective stories use the same form as

100

classic comedy. We all have these innate desires, greed, lust, and the crime in the story is a symbolic enactment of them. The detective's job is to solve the crime, and in doing that he's helping the personality to reintegrate with the community.'

'You just destroyed Hammett for me.'

'Don't say that, he's a classy writer,' she said. 'I loved the opening.'

Stone took the book from her and read the first few lines of chapter one. He smiled as he read, then looked back at her. 'Real style,' he said. 'I love it. They put him in prison when he was an old man, and he said he had more in common with the prisoners and the screws than with other people.'

'D'you feel like that?' She picked up a magazine, took some green Rizlas from her bag and started a ritual.

He shook his head. 'Not really. All the time I was in there I felt like I was in the wrong place. I didn't know where the right place was, but I knew I wasn't there. I think Hammett said that about prisoners because he was a writer. If he hadn't been a writer he'd've known that prisoners and screws just drag you down.'

'He might have enjoyed being down,' Ginny said. 'Some people are like that.'

'Yeah,' Stone said. 'Or they're afraid of happiness. I think he was like that. He said he had the same roots as the prisoners, talked the same language, but he didn't, not really. Only in the books. In his real life he was interested in literature and art. Lived with Lillian Hellman.'

'I thought he was a womanizer,' Ginny said. She split open a Silk Cut and sprinkled the tobacco on top of the crushed dope in the cigarette papers.

'Yeah, that as well. He had the clap a couple of times when he was young. Always had tarts around, liked black women and Orientals.' He stopped himself.

Ginny laughed. 'Don't worry. An innocent enough *faux pas*. I can just about concede that all racial groupings have their whores. But don't stop now. You were getting to the interesting bit.' She ran her tongue along the gummed edge and rolled up the joint.

'Yeah, he always had whores around, even when he had a regular girlfriend. There was this time, I think it was in thirty-six or thirty-seven, when he checked into a New York Hospital with gonorrhoea. One of the ways they used to treat it in those days was with fever treatment. They put him in an oxygen tent, and heated him up until one of them died, either Hammett or the gonococcus.'

Ginny shook her head. She spoke as she popped a roach into the end of the joint. 'I think they designed those treatments to punish people rather than cure them.'

'Yeah. Like prison,' Stone said. He watched her light up. The twisted end of the joint flared up in a two inch flame before dying into a glow. 'Anyway, they started heating him up around eight in the morning, and his temperature went to 104, by mid-afternoon it was up to 107. Old Hammett was delirious. They took samples of the germs from time to time to see how they were doing, but *he* was out of it, mumbling away to himself, still breathing, giving it plenty of mouth but not making much sense. And they kept him there for three days and nights before they were sure all the germs had croaked. Hammett survived it.'

'And he was OK?'

She passed over the joint and Stone took a deep pull, holding the smoke in his lungs and shaking his head from side to side. He let it go, and when he spoke he was short of breath. 'OK? Yeah, but it was a couple of days before he went looking for another tart.'

'Is it true? Or is it a good story?'

'I think it's true,' Stone said. 'The guy who told me was

an honest crook.' He had a broad smile on his face and his eyes picked up and reflected the light.

Ginny realized she'd begun to trust him again.

'That's the first time I've told anyone that story,' he said. 'Since I came out of the joint, apart from my family, you're the only person I've talked with. I mean, really talked. I'd like to register that.' He tapped his head. 'So I don't forget.'

'I've done nothing since I got here,' Ginny said. 'Before the plane landed I realized I didn't know where to start. After I talked to Beige, I went to see my mother, well, my stepmother really.'

'You gonna tell me a story?' he asked.

Ginny smiled. She said, 'I was born in Vietnam. I don't remember my natural parents; I was a refugee orphan wandering around Saigon. My adoptive father was a Scot, and my mother from Yorkshire, Rosedale. Dad died when I was sixteen, and a couple of years later, when she saw I was managing by myself, Mum ran away to join the circus. She trains lions now. Helps someone else to.'

'Is this for real?' he said.

'I'm telling you. My mother's an assistant lion-tamer. I'd always thought I'd go back to Vietnam, but it was a dream. I didn't have enough of the language, and the authorities there didn't want to know. A few months after Mother left I went to America for a holiday, met a Tibetan-American boy and got married.' She shrugged her shoulders. 'There you have it, the story of my life.'

'Married?' He was cool about it, but she watched the light disappear from his eyes. Husbands were undesirable traits in his female companions. 'You don't have a ring.'

She looked at her finger. 'I don't wear one.'

'Not a love match, then?'

She pursed her lips. 'I still live with Sherab. We're trying to make a go of it. He loves me.'

'But you don't love him?'

'I don't know,' she said. 'I still remember the night we called it a day.'

'Sounds final.'

'It was, then, for a while. But we've committed ourselves to trying again.'

Ginny tried to float to the surface of the tension that enveloped the room. 'Seems like confession time,' she said.

'When you're in prison,' Stone said quietly, 'you imagine that on the out people don't have problems. It's like everyone on the other side of the walls is in paradise. You can't imagine what they've got to worry about.'

'Only money and relationships,' she said. 'Sex and religion. Or lack of them. I'm almost broke now. When I went to see Mum, we got into drinking, so I've spent up on hotels and booze.' She sighed. 'If I start drinking, I have a habit of falling into the whole jug. I haven't got very far with my search for Juliet.'

'I don't have much spending,' Stone said. 'But you can stay in the flat for a while. I can borrow a mattress from the woman next door. It'd be nice to have something pretty around. I won't try anything on.' He stopped talking and looked at her, then had another thought. 'But I don't want you drinking. That'd have to be a rule. This flat's my squeeze, I don't want it turning into a jacket job.'

She shouldn't drink anyway, not if she wanted to keep the baby. For a moment she thought she might tell him she was pregnant, but something stopped her. The thought of living under someone else's regulations was a joke, but at the same time the no-drinking rule was exactly what she needed. With Juliet missing, after travelling halfway around the world to get here, the beating, and the growing fear that she might lose her baby, Ginny was tempted to think that a limiting factor on her actions could only be for the good.

She returned his stare for a long time. Then she nodded.

'I'd like to stay,' she said, 'for a while. I need to know what's happened to Juliet.'

'I'll go get the mattress,' he said.

Ginny thought about Juliet while he was out of the room. She wondered if her friend was dead. Juliet's mother was dead, but her father was still alive. Perhaps she could start with him. He might know something.

Stone lumbered back into the flat with a mattress on his shoulders and a grin on his tattooed face. So, he thought she was pretty, did he?

18

WAITING ANGELS

When they left the flat the next day the black Scorpio was parked fifty yards down the road, the outline of a man at the driving wheel. Stone and Ginny set off in the opposite direction. Stone walked close to her. He handed her the plastic bag he was carrying and asked her to hold it. He said: 'Wait for me.'

He turned and ran towards the car. The figure behind the wheel showed no signs of panic, but by the time Stone was within twenty metres of the car it was pulling away from the kerb. The windows were tinted, but not enough to hide the figure of a thirty-five to forty-year-old man, suited, short-styled red hair, and a slim, athletic figure. He didn't look at Stone, and even for Stone himself there was some ambiguity in the situation. He couldn't be sure that the car had driven away because he was running towards it.

'You seen that car before?' he asked Ginny.

'No, I don't think so. What was that about?'

'It arrived about the same time you did. There might be a connection. Look out for it. Don't walk past it on your own.'

She stiffened. 'You trying to frighten me?'

He took her arm, shook his head. 'Trying to keep you safe.'

On the way to the hospice Stone dropped his plastic bag off at the HOPE shop. Before they'd left the flat, he'd stuffed it with a few items that were slowing him down. An old street map of Hull. A Scotch video tape that had come through the post. A wind-up watch that didn't work and that Sally had told him once belonged to his natural father. A pair of jeans from a previous life and an unopened can of Avon Black Suede talcum powder, origin unknown.

The old boy was gaga. His teeth were long gone and his head moved jerkily on a long, scrawny neck. His eyes were bright and watchful, and looking at him you could kid yourself there was intelligence there. But within seconds you'd start suspecting his porch light was out, and by the end of the first minute you knew you were being fazed by a collection of chemical and cellular reactions. Consciousness had degenerated into confusion.

Stone took a chair a few inches behind Ginny and watched her go to work. 'Do you remember me?' she asked the old man. 'I'm Ginny, Juliet's friend.'

He didn't look at her. You could see her words making their way through the soup of what had once been his brain cells. They entered him as words, and there was a part of him that knew he was expected to do something with them. But he didn't know what it was. He tossed them around in the bowl of his mind, like a mad cook, finally whisking them up into a froth of nothingness.

'Was it Debbie?' he said.

Ginny looked round for an interpreter, and the nurse came and smoothed his collar, wiped an imaginary fleck of food from his cheek. 'We think he had an affair,' she said. 'And he's trying to remember her name. That's all he does now. It's difficult to get anything else out of him.'

Ginny tried again. 'I loved coming to your house,' she said.

They'd had to wait in the reception area of the hospice for twenty minutes because he was eating lunch when they arrived. When they were shown to his bedside he was having the remains of a chocolate pudding spoon-fed into his mouth. Crumbs down the front of his dressing gown, streams of custard forming small volcanic falls at the end of his bony chin. And everywhere the scent of death. Urine and disinfectant, polish and cut flowers, the feathery whiff of waiting angels.

It was like prison, being in there. It didn't look like prison, and the nurses didn't look like screws. But the people in there, the inmates, they were never coming out under their own steam. The next time Juliet's father went for a walk, it would be in a box on the shoulders of professional bearers. That's why he looked permanently startled.

'Was it Caroline?' he said through the muffled drum of his head.

Ginny gave up. She looked over at Stone and raised her shoulders. Then she took the hand of the old man and sat with it in her lap. Her make-up was flawless, like the pancake masks you see in Chinese theatre productions. Her real beauty was hidden beneath it. The make-up was like a veil, there to conceal the physical beauty of a married woman.

I won't try anything on. Why had he said that? Now, when he tried something on, he'd be a liar. Big mouth. Watching her there with the old man, he'd like to reach out and put his arms round her. Just say excuse me to the old man and the nurse and take her into one of the side-wards, give her the treatment, hope she responded, give him the treatment back.

'Linda,' the old man said. 'Linda?' Those few remaining memory cells were as relentless as a debt collector.

'He doesn't understand why he can't remember,' the nurse said.

Stone shook his head. The guy's brain was a passing bell.

He didn't remember that he had a daughter. The working brain cells still under his command had no memory of her.

When they got outside Ginny looked as though her jam pies were gonna start leaking. 'That's so sad,' she said. 'I remember him being full of life.'

Stone put his arm round her shoulder. She didn't pull away, accepted him as a support. They walked through the hospice grounds together. Passed a seagull sitting on a post waiting to be photographed. Jesus, I've got my arm round her, Stone thought, feeling the warmth of her body. The closest he'd been to a woman since he was little more than a boy.

'I hope I never get like that,' Ginny said.

'You know what you were saying about when the detective solves the crime he's symbolically reintegrating the personality with the community?'

'I was just showing off.'

'I know, but it doesn't work in Hammett, because he doesn't have a community that's worth being a part of. That's why he's so great. He tells it like it is, not Miss Marple, Hercule Poirot, all that crap. The community isn't a dreamy little hamlet, it's a crock of shit that suffocates and alienates.'

'Sometimes I think it's like that,' she said. 'Other times I think there's hope.'

'Hull's like that for me,' he said. 'I need a new city in a new country. For a while at least. Somewhere I can stretch and grow.'

'You could come see me in America,' she said. 'Should be big enough for you.'

Stone held her tighter. Might as well make the most of it. Could be another eleven years before he got as close as this again. When you're in prison, he thought, you learn to live with nothing except hope that one day you'll get out of there. You live without desire, and you live without love, and when you come out, your soul is as wrinkled as a plucked bird.

The plan had been to earn a reputation in Shooter's organization. Stone had been preparing himself for a long haul. He would progress from errand boy and general dogsbody, move up the ranks until he was in a position to take Shooter out. First humiliate him, hurt him as badly as possible, and then take his life.

But the arrival of this girl on his doorstep had changed all that, because Shooter had an interest in her. According to Heartbreak, Shooter had been behind the girl's beating, and if he didn't know already, sooner or later he would realize that she was living with Stone.

Stone's initial reaction to the news was to get rid of her. She could jeopardize his plans, stand in the way of his revenge on Shooter. But there are no accidents. On reflection he saw that his revenge could be brought forward by several months, if not years. Because when Shooter realized that Stone was harbouring the girl, he would come for her. And he would come for Stone. And that would be the time when Stone would kill him.

19

DARK AND PRIMEVAL

Aunt Nell was listening to *Sixties Souvenir* on Radio Humberside when Sally knocked on the wall. She hadn't enjoyed the programme today, too much Jimi Hendrix and not enough Joni Mitchell. Not that there was anything wrong with Hendrix, if you were in the right mood. Today she'd been in a Joni Mitchell mood, could have turned it around to Joan Baez or Paul Simon, early days Neil Young, even Leonard Cohen at a pinch. But not Jimi.

Could mean almost anything, Sally knocking on the wall. Usually meant that her sister had put the kettle on, or she was feeling depressed and weepy. Sally was one of those people who spend so much time watching their health that they haven't the time to enjoy it. But it could be a call for help, like Sally was ill or some neighbour had come round and wouldn't leave, or there was a rapist at the front door. Whatever, it was definitely a summons for Nell to switch off the radio, go outside and down the path, then round into Sally's garden and Sally's house.

Aunt Nell was fifty-six years old and tiny. One metre forty in her stocking feet. She had gone through the menopause while still in her twenties. Some rogue gene with a dicky timing mechanism had given the signal thirty years too early, triggering a butterfly effect in the form of a host of doctors and specialists and medical technicians over the course of the next four years. They'd stampeded through her life, made copious notes for a dozen different theses, and disappeared. None of them had done anything to help. They'd been voyeurs, spectators, tourists at the site of an ancient monument.

At the end of her path she stopped to rub a speck of dirt off the bullbar of the Lump, her Mitsubishi Shôgun. Aunt Nell might be tiny in her stocking feet, but when she was in the driving seat of the Lump, she had a certain altitude. No driving licence or insurance, and not a whole lot of road sense, but it certainly did make her taller.

As she rubbed at the grease, Heartbreak came along the street. She heard him before she saw him, the sound of his footsteps on the pavement. Heartbreak walked like Ratzo in *Midnight Cowboy*, as though he couldn't bear to put his whole weight on either foot. As soon as he put one foot down it was like he was stepping on hot coals, so he immediately hopped to the other foot. Same problem: hot coals, so he hopped back again. He moved forwards though; if you walked along beside him, you had to move to keep up.

'Hi, Nell,' he said. 'What's happenin'?'

She looked up into his busted face. 'Sally's got some tea on, I think. You wanna come in?'

'Never say no to a cuppa.' He touched her arm. 'You've got goose pimples. Should've put a cardy on.'

Everything about him was thin. His body, his limbs. He had a thin nose and long thin teeth, thin patches of hair on his head. He was sixty-one, but if someone told you he was ten years older, you'd have no trouble believing it.

Everyone called him Heartbreak because he'd been heart-broken most of his life. Some floozy had let him down when he was a teenager and he'd never got over it. He'd talk to her on and off, this phantom from his past. Disconcerting, because you'd look around for her, but she was never there.

Heartbreak had been on the scene for ever, on and off,

but lately he'd gone soft on Aunt Nell and turned up regularly, like a bad penny. Brought presents. Offered to clean the Lump or weed her garden. Aunt Nell didn't think she fancied him. He was too old and miserable, and he had bad feet. On the other hand she was flattered that he thought about her. Yesterday when he brought flowers she'd kissed him. Couldn't help herself. Planted a big wet one right in the middle of his cheek. That was the first time he asked her to go dancing at the Rock'n'Roll Club, and Nell said she'd go because she couldn't believe that Heartbreak was a dancer. Proved it all over again to herself last night: you can't judge a book by its cover.

Nell had been off sex for years. When the premature menopause happened, she was just getting into it. Then everything came to a halt, and men ceased to be objects of desire. At that time her sister and all their friends were getting hitched and having babies. Nell got into travelling as a substitute and to stop herself thinking about the injustice of the world. Ended up working in advertising, promoting rock'n'roll and country music bands.

Now, Sally and all their friends were menopausal, or post-menopausal. Their families had grown-up and left, as had most of their husbands, while Nell herself was beginning to take a late but swelling interest in the opposite sex. She was beginning to realize what people meant when they said, What goes around comes around.

'Must be the HRT,' she'd said to Sally.

'No, it's ironic, innit?' her sister had replied.

Nell gave the bullbar a final rub and opened the gate to Sally's garden. It was covered with paving stones to stifle vegetation. Occasionally a heroic weed would force its way through the mortar that held the stones in place, but Sally would be waiting for it with a spray of poison. Heartbreak followed Nell up to the house. She opened the door and pushed her head through the gap. 'Yoo-hoo,' she shouted.

'We're in here.' Sally's voice came from the kitchen.

'Who's we?' said Nell, walking along the passage and entering the kitchen. 'Stone,' she said. 'And who's this?'

'Ginny,' said Sally. 'She's called Ginny.'

Stone got out of his chair and gave Aunt Nell a hug. Then he turned to the girl. 'Aunt Nell, this is Ginny,' he said. 'Ginny Bradshaw. And, Ginny, this is Aunt Nell.'

Nell took the girl's hands and looked up into her face. 'Exquisite,' she said. She winked. 'Wonderful. Gorgeous.' She turned back to Stone, still holding the girl's hands. 'Really lovely.' She smiled a deep leathery smile. 'Almost makes you want to believe in God again.'

Ginny was looking over Nell's shoulder, where Heartbreak was standing in the doorway. 'Oh, this is Heartbreak,' Nell said. 'This is Ginny, Heartbreak. Stone's friend. Isn't she lovely?'

Heartbreak agreed. He agreed with everything Nell said. He edged his way around the room, took a chair next to Stone and sat at the table.

'Stone,' he said.

'Heartbreak.'

'Stone.'

They'd got into a loop that could have taken for ever, so Stone parked. He touched Heartbreak's shoulder. 'All right?' he asked.

'Yeah, great.'

'Plenty of work?'

Work was a reference to Heartbreak's trade and profession, which was now freelance odd-jobbing for the town's criminal fraternity. In the past he'd been a tearaway, involved with prossies and the protection game. He'd always been a soldier for one of the big boys, though, never got anything going for himself. He'd done a couple of stretches at the pleasure of Her Majesty, the last one coming close to breaking his spirit. He'd gone in as a hard nut and come out three years later with the shakes.

That's what prison did. That's what it was good for.

'Bin working nights for Shooter,' Heartbreak said. 'Watchman. Feedin' the chickens.'

'Treat you right?'

Heartbreak smiled wryly. He shook his head. 'You know Shooter,' he said. 'Thinks more of his dogs than he does people. You?'

'Apart from System.ini, Shooter throws me a few scraps. Moved some gear last week, got a driving job coming up in a fortnight. Never see him, though, I get messages from one of his cousins. Guy called Brian?'

'Don't know him,' said Heartbreak. 'Can't imagine Shooter having family.'

'You don't have to work for him,' Aunt Nell said. 'There's lots of other things you could do.' But she bit her tongue as soon as the words were out, because there wasn't a whole lot of other things Heartbreak could do. In fact she couldn't think of anything. Still, working for Shooter Wilde was the pits. Life didn't get lower than that.

Nell watched Sally looking at Ginny. The young girl moved around the table and took a chair next to Stone. She was clearly embarrassed by all the attention. But she moved like a willow, with a natural grace that was almost hypnotic. Sally smiled as she watched her, as though for a moment she'd almost forgotten her varicose veins. But her scarred face was beginning to crumble, and it wouldn't be long before the first tear slipped down her cheek. She already had Stone and the girl hitched. Nell shrugged and shook her head.

It would be nice, of course, if it happened, but Nell knew all about counting chickens before they were hatched. She dearly loved Stone, as much as Sally did, and with more objectivity. But he had been damaged by his time in prison, and, although he had managed since his release, she seriously questioned his ability to keep it up indefinitely. He was carrying something around inside himself that was crippling, something dark and primeval that didn't properly belong in the realm of men. With Ginny, on the other hand, with someone so poised and vulnerable and intelligent, if they were a partnership...

Ginny and Stone exchanged a glance, and Nell watched him melt like chocolate over a high flame. She sighed. A mother takes twenty years to make a man of her boy, and another woman comes along and makes a fool of him in twenty minutes.

Stone was speaking. 'Ginny's here to look for a friend who's disappeared. Juliet Gurney.'

'I watched a programme on the television,' Sally said. 'About people who disappeared. Their families had placards with photographs: "Have you seen this person?" And they walked round the streets with them. The placards.'

Stone looked at her as though he wished she'd disappear through a hole in the dimension. 'D'you wanna do that?' he asked, glancing at Ginny.

'Not placards,' said Aunt Nell. 'But we could make up posters with a photograph. We could fly-post them over the town. Illegal, but if we do it at night. Somebody must know what's happened to her.'

Ginny smiled and turned to Stone.

'OK?' he asked. Then to Aunt Nell, 'You could drive us round in the Shôgun. If we all pile in, we could cover the town in a night.'

'I've got a photograph here,' Ginny said, opening her bag.

'Right,' said Aunt Nell. 'I'll go and design the poster, get a couple of hundred copies run off.'

'Don't worry about it, there's no place to hide in this town,' Sally said to Ginny.

'What do you say, Heartbreak?' Stone asked. 'You gonna help?'

Heartbreak looked up when he heard his name. But his face was blank. 'Sorry,' he said. 'I was miles away. Thinking about somebody I used to know.'

20

A PRISON SMILE

Stone ushered her into the café and went to the counter for a couple of coffees. She had her thick black hair brushed back above her ears, and it hung in a loose plait down her back. Her make-up was pale frosted blues and pinks and contrived to make her eyes seem wider apart. He brought the coffee to the table and sat opposite her. 'That was my family,' he said.

'I like them. The poster's a good idea. It could just work.'

Stone shrugged. 'I like you,' he said. He'd been looking at her ebony eyes. The words had left his lips without effort. Without thought. She looked down at the table. Too quick. He was moving too fast.

There were a couple of rubber plants in the café that had grown out of all proportion, covering the ceiling. He remembered them being much smaller before he was put away. He wondered if the plants had grown in a similar fashion to him, or if they'd grown in a different direction. He didn't quite know what he meant. Had he grown wild? Or was his growth controlled? Was it stunted?

'Is your mother religious?' she asked.

Stone shook his head. 'Not specially. We're lapsed Methodists. Sally isn't strong on concepts. Sometimes she gives you the impression you're having an interesting conversation, but she'll always end up talking about feelings.'

'Nothing wrong with feelings. I like to talk about feelings. All women do. They're interesting.'

'Sometimes,' Stone said. 'They don't last, though. First you feel this, then you blink and find you're feeling the other. But Sally wallows in them. Her feelings swamp everything else in the world. Makes for heavy going.'

'What happened to her face? Her cheek. That's a bad scar.'

'She upset a guy. He took a razor to her.'

'God, that's awful.'

He waited for two beats. 'What about you and religion?'

'I try to be a Buddhist, but I can't keep it up. Aren't Methodists against drink?'

'And gambling,' he said. 'They're against everything.'

'Are you an agnostic?'

'I'm not sure.'

It was a joke, but there must've been a following wind because it sailed right past her.

She spilled coffee on the table. She wadded a paper napkin and watched as it soaked up the liquid. The waitress came from behind the counter with a grey dishcloth and wiped it up. The dishcloth smelled of grease and decaying food. She scooped the sodden napkin on to a tray. She looked at Ginny and turned up a corner of her lip. As the woman walked back to the counter, Ginny spoke loudly: 'A woman like that should carry a health warning.' The venom of an age of colonial oppression was embedded in the tone of her voice. The waitress hesitated, but she didn't reply or turn around.

'Did I miss something?' asked Stone.

Ginny shrugged. Her lips quivered, her eyes shone like diamonds. She shook her head. 'I think it's easier to deal with in the States,' she said. 'There they just tell you to your face that you're not white or black, or whatever it is they consider themselves to be. That you aren't the same as them, and therefore you're a pile of shit. But here they don't say anything, they zap you with silence or a superior attitude. You know they'd like to put fire-lighters through your letterbox, but they're not gonna lower themselves to tell you what they think.'

Stone looked over at the waitress, who glared at him. He gave her his cold killer look. He turned back to Ginny. 'D'you want to leave?'

'I wouldn't give her the satisfaction.'

'It's the same when they find you've been in prison. People clam up. All the pretence falls away, and you know you're on your own.'

Ginny threw a final, javelin-shaped look at the waitress. It went through her and carried her backwards, pinning her to the cupboard behind the counter. Ginny turned back and looked closely at the teardrop tattoo under Stone's eye, and at the rest of his face.

'Is that a wedding ring in your ear?' she asked.

'No. I've never been married.' He fingered the ring in his ear. 'This is to remind me that I nearly was. It was before I went to prison, she had different ideas to me, we couldn't see eye to eye on most things. So we called it off. Saved a lifetime of arguing.'

Stone looked at her over the table. Watched her sip coffee from the cup. 'That was a lie,' he said. 'She sent me a Dear John three weeks after I drew the life sentence.'

'Marriage isn't easy,' she said. 'It was probably as well you didn't do it.'

'Is that the voice of experience?'

She shrugged. 'Yeah. If I'd known then what I know now, I would still be single.'

'What's he called? Shadrack?'

'Sherab. It's Tibetan.'

'When I read Juliet's letters,' he said, 'I couldn't understand why you come running over here to look for her. I mean, she's not a relative or anything, not a sister or anyone particularly close.'

'We shared a flat together, before I went to America.'

'Yeah. I picked that up; but even so, she's very different to you, and you haven't seen her for a long time. There has to be something else in the equation. Juliet's not the only reason you're here.'

'D'you know more about me than I do?'

He shook his head. 'No, you know as well as I do that you're running away from Shadrack.'

'Sherab.'

'Whatever. Juliet's disappearance is the excuse you used to get on a plane. Oh, sure, you're concerned about her, and it certainly looks as though she's gone AWOL, but if your life back in LA was settled and happy, I reckon you'd still be there.'

She looked him in the eye. 'I bet you were the prison philosopher.'

'No, I wasn't,' Stone told her. 'But I learned to distinguish between the wood and the trees. I don't mind helping you look for Juliet, but I don't want to help you kid yourself there's nothing in it for you.'

'I can accept that,' she said. 'We all have agendas that we don't know about. That we keep secret from ourselves.'

'I don't,' he said. 'I used to, but I don't do it any more. You do that inside and you don't survive.'

Ginny shook her head. 'What was it like inside?'

He took a breath, held it as long as he could. Then he let it go slowly, evenly, quietly. He had done that with parts of his life, held them close for as long as he could, then blown them away.

He had seen the crucifixion of a young Pakistani during the first month of his sentence, while he was still a fish. A crowd of inmates had drawn a cross on the wall and nailed the guy to it. They'd put a wicker basket on his head and one of them had speared open his side with a banger so he'd bleed to death. They said he'd thieved Jack and Jills from the wrong corner.

Half the bedbugs were on snot-balls and lucky charmz, the other half were amped-out, capable of anything. A bunch of loused burnouts on an interplanetary mission. Prison and drugs went together.

'I got the tattoos inside. Guys need something to do, and they don't care about the consequences. Shooter, the guy Heartbreak was talking about, he was running D wing for the last three years I was there. The screws left him to it. The rest of us did as we were told. Shooter said I needed tattooing, so they held me down.'

He fell silent. Waited for Ginny to say something, but she didn't, so he tried again. He was aware of a prison smile on his face but felt powerless to get through it.

'Not much to say, really. Every day is the same. I don't remember what happened yesterday. Due to general lack of interest tomorrow has been cancelled. You're either depressed or numb.

'Or you're kicking off, fighting, having punch-ups, causing trouble, getting yourself on punishment.

'The screws are screws because they're too thick to be anything else. And no one'd give them a decent job.

'If you're a lifer, like me, they move you around from prison to prison, try to lose you. Someone asks your address to write to you, and they can't tell them because they're not sure where you are. *I* didn't know where I was most of the time. Pink walls on the wing, this must be Lincoln, then, or is it Portsmouth?

'What I learned, what it taught me was that you're no better than the company you keep.'

She said, 'Who sleepeth with dogs shall rise with fleas.'

'Yeah.'

She waited a while, make sure he'd finished. She said, 'Thanks.'

He tried a real smile, didn't know if it worked or not. 'That enough for you to be going on with?'

'Yeah.'

She was easily satisfied. He'd not told her anything. Just thrown her a few bones. 'This place is as squalid as a ten-pound whore,' he said. 'D'you want another coffee?'

'No.' She shook her head from side to side. 'I'm glad you like me, Stone.' She squeezed his hand. 'I like you, too. But I have a husband back home.'

'I don't wanna hear about husbands,' he said. 'It's like having a shit sandwich for breakfast.'

21

SHE'S A MULE

Ginny was barefoot in the kitchen making coffee and singing *Trista Pena* loudly in Spanish. She'd taken off her make-up because Stone seemed to like her better without it, and there was no one else there to see. Stone was standing in the doorway watching her like she'd just stepped out of heaven. They'd been to the Willows Hotel and collected her things, and she'd put on a pair of black jeans that fitted and a sleeveless silk blouse to match. She loved it that Stone appreciated every move she made. Some guys felt threatened when she spoke Spanish or French or any language they weren't familiar with. But Stone just opened his eyes wider and swallowed hard.

'Aw-riiight,' he said when she'd finished. 'What's it about? We could sing it together.'

She talked him through the first lines of the song, articulating the consonants, dragging out the long vowels, and he stayed with her, his ear picking out the homoeopathic alternations of accent and rhythm. Eventually they tried the first couple of verses, harmonizing together, and he didn't stop at his mistakes, but picked it up again immediately so the sense of the continuing song was not lost. Ginny danced around him, twisting and twirling to the rhythm, her arms high in the air, fingers responding to the final nuance of each musical phrase, while her feet tapped out the muted flamenco beat.

Stone poured the coffee and carried it through to the

other room. They sat together on the couch and Ginny put her feet on his shins. He cupped the mug of coffee in both hands and looked sideways at her. The moment lasted a long time. Ginny wondered how it would end. She thought he'd put the mug down and reach for her, his fingertips straining towards her face. That, or, if he didn't get a move on, she'd have to take the mug away from him and do a pounce.

Come on, Stone Lewis, you haven't got there yet.

Still, no need to rush the man, there was plenty of time. But it felt like God resting on the fifth day.

There was a knock at the door and Stone widened his eyes in disbelief. As he left the room Ginny's womb contracted. It was as if a tool with a thin cutting edge and sharp point had been inserted into her. She took in air, bracing herself for a still sharper pain to follow. But nothing happened. She felt giddy and laid her head on the back of the couch. She explored the lower regions of her stomach with the fingers of both hands. Everything seemed to be all right. A sense of nausea, rapidly receding, and a cold sweat on her forehead. She'd have to see a doctor.

'Is Ginny here?' When she heard Beige's voice, Ginny got up from the couch and joined Stone at the door. He was helping Beige into the flat with a pushchair, a child sleeping inside. Beige was the product of a grocer's daughter from Beverley Road and a Tanzanian prince. After she was conceived her father had become impotent, and her mother had been forced into a reluctant celibacy for the next five years, until she found a substitute. During that time Beige's mother had sung *Someday My Prince Will Come* at least once a week, but he never managed it.

Beige was the colour of milk chocolate, with frizzy hair, and she must've been stunning up to the age of eighteen. But being at the bottom of the food chain, living with poverty had ravaged and coarsened her features, and her eyes had the feel of something cold and withering. She tended the child gently and lovingly when he whimpered, pulling the cover up to his chin and letting him hear the softer tones of her voice.

When he was settled they left the pram in the hall and went through to the main room. Beige took the couch, and Ginny sat on the bed. Stone settled in a chair at the table. Beige glanced at Stone, card-indexing him, then looked questioningly at Ginny. 'Are you two . . . ?'

'Yeah,' Stone said. 'We live together as wife and wife.'

Ginny laughed. 'It's all right to talk in front of Stone,' she said. 'D'you have some news?'

Beige shook her head. She wore a sky-blue shirt with long collars and black leather pants. 'I haven't heard anything. But I talked to Harry and we thought you ought to know the whole story.'

'The whole story?'

'Juliet was in trouble. I didn't say before because I thought she might come back. But now she hasn't, and . . .'

'Start at the beginning, Beige,' Ginny said. 'What kind of trouble?'

'She used to go to London now and again,' Beige said. 'Once, sometimes twice a month. She'd stay with Harry and Josephine, and sometimes she'd score dope as a present for him. She wasn't a user herself.

'Three or four months back she was busted on the station. She was carrying crack, not much, I don't think, but the cop put the frighteners on her. He could arrest her for dealing, in which case she'd get involved with social services, probably have her son taken into care, or he'd give her the crack back and she could do some jobs for him on the side.'

'Cops are real sweethearts,' Stone said. 'They invented free enterprise.'

'There was no choice as far as Juliet was concerned,'

Beige continued. 'She had no idea what the jobs on the side might be. She thought she might have to screw the guy, something like that, but she didn't care. She said she'd screw him and all his friends if necessary. She couldn't've stood losing little John.'

'D'you know anything else about him?' Ginny asked. 'His name?'

Beige shook her head. 'I asked Juliet what he was called, but she wouldn't tell me. The only thing she said was he didn't wear a uniform. So he was something in CID.'

'Drug Squad?' Stone said.

Beige shrugged her shoulders. 'Maybe. If I knew, I'd tell you.'

'What were the jobs on the side?' asked Ginny.

'She's carrying little parcels round the town, delivering. Juliet makes the drop and she gets an envelope back, which she gives to the cop.'

'She's a mule,' Stone said.

'Yeah, she knows there're drugs in the parcels, but she doesn't have to worry about it because she's working for the cops. The drops around the town might've been dummy runs, but after a while she's making drops in other towns. Sometimes three or four a week. One day she's in Manchester, the next she's in Glasgow. And she gets paid for it.'

'And one day she didn't come back,' said Ginny. 'She could be anywhere.' She looked over at Stone. 'Where do we go from here?'

'We go slowly,' he said. 'If it's a police racket, there's nowhere safe to run. We don't know how to shovel it as fast as they do, so we don't try. For the time being we stay out of their hair. Might be an idea to talk to Harry, see if he knows anything else. And Juliet's landlord, her neighbours. The more we can turn up without involving the fuzz the better.'

*

It was late when Beige left. Ginny got into bed and closed her eyes. She listened to Stone moving around the apartment. Eventually he settled on the mattress and said good night. She peered up into the darkness and listened to his breathing. She thought about Juliet and wondered if she was alive or dead. She couldn't conceive of her dead, and yet the more she learned of what her friend had been involved in, the more likely it seemed.

She thought of Sherab, her husband back home in LA, and she thought of Sherab's mother. There'd been a moment, just before Beige arrived, when she would quite happily have jumped into bed with Stone Lewis. Sherab would say that Beige's arrival at the door at that moment was not fortuitous, that it was an intervention by the Great Loving One. Ginny didn't know. Everything was changing.

On the other side of the room Stone stirred on the mattress, but his breathing soon returned to normal. She wondered if Sherab was thinking about her, wondered if he was faithful. But she knew he was. Sherab was always faithful.

Ginny knew that an improper mind is a perpetual feast. She imagined herself getting out of bed and walking over to Stone's mattress. She would lift the corner of the quilt and slip in beside him. He'd probably think it was a good idea, not even consider throwing her out.

'Jesus,' he'd say. 'It's been a long time.'

'OK?' she'd whisper back. 'Methodists aren't against sex, are they?'

'Don't know. Can't remember.'

Then he'd touch her gently. Going slowly at first, hesitantly, using only the tips of his fingers.

22

HARRY

They got on the train at nine in the morning and arrived at King's Cross at noon. Harry Hellier met them on the station. He was young with spiky blond hair, liberally pierced with several rings in both ears, two in his nose, singles in upper lip, eyebrow, and right cheek. He had large eyes in a round, rosy-cheeked face, and appeared to be on the crest of a permanent smile. He was the first person in the whole world to make Stone Lewis feel avuncular.

He shook hands with a natural effusiveness, and Stone hoped that he'd never see the inside of a prison. He was the kind of boy the system loved to destroy. Cons and screws together would corner him and roast him down to the white of his bones.

Harry led them to a greasy spoon off the Gray's Inn Road and introduced them to his girlfriend, Josephine, who worked behind the counter. Ginny and Josephine both smiled as they inspected each other with microscopic carelessness. Harry settled them at a table and brought over a tray with coffee and toasted sandwiches. Stone wondered briefly what trade was like back at System.ini, and if Eve was managing without him. But Eve managed whatever the world decided to throw at her, and she'd promised that unless the place was over-run with punters, she wouldn't miss him at all.

Ginny was speaking to Harry through her toasted sandwich. It was as if no one had ever told her not to speak with food in her mouth. Or, if they had, she'd decided to ignore it. Stone wondered what it felt like, just to go ahead and talk and not apologize for blowing crumbs on the tabletop. He had a go with his own sandwich, but it didn't feel comfortable. Sally had done too good a job on him way back when she had him in short trousers.

'You know what Juliet's been doing?' Harry said.

Stone looked out the window. 'Moving gear.'

'Yeah. That's how it started. Her contact is a guy in Hull CID. Really laid-back op. She gets expenses, and when she hands over the bread the guy lays two, three hundred notes on her. If it's been a long trip she can come out of it with five.'

'Any pattern to it?' Stone asked. 'Do we start looking here, or do we look up north?'

Harry shook his head. 'She only gets a day's notice. She'll pick up the gear one day and deliver the next. She doesn't know where she's going until she makes the pick-up. London, Glasgow, Manchester, Nottingham, it could be anywhere. She had a drop in Stroud once, Aberdeen, even Kendal.'

'Crack?'

'Mainly, yeah, but sometimes it's black or acid. A lot of H lately.'

'How d'you know?' asked Ginny.

'How d'you think?' Harry said.

Stone was nodding his head. 'She got greedy. Started skimming off the top and cutting what was left to make up the weight.'

'I've been helping with the cutting,' said Harry. 'As soon as she knows where she's going, she rings me and we arrange a meet. Then we open the packet and skim off as much as we think we can get away with. We cut the rest with talc or parsley or benzocaine or whatever, then Juliet makes the drop and goes back to Hull.'

'And you,' said Stone, 'bring the skimmings back here and sell on the street.'

Harry nodded. 'We split, fifty-fifty. Whatever I make, Juliet gets half.'

'What about other couriers?' asked Stone. 'Is she the only one? Now she's gone missing, who's delivering the stuff? We need a name. Something to get us started.'

'She never mentioned anyone else. Just the cop.'

'Where did you last see her?' asked Ginny.

'Here,' said Harry. 'She was dropping a parcel of H off in St John's Wood High Street. We skimmed it and cut the rest with powdered milk.'

'Isn't that dangerous?'

Harry glanced across at Stone with a hint of amusement around his eyes, then he snapped his focus back to Ginny. 'Dangerous?' he shrugged. 'Milk?'

'I can't imagine Juliet coping with the pressure,' said Ginny.

'She was frightened,' Harry confirmed. 'She thought he might've rumbled her. The guy hadn't said anything, but he was suspicious. She was thinking of running to the States.' He looked at Ginny. 'Going to stay with you.'

'But she didn't make it,' said Stone. 'That was the last time you heard from her?'

Harry shook his head. 'It was the last time I *saw* her. But the last time I heard from her was about a week later. She had a drop to make in Glasgow, and I arranged to meet her there the next day, the same place we'd met a couple of times before. I got an early train, but Juliet never showed. That's when she went missing. I tried ringing a couple of times, then I contacted Beige and she told me Juliet had disappeared.'

Stone held eye contact for a full minute, see how much the guy was holding back, but he seemed to've let everything come. 'What d'you think happened to her?'

Harry shrugged. 'She might've decided to split with the whole package. It was a big delivery.'

'Except she depended on you to do the selling,' said Stone. 'Did she have some other way of unloading?'

'No. You're right, she depended on me. But she might've delivered the dope and split with the spends. Maybe she's in Spain or somewhere, living it up on the Costas. I keep expecting a card from her. "Dear Harry, Wish you was here."'

Stone said, 'If she was gonna do that, why didn't she show in Glasgow? She arranged to meet you.'

Harry shook his head. 'That's the bit I can't explain.'

'No,' said Ginny. 'Something must've happened. She obviously intended to meet you. Something stopped her, made her change her mind.'

'There's nothing to explain,' said Stone. 'She never got to Glasgow. If she was there, she'd've met you. Even if she'd changed her mind about the skimming, decided to play it straight, she'd've had nothing to lose by meeting you.'

'So where do we go from here?' asked Ginny.

'Back to Hull,' said Stone. 'Harry's given us a few answers, but the real solution is back there where Juliet lived. We're gonna have to find out who the cop is. When we find him, we find what happened to Juliet.'

When you put drugs and Hull together there was another name you couldn't rule out. Shooter Wilde. There must be a connection between Shooter and the cop. Stone didn't quite know how, but he was going to stay with it until he did. If Juliet had been ripping off some dumb cop she might have had her hand slapped, but if she'd been ripping off Shooter, she'd probably be dead. That would explain why Shooter didn't want Ginny sniffing around.

Whenever he thought of Shooter, Stone could feel the rage burning inside him. He'd fantasized for months about how he'd deal with Shooter when he got the chance. He'd thought of tattooing Shooter's face, or of taking a razor to it, like Shooter had done with Sally. He'd thought of castrating him with a couple of bricks, or of slowly bleeding him, the death of a thousand cuts.

That was in the early days, while he was still banged away in stir, and when the revenge fantasies were still fuelled by an internal fire. Stone had cooled down considerably since those days; at the heart of his revenge now there was still a fire, but it was heading in the direction of ice.

He no longer required Shooter to cry out in pain. He didn't need the guy to be disfigured or mutilated in any way. He only wanted to be close enough to see his eyes when the sadistic bastard realized that Stone Lewis was going to kill him.

He sat opposite her on the train and undressed her in his head. Couldn't stop himself and didn't want to. After Doncaster he went for a slash and completely missed the pan. It's never easy trying to aim when you've got a hard-on.

They stopped off at the Botanic when the train arrived in Hull. Stone's idea. He didn't want to take any chances, thought he'd have to get her well oiled before making his move. He got a couple of pints and walked back to the table with them. When he'd finished his, Ginny supped the dregs from her own glass and put it down on the table.

'Same again?' she asked.

He nodded, watched her collect the glasses and go over to the bar. He watched her return, being careful not to spill the ale. He thought about the Ten Commandments and remembered the best advice he'd ever been given: no more than six of them should ever be attempted.

She sat opposite him and took the top off her pint, licking the creamy foam from her top lip. She was flushed from the day, the travelling, and the alcohol. Three or four pints should do it, he thought. Hops and yeast. Just pour it down her and wait. Mr Integrity.

He watched her drinking her way slowly down the second pint, and was getting ready to buy a third when he changed his mind. Didn't have a reason for it. 'I'm going for a slash,' he said. 'Then we should go home. I've got to be at work in the morning.'

What it was, he mused as they walked from the pub back to the flat, he didn't want to fuck her when she was drunk. When he'd undressed her in his head, back on the train, she'd been sober, she'd been smiling and happy, and what they'd done together, though it was a fantasy, had been fun.

He put his arm around her shoulders as they approached the flat, and the diamond-black Scorpio Granada pulled away from the kerb and vanished into the night.

23

BLOOD BUBBLED TO THE SURFACE

When Stone had gone to work the next morning, Ginny washed the breakfast bowls. She straightened the sheets on the bed and on Stone's mattress, and wondered how it was possible they'd slept through another night in separate beds.

Stone thought they should stay away from the police for the time being. It seemed incontrovertible that at least one cop had embroiled Juliet in the drugs trade, and it was a reasonable assumption that others would be involved. 'Why draw the heat?' Stone had said. 'Until we find out who they are, we assume they're all bad.'

Ginny could see the logic, but she wasn't convinced that Juliet's cop was authentic. 'He could've just told her he was a policeman,' she'd argued. 'We don't know he was a cop. All we know for sure is that Juliet *thought* he was.'

'From where I stand,' Stone had said, 'cops are the enemy.'

'I know that.' Ginny had turned to face him on the couch, slipped her arm around his shoulders. 'But you don't have to be involved. I'll go to the police station by myself. All I'm doing is following up a previous enquiry. Let's see what happens?'

'And if you get beaten up again? I come home from work and find you concussed in the doorway. Or worse. What then?'

'You can be my avenger.'

'Jesus. Thanks a lot. Leave the cops out of it for now,

Ginny. We'll have the posters tomorrow. Somebody'll've seen her. Somebody might even've seen her with the cop. We could get a description of the guy.'

'All right,' Ginny had said. 'I'll give it another couple of days.'

But that was last night. This morning Ginny couldn't think of a reason for not going to the police station. It was understandable that Stone was paranoid about the cops. He thought they were all torturing nuns in the cells. But she couldn't let that stand in the way. It wasn't like answers were falling out of the sky.

She walked into town and across Queen's Gardens. There was a new cop at reception, no sign of the racist with the big nose. He wrote down the details and told her to take a seat for a minute. Twenty-eight minutes later a WPC told her they had no news of Mrs Gurney's whereabouts. 'Her description's gone out to other stations,' she said. 'But you do realize that we can't interfere. If someone wants to disappear, that's perfectly legitimate. Not against the law.'

'I'm worried that she *didn't* want to disappear. What if she's being held somewhere?'

The WPC gave her a patronizing smile. 'Why would someone do that? If she'd been abducted, there would be a ransom demand. Like in the movies.'

'But you are looking for her?'

'Well, yes, of course. But if we find her and she doesn't want anyone to know where she is, that's her right. We can't compel her to let her friends know where she's moved to.'

'Do you know something?' Ginny asked. 'Can you at least tell me if she's OK?'

'We don't know anything,' said the WPC. 'There've been no sightings. We're as much in the dark as you.'

Ginny walked down by the side of Princes Quay and

ordered a Scotch at the bar of a tiny snug. She put it down her throat and ordered a double. The overweight landlady, fifty trying to look seventy, gave her a cold eye and watched while Ginny carried her glass over to one of the two empty tables.

Juliet as a drugs courier was another thought to take on board. This was Juliet, her friend since school days. And yet it seemed impossible to deny, both Harry and Beige were witnesses. So how well did Ginny know Juliet? How well was it possible to know anyone else? If she knew next to nothing about Juliet after all these years, then how much did she know Stone?

Ich kenne mich auch nicht und Gott soll mich auch davor behüten. Goethe didn't know him*self* and thanked God that he didn't.

People projected images of themselves. The reality was something else entirely. Image and reality were separate phenomena. What lived and lurked beneath the surface of a beautiful face did not necessarily bear any resemblance to the face itself. There was no correspondence between what people said they were and what they really were. Everyone wore a mask or a series of masks. The persona was an instrument of deception, because the picture that people projected out into the world was not reality, but a distortion of reality.

A man came into the bar and ordered a pint of bitter and a rum chaser. He looked out of it, like he might not be playing with a full deck. He was a walking splodge of cholesterol, wearing a dirty vest and track trousers, trainers without socks. He brought his drinks over to the next table and nodded at Ginny without smiling. Carefully, he lowered the small glass of rum into the bottom of his pint and watched as it clouded up into the beer. He let a long fart happen, raising his buttocks slightly, giving it free expression. Didn't do much to melt her chocolate bar.

Ginny thought about the secrets she'd shared with Juliet, the ways in which, over the years, they had revealed more and more of their personalities, their hopes and their fears to each other. She thought of Juliet's breakdown and its aftermath, the way in which her friend had explored the depths of her consciousness, and she flipped the coin and saw Juliet's shallowness. That's how people were, shallow and deep at the same time, in the same breath.

So where was this shallow-deep person? Holidaying in the sun or rotting at the bottom of a ditch? For a moment Ginny was convinced that Juliet was dead, but the thought was too real and it brought horror in its wake, so she let it go. Watched it skittering off along a dark avenue of imagination.

The glow started when she'd taken the last swallow of the fifth double. She picked up the glass and went back to the bar, staggering against a chair. 'Same again,' she said. The landlady raised her eyebrows.

Ginny shrugged. ' "*Freedom and whisky gang thegither.*" Robert Burns.'

'You've had enough,' the landlady said.

'Come on, it's the only thing that clears my head.'

The man at the table put his glass down and made a sound like an animal.

'Do you belong to a cult?' she asked him.

On the way to System.ini the weather was sulking. Ginny stumbled a couple of times. The second time she saved herself by reaching out for the brick wall of a house. She scraped the back of her hand along the wall, tearing the skin. She watched blood bubble to the surface, and had to staunch it with a handful of tissues.

Stone brought black coffee to the table by the window.

'Drink it,' he said. 'Getting pissed's a really good idea. You wanna spend the rest of the day in the khazi?'

Ginny tried to make eye contact. 'Don't get mad at me. I'm not in charge of the world.'

Stone shook his head.

She found it amazing that you could leave LA and end up in a city with even more stupid people.

'I went to the police,' she said, aware that she was slurring her words. She tried to enunciate each syllable separately, but it wasn't easy. The sentences buckled. 'They were no help.'

'Come through the back,' he said. He led her behind the counter, into the rear of the café. He put her hand under the cold tap and let it run.

'There was a man in the bar,' Ginny said. 'The kind who thinks if you're not white you must be a nymphomaniac. I wanted to put my fingers up his nose and yank his fuckin' face off.'

Stone said, 'What's a sweetheart like you doing in a dump like this?'

Eve Caldwell came over to the wash basin. 'What's all this?' she said.

'She's elephant's trunk,' Stone said.

'I can smell that,' said Eve. 'I mean all this, on the floor.'

Stone and Ginny both turned. 'Jesus,' said Stone.

Ginny could see what appeared to be liquid, but it took her some moments to realize what it was. She sashayed towards a dark red stain on the floor tiles. There was another one near the door, and still another by the wash basin. 'Oh! God!' she said, remembering a line of Thomas Hood, *That bread should be so dear, and flesh and blood so cheap!* Her DMs and tights were covered in it. She reached down to her knee and rubbed lightly at the substance that was coming from under her skirt. A viscous vermilion clot attached itself to her fingers like an alien flower.

'You'd better lay her down,' said Eve, a note of authority in her voice. 'I'll ring for an ambulance.'

24

NOT FOOTBALL

Aunt Nell was sizing up Heartbreak, wondering where he'd got a sixties-style lilac shirt, when she heard the car engine. The taxi stopped outside her house, neatly tucking itself up against the curb in front of the Shôgun. Stone got out and Nell thought he was going next door to his mother's house. But when he'd paid the driver he walked up Nell's path. His shoulders were slumped and his face was a shade or two paler than normal. 'Something's wrong,' she said to Heartbreak.

By the time she met Stone at the door she was shaking, her voice pitched high. 'What is it, Stone? What's happened?'

'It's all right,' he said. He took her by her forearms and pulled her close to him. 'It's Ginny. I've just come from the hospital. She's gonna be all right.'

At the mention of the word 'hospital' Nell felt herself begin to panic. Thirty-six years after they'd taken her into a hospital for the first time, she was still capable of picturing the series of horrors that had been her life at that time. 'What happened?'

'She miscarried. I thought she was dying, there was blood all over the place. But they say she'll be OK. They're gonna keep her in overnight.'

Nell's panic began to subside. 'Poor kid,' she said. 'Pregnant?'

'I didn't know. Didn't have a clue.'

'I'll make some tea,' she said. 'Something to calm us down.'

Heartbreak followed her to the kitchen. She was overcome with relief, and when she turned to look at Heartbreak she thought she could've cuddled him if he'd had any hair and a personality. His lilac shirt had rounded collars and must've once belonged to a mod. There were not many men like Heartbreak around. He should be on the endangered species list.

'Show 'im the posters, Nell,' said Heartbreak. 'Cheer 'im up.'

'Tea, first,' Nell replied. 'Bang on the wall for Sally.'

She used the big teapot out of the china cabinet and found some chocolate-chip cookies and half a Dundee cake. Heartbreak helped her pile cups and saucers and side plates on to the hostess trolley, but Nell pushed it through to the sitting-room. Sally was there. Looked as though she'd already had one cry and was working herself up for another.

'Mother, she's gonna be all right,' Stone said. Nell detected the frustration in his tone. He'd come for sympathy for himself, but Sally had already hijacked it. She was so needy in the sympathy department that no one else got a look in. If anything, Sally had got worse since Stone's release. She'd always been emotional and tearful, but now she seemed ready to howl at an approaching cloud, and to anyone who happened to be around. She was happy to let it ooze out over anyone who was prepared to listen. Seemed to be in perpetual crisis.

There had been a time when she tried to help herself, planning to take a cure in a mental hospital, or having acupuncture or homoeopathic treatment. She'd even gone to a feminist therapist for a while, but she'd always return to the same point of despair. For the last year she'd been overeating and put on around fifteen kilos, but a fortnight ago she'd declared that she needed to lose weight, and was currently living on a tin of soup a day. Had more soups than Mr Campbell on her kitchen shelf. But she hadn't given up on the red wine or the white wine or the whisky, which she used to blot out the world.

She pulled a large handkerchief from the pocket of the tent she was wearing and blotted her eyes. 'My God, what a life,' she said. 'There's never any relief.' She blew into the handkerchief. She picked up her cup and sipped the tea.

'It's orange pekoe,' Nell told her. 'You might want sugar in it.'

'We've got the posters,' Heartbreak told Stone. 'Show 'im, Nell.'

Nell brought the posters through and handed one to Stone. He looked at it and a smile passed over his face. 'I'd like to get these put up,' he said. 'Can we do it now?'

'Don't see why not,' Nell said. 'The Lump's outside. It's about time it had a run out.'

'Yeah,' said Heartbreak. 'Let's do it. There's noffin on the telly.'

They trooped down the garden path to the Shôgun, Sally bringing up the rear in her tent-dress. The two men got in the back, and Nell drove, with Sally in the front passenger seat. Whenever Nell drove the Shôgun, it acted as though she had no control over it. It leapt forward as if it had a mind of its own. Like an unbroken stallion, it bucked along the streets in a series of acrobatic manoeuvres, the exhaust cracking, popping and detonating in a pyrotechnic display. When Aunt Nell drove the Lump other drivers pulled in to the kerb.

They posted both sides of Spring Bank, then Nell bounced them over to Anlaby Road, where Juliet's house was. They slapped posters up around Gipsyville and Hessle Road, and Heartbreak suggested they do Beverley Road as well. On the way back they stuck the last ones on shop fronts and lamp-posts along Sculcoates Lane and Princes Avenue.

Sally was nodding off by the time they'd finished, looking as though she'd been extracted from a tumbler-drier, held upright only by her seat-belt. Nell glanced across at her and wondered where she found the energy for such an active emotional life.

She had at least three men on a string that Nell knew about. This was a woman with a four-inch scar travelling the length of one cheek. Didn't seem to affect her pulling power. Nell sometimes thought it enhanced it. There was a huge, uncouth, hairy lorry driver who lived in London but who had regular runs through to Hull. He drank massive amounts of beer and cursed every time he opened his mouth. Sensitive type, though, the sort of guy who, when you were introduced, shook so hard he broke every bone in your hand. He was the only one who could make Sally forget herself for more than an hour at a time. But when he'd gone back home to his wife and kids, she came crashing down again.

She also had a wimpy, immature trainee teacher called Greg who was thirty years younger than her. Greg thought Sally was his Cleopatra, and he followed her around like a lapdog. She treated him with contempt, which seemed to hit the spot and maintain his tumescence.

Finally, there was Mikey, a man only a little younger than her, who managed a small theatre company. Mikey was intelligent, thoughtful and unmarried. He was strong without being abusive, sensitive without being a wimp. He made no bones of the fact that he'd like Sally to move in with him, or he with her. If she wanted, they could get somewhere new together. But Sally wasn't interested. Not really. She managed to string him along with a series of vague promises, and she enjoyed their conversations. But for some reason that Nell couldn't understand, what Sally really wanted in a man was danger. That's what she'd found in Shooter Wilde, and that's what she loved about her lorry driver. Mikey didn't have it. He was too decent. A loser.

She knew how to pick 'em, did sister Sal. When it came to men, her critical faculties were as accurate as tea leaves.

When Nell brought the Lump to a standstill outside her house, Sally opened her eyes and yawned. She smiled and chatted with Stone as they walked up the path to the house, but she still managed to portray a woman standing on the edge of the world, waiting for someone to push her off.

Stone asked Heartbreak if he was going to see the Tigers on Saturday. 'That's not football,' Heartbreak said. 'A team like that. Wouldn't waste money on 'em.'

'Thought you was keen.'

'A long time ago. They used to be Tigers, now they're just pussy cats. In the old days, when Raich Carter was on the field. I never missed a match then. I'd travel anywhere to see Raich. That was a real footballer. And later, when Stan Mortison came back, him and Billy Bly. I'd go get me hair cut on Friday down at Billy's barbershop on the Priory roundabout, and then on a Saturday we'd walk past again, and along Calvert Lane to Boothferry Park. I remember when they signed Vigo Jensen, the Scandinavian lad, used to do the scissors kick. Them was the days. Never missed a match. Standing up on Bunker's hill watching the lads do their stuff. Now it's not the same. If they were playing out there in the street, I'd draw the curtains.'

25

FORMICA HEAVEN

Stone went to the hospital at noon the next day. Ginny was pale but relatively undiminished by what had happened to her. He put a copy of *The Dashiell Hammett Omnibus* on the bed, and she picked it up and stroked his hand. 'Thanks, Stone.'

She smiled and sat up in the bed when he told her about the posters. 'One thing I thought,' she said. 'If Juliet's in trouble, she might have gone into hiding. It's possible, don't you think, that she's somewhere close by.'

'Anything's possible,' Stone said. 'But there's been no sightings. If she's still around, at least Beige would've heard. They saw each other every day.'

'You think she's dead, don't you?'

'I don't know, Ginny. She was in with a violent bunch, and we know she was ripping them off.'

'First Juliet, then my baby. Everyone around me is dying. Around me and inside me.'

Stone couldn't think of the word that would comfort her. He took her hand and held it while the tears spilled silently over her face. Last night the flat had been empty without her. He'd sat and looked at her drawing of the swallow on the wing, and thought about how close they'd become in just a few days. Apart from Sally, Stone had never lived with a woman before, and he'd never really wanted to in case she turned out to be like his mother. And the way guys in prison talked about cooze and fanny, and the mess they were gonna make out of buggering a piece of ass if they ever got out of this place, it all turned a woman into something else. A collection of disparate bits and pieces of meat that didn't necessarily belong to each other, the only defining factor being size. Bigger was always better. Bigger was always more.

But reality was something else. It was to do with watching Ginny put on her make-up because she didn't believe she was fit for the world without it. Hearing Robert Johnson and that driving guitar on *Preaching Blues*, seeing the whole evolution of blues and rock encapsulated in that one song, and then remembering that Johnson got himself killed by some woman's boyfriend. And it was to do with not touching this woman at all, but of talking together and laughing, trying to think of new ways to make her laugh. The touching was out because she was concussed or having a miscarriage or the time wasn't right. But one day it would be right, it would be more than that, because it would be a time when nothing else was possible.

After a couple of minutes she turned away from him. 'Don't look at me,' she said. 'I'm ugly.'

He squeezed her hand, shook his head from side to side. 'You look like a wet peach.'

She pulled her hand free and covered her face. 'Go away,' she said. 'Leave me alone.'

He stood and took a step back from the bed. 'I'm going,' he said. He walked towards the exit, but stopped short. 'When I've gone, I've gone,' he said. He waited a moment, then stepped through the door and round the corner. He took two steps forward and two steps back and returned to her bed. 'Another thing. This husband of yours, fuckin' Shadrack, whatever his name is. Why'd you marry a guy like that? He's not your kind.'

That evening he borrowed a key from Beige and walked

round to Juliet's house in Greek Street. Working-class shams, two-up and two-down, originally with an outside bog and a coal house, but now upgraded into two-up and one-down, with a leaky extension built on the back to house a kitchen and a bathroom. Whatever happened in these houses was shared with the neighbours on either side. You picked your nose and the woman on the other side of the paper-thin wall would smack your hand.

Juliet's house was identical to the others in the block, except it had a green door instead of brown, and blue drape curtains instead of white nets. From the upper window of the house opposite, a woman in a yellow dressing-gown and curlers in her yellow hair watched him fumbling with the key.

He'd passed a gaggle of women on the pavement at the top of the street. They were congregated around a blue pick-up with an old white bath in the back. Free enterprise again. It was everywhere you looked. The women were all young, but didn't look anything like the girls in magazines. Around here they looked as if they'd been working since time began, and no one had ever appreciated the efforts they made.

He'd have to ask Aunt Nell what a D and C was. Or was it DNC? He knew it meant they scraped the womb out, got rid of anything in there that could putrefy and cause complications. But what did the letters D and C stand for? Was it something so obnoxious they had to hide the words that described it?

Stone was playing detective, looking for clues, except he didn't really know what he was looking for. He'd recognize it when he saw it. For now he'd do a quick recce of the house.

There were no chairs on the ground floor. There was a huge mirror on one wall and a picture of a peasant on another. There was a low bookcase stacked with videotapes and magazines. The house smelled damp. In a corner was a television and VCR, and in front of them, a mound of cushions. A child's shoes and shorts were behind the door.

The kitchen was thrilling, a Formica heaven, wiped to a high sheen beige. There was a third of a bottle of white rum. The shelf was lined with canned foods, soup, beans. The fridge was packed with mouldy cheese and dried ham, coagulated milk, butter, and a bag of tomatoes, the secret store of a culinary master gone rancid. The drawers contained cutlery, tin foil and paper bags. The cupboard housed glasses and cups, plates and saucers, a candlestick. Pans, aluminium, with their lids. High on the wall was a clock that had stopped at three-eighteen. That could be a clue. Stone looked to see if a myopic gunman had shot it, but there were no bullet holes. It seemed more probable that it had been suffocated by years of old fly shit. All in all, then, not a lot to go on.

What he'd do if he lived here, he'd throw everything out and start again. Throwing something away every day wouldn't make a mark on the place for years. No, hire a skip and put the lot in there, pay the man to take it away. Pare it down to the simple furnishings of a prison cell. A place in which a man could die to the world so that he could begin to live again.

Upstairs was an exercise in contrasts. The child's room was immaculate, everything in its place, the surfaces dusted, and the carpet swept clean. Juliet's room looked and smelled like a charity shop whose ship had come in. It wasn't possible to walk on the floor without treading on her clothes. All the surfaces were littered with knick-knacks and souvenirs, and dirt and dust and condensation had welded them in place. Her stale sweat clung to the sheets on the bed. A waste bin contained used sanitary towels, folded once, and the radiator supported a line of faded knickers. A real classy piece lived here, no doubt about it, the kind of girl a man'd give his right mind for.

Juliet, although he'd never met her, reminded him of Sally. Of his memories of Sally when he was a small boy and Sally was the whole world. Back when the earth was flat. Except it had never really been like that because there had always been Aunt Nell. Thank God. Stone couldn't imagine what life would've been like if there'd only been him and Sally. She'd have worried him into the ground. Because there was a sense in which Stone had always been older than his mother, a way in which he'd always had to be older than her. Because she was a perpetual little girl. Even now, with her boyfriends, and her pouting and posing. What it was, she was always trying to be kooky, like she'd picked up this image, probably from some film in the sixties, of a really dizzy woman. An original bimbo, who acted the little girl. She couldn't help herself, especially if there was a man around. But she wasn't a little girl; she didn't know anything about being a little girl. Sally had probably never been a little girl, but always a neurotic old woman putting on an act.

She was his mother, though. The one he'd been allocated this time round.

What he'd wanted to say to her, to Ginny, not Juliet; he'd wanted to ask her: What if there is a God? What if everybody has got it wrong and there is some being in a different dimension with an evolutionary plan? It was when they talked about religion, when she told him she tried to be a Buddhist. He should have said it then, see what she thought.

The prison philosopher'd said there was a theological argument about how many angels you could get on the point of a needle. What he hadn't said was how those angels sorted it amongst themselves. What were the upper and lower limits? Stone couldn't imagine angels squabbling, the ones on the needle point telling the others to fuck off and find their own needle point. If you accept that angels exist in the first place, you've got to think they'd find a way of being on a needle point together. These're angels, after all. If *they* can't get it together, what chance is there for the rest of us?

And he'd wanted to tell her the joke about the old Methodist preacher haranguing his flock: 'On the day of judgement there'll be weeping and wailing and gnashing of teeth.' And a voice from the congregation had asked: 'What about people who've lost their teeth?' Grimly, the preacher had replied: 'On that day teeth will be provided.'

And what would God think about Stone killing Shooter Wilde? Actually planning the deed and then going out and doing it. Not like the guy he killed before, which was an accident. No, this time it would be premeditated murder.

What would God think about it? He'd love it. He'd be up there now sorting out second-hand harp and halo sets, talking to the devil on a new mobile. 'I'm sending a right miserable bastard down there. Be really useful in the stoking department. Let me know how he's getting on after a couple of thousand years.'

Since Ginny had arrived on his doorstep, Stone had modified the master plan. He didn't have to work his way up in Shooter's organization. He had to stay close to Ginny and wait. That was all. Shooter wanted Ginny out of the way, and sooner or later he'd have to come for her. That would be the time when Stone would take him out.

He smiled to himself. There was nothing to find in this house. You looked at it and you knew life was a series of wringers. Juliet was no longer here, but he'd known that before he arrived. He was no detective, anyway. He didn't know what he was looking for; just hoping that something would gel. He'd never been any use at finding things, quite the opposite. Could've been a good loser if he'd put his mind to it.

26

A MAN WITH CARROT-COLOURED HAIR

The day after Ginny was discharged from the hospital, she received a letter from Sherab in LA, passed on by the Willows Hotel. He asked her to telephone him immediately. He was worried there was no word from her since she'd left. Ginny spent half an hour getting made up, then hobbled along Spring Bank to the telephone box.

'Aw, Jesus, hon. I thought you was dead.'

'No, I'm still in Hull. Sorry; I should've rung you.'

'You should've rung me every day. Half-assed idea in the first place, going to England. I need you here.'

'It won't be long, now,' she told him. 'Soon's I've got some word about Juliet.'

'You get your ass on a plane today. What kind of marriage is this? Every day I come home from work and my wife is in another country. I'm living out of cans, here.'

'Sherab, I'll come when I've got some word about Juliet.'

'What does that mean, hon? Does that mean what I think it means?'

'I don't know what *you* think it means, Sherab. It means whatever. It means I'll be home later, when I've got some word about my friend.'

There was a silence down the line while Sherab gathered his thoughts together. Then he said. 'It means, basically, fuck you, Sherab. That's what it means. It means that Ginny is going to be her selfish old self and if that is inconvenient to anyone else, like, for example, her husband, then fuck him. That's what it sounds like to me, hon. Wouldn't you say that's what it sounds like to you? If you was me? If the boot was on the other foot?'

'No, Sherab. It's not like that. Juliet is my friend, if something'd happened to me, she would've done the same. I owe her this time.'

'You owe *her*? What about owing me, hon? Wouldn't you say you owed me some time? Just occasionally to spend a little time in the same *country* as your husband. Now listen here, hon; I want you here tomorrow. I'm not *asking* you to be here tomorrow, I'm telling you that that's how it's going to be. You hear that. I want your ass on a plane today, latest tonight, then you give me a ring and let me know when to meet the flight.'

'No, Sherab.'

'Don't give me no more noes. We've talked about this enough. Either you get yourself here by tomorrow, or I'll come over there and get you. You hear that?'

'You're right, Sherab,' Ginny said.

'You'll let me know when your flight gets in?'

'No, you were right earlier, about what I meant.'

'Say what?'

'Stop ordering me around.'

'I've told you how it's going to be, hon.'

Ginny lost it. 'I hate to disturb your coma, pencil dick, but you've no more brains'n a dog's got feathers.'

As she put the handset down it sounded like there was a bee trapped in there.

Jesus, she said to herself, as she left the telephone box. He didn't even ask how she was. She hadn't told him about the beating, about the miscarriage, the hospital, the D and C. He was only interested in someone saving him from eating canned food. She hadn't told him about Stone, the police, the trouble that Juliet had got herself involved in. Nothing.

He hadn't given her a chance. *Get your ass on a plane.* Who did he think he was?

Men occasionally stumble over the truth, she thought, but most of them pick themselves up and go on their way as if nothing had happened.

Ginny was almost into the city centre before she realized she was walking in the wrong direction. She turned around and made her way back towards the flat. She slapped the telephone box with the flat of her hand as she passed it, imagining somehow that the vibrations of the slap went all the way to LA. It would be easy to make this marriage work; all she'd have to do is exactly what her husband told her to do. Nothing more. She wouldn't need initiative, any thoughts of her own. She'd just have to toe the line and everything would be perfect. It'd work wonders for Sherab, he'd be attentive and gentle and generous in return. Their friends would marvel at it, how they managed everything and still remained the perfect couple. Sherab wasn't a bully by nature, when the world lived up to his expectations he was a giving and sensitive man. Only his world happened to be Ginny, and she was her own woman.

Ginny hoped that one day he'd find someone who wanted to have his baby more than anything in the world. Someone who wouldn't judge him or feel judged by him. A real womanly woman who would be a mirror for him and bring his humanity and his confidence out of the dark place in his soul in which he kept them hidden. She knew she would never be able to do that for him, and for as long as they remained married, her own life and destiny would be on hold. She would manage from day to day, but she would manage as a corpse, in a cold way, alive to the world, but dead inside, down in the core of her being.

The old truth about altruism came back to her as she neared the flat. Stone was right, she wasn't here to find Juliet; Juliet's disappearance had served as the excuse to get

Ginny out of LA, and away from her failing marriage. Oh, she loved Juliet; there was no doubt about that, but the truth wasn't that simple. And it never had been. Ginny Bradshaw was not here for Juliet alone. She was here for herself.

He was standing by the iron railings outside Stone's flat. She'd never seen him before, but it was obvious by his stance, by the way he watched her approach, that he knew who she was. He had cop written all over him, in fact it was written all the way *through* him, like seaside rock.

They'd found Juliet, that was her first thought, and she increased her pace so she could get to the news, get to her friend quicker.

He was thirty-five, forty years old, in a dark grey single-breasted suit. He had a slim, athletic figure, but a rather bony face with a ridged forehead. His hair was carrot-coloured, cropped short, and his shoes were buffed to a high shine. He took a step away from the railings as Ginny approached.

'Is it about Juliet?' she asked. 'D'you have some news?'

'Virginia Bradshaw?' he asked. His voice was thin, and now she was close to him Ginny could see that his eyes had translucent webbing at the corners. You wouldn't smile at him. It would be a waste of time.

He looked down at her. 'I'm from Special Operations,' he said. 'I'm only going to say this once, miss, so do pay attention. You've reported Juliet Gurney as a missing person, and put up posters in the town asking for information about her whereabouts.'

'Yes, she's my friend, I want to find out . . .'

'Listen,' said the man, fractionally raising his voice. 'I shouldn't tell you this, but the woman in question is helping us in a sensitive investigation. She's working under cover. Your meddling could blow that and leave her exposed, in danger. If you're interested in her welfare, you'll stay out of it.'

'Juliet? Under cover?' Ginny watched the man's inscrutable face. There was a tick under his left eye, but otherwise he didn't flinch. His clothes smelled of tobacco smoke and a stale, musky body odour. 'I don't believe you,' she said. 'Show me some ID.'

'It'd be best if you forgot about Juliet Gurney for the time being. Go back to America. When the operation's finished she'll be in touch.'

'When will that be?'

'Couldn't say. Weeks? Maybe a month or two. Depends.'

'If Juliet contacts me,' Ginny told him. 'If she asks me to go home, I'll go. But otherwise I'm going on searching for her.'

The man shook his head. 'Think carefully about your next move, miss. You could put your friend in danger, and goodness knows what you might bring on yourself.' He turned quickly and walked away along Spring Bank. Ginny watched him go, his carrot-coloured hair remaining visible long after the rest of him had become a blur. Ginny opened the door to the flat and closed and locked it behind her. She shivered, felt as though the man had reached out and touched the vulnerable and private parts of her body. And that was the second time today she'd been told to go back to LA. First by Sherab, and now by carrot-top. Two men, both of whom'd lose a popularity contest with a snake.

27

SOMETHING OUT OF HAMMETT

Heartbreak said, 'The cop who comes down to Shooter's place is a red-head. Name've Harvey, something like that. Doesn't wear a uniform, but he's filth. On the payroll.'

Ginny turned to Stone. 'Who are these people, Mafia?'

He shook his head. 'Different league. They're not Italians. Shooter runs whores, always been involved in porn, protection rackets. Trying to out-Kray the Krays.'

Anyone who got in Shooter's way would suddenly disappear. He was an average heavy in the early days. His manor was west of the river, and he ran a tight ship. But when the drugs scene escalated, all the old rules went out the window. There was too much at stake, and everyone wanted a piece of everyone else's territory. After they'd finished with their alliances and betrayals, chopping each other up, when the scene settled down again, there were less than half as many players as there'd been to start with, and Shooter found himself at the top of the pile.

'He wasn't the sharpest tool in the box, far from it, but he was left with the power and the guys around him were too busy out-manoeuvring each other to stop him consolidating his position. By the time they caught on what was happening, Shooter already had them marked out for Jesus.'

Ginny shook her head. 'This is like something out of Hammett.'

'Not quite. There was a time, in the early days, when Shooter was involved with Sally, he still had some feelings. I think he cared about her, but he was never a liberal; you wouldn't've called him sensitive. And that was a long time ago. He kills people.' Stone turned back to Heartbreak. 'Explain Shooter to her. The guy's a cracker. He likes killing people.'

Heartbreak didn't reply. He was staring off into the past.

Nell came to the table and ran her hand over the top of Heartbreak's head, letting it come to rest on his shoulder. He picked it up in both of his own and absent-mindedly took it to his lips. Nell raised her eyebrows at Stone and Ginny. 'He hasn't had his breakfast,' she said.

Stone looked along the garden to the Shôgun parked at the kerb. 'Could be a coincidence,' he said. 'Hull's a big place, there's more than one guy with red hair.'

'D'you remember Carver's?' Heartbreak asked.

'Fish shop, in the town?'

'No, that's now. In the old days they used to have a stall in the market. They had a tent with benches, a narrow shelf that went all the way round. You'd go in there and buy a plate of chips and peas. Sawdust on the floor.'

'I don't remember,' Stone said. 'Sally says she took me once or twice when I was small, but I don't remember.'

'They had those thick glass plates. Proper forks. Fuckin' good chips. Anyway, walk through to Queen Street from there. Shooter's got a bar on the right-hand side, place called Buba's. He's in there mornings, collecting debts, paying off people who've done favours. Your man might show.'

They were turning into Trinity House Lane when Ginny stopped. 'That's Juliet,' she said. She turned and set off along Silver Street and across into Scale Lane. 'Juliet,' she shouted. And then again, 'Juliet.'

'Which one is she?' said Stone.

'With the short hair, just turning the corner.'

When they reached the corner of High Street there was no one in sight. 'The pub,' said Ginny. 'She must have gone in here.' Stone followed her into the Black Boy Inn. A few business people were sitting around, and Ginny checked the features of each of the women. But Juliet was not there. She asked at the bar. 'Did a woman just come in? Short hair, red skirt, black jacket?'

The barman shook his head. 'Didn't see anyone, but the place's haunted. So I wouldn't, necessarily, would I?'

Ginny insisted on walking further along High Street, but by the time they reached Wilberforce House, she was beginning to wonder if she had made a mistake. 'Let's go back. See if we have better luck with the redhead.'

It was an apparition. An illusion. Stone kept his thoughts to himself. When someone disappears, someone close, we miss them so much that our unconscious conjures them up. People can do that with the force of their will, but they can't clothe the apparition in real flesh and blood. We can create the visual illusion, give it a comforting scent and make it act out a perfectly recognizable body language. But we're not allowed to touch, unable to get close enough to reach out and grasp it.

In Queen Street he recognized Shooter and pointed him out to Ginny. The man got out of a Mitsubishi Shôgun like Aunt Nell's, same model and colour. Only this year's instead of last year's registration. 'Look at that,' said Stone. 'One of the biggest hoodlums in the north-east, and he's got wheels just like my auntie's.'

'That's the good thing about modern technology,' Ginny said. 'It brings everyone down to the same level.'

Shooter'd put on several pounds in weight since his release from prison, but the only flabby thing about him was the wrapper he came in. There was a leery confidence about his checked three-piece suit, the flash of gold at his cuffs, the tie that was so far past bad taste it was ready to come back down on the other side. His walk was jaunty and did nothing to disguise his insolent and overbearing nature. He carried a tightly rolled tabloid newspaper, whipping it along his thighs like someone who'd been riding to hounds. He looked to neither left nor right until he came to Buba's, then he scanned the street quickly before disappearing inside, his trendy crew-cut hair shimmering in the rays of the sun.

They watched the comings and goings for another hour. A succession of thieves, bandits, pushers, thugs, pimps, accountants and general muscle. Buba's seemed like the place to be for upwardly mobile scum. They watched the arrival of a Jamaican stud wearing a suit you could practically hear from across the street. Then a tall, statuesque blonde glided along the pavement and spun around on a stiletto heel as she turned into the bar. Stone looked at Ginny and raised his eyebrows in a question mark, but she shook her head. The blonde was nothing like Juliet, about a foot too tall and with a figure only as full and voluptuous as Juliet's dreams.

Stone took Ginny's hand and pulled her into a doorway as the diamond-black Scorpio Granada came around the corner. It double-parked for a moment while the driver waited for a free metre, then the window came down and a cigarette end was tossed into the street.

When it was parked, the door opened and Stone felt Ginny tense beside him as the driver emerged. 'That him?' he asked.

'Yes.'

Harvey, the cop, was slim and indistinct apart from his crop of carrot-coloured hair. He stood on the pavement with his arm on the roof of the car while he examined the street. He put a fresh cigarette in his mouth and set fire to it with a gold Zippo. He stood there smoking until the cigarette was finished. He flicked the butt into the middle of the road. Then walked towards the door of Buba's bar.

A gigantic truck came to a stop in the road, obscuring their view. The truck farted heavily, then continued on its way. Harvey had disappeared into the bar.

'I was sure he'd see us,' Ginny said.

'Yeah. Me, too. It was like he was waiting for someone.'

'Or making sure no one was watching him.'

'Paranoid man.'

Stone took her back to the flat. Her picture of the swallow on the wall, beautiful, a composition of red and blue in movement. Stone couldn't get used to it being there every time he opened the door. He would come to hate it, he realized, if Ginny wasn't there, if there was only the swallow and a memory of her.

He made her lie on the bed. 'You're supposed to rest,' he told her.

Shooter was behind it all the way. Shooter was always there in his life. Whatever Stone valued, somehow Shooter would put his dirty hands on it. The disappearance of Juliet, the beating of Ginny, they were both the responsibility of Shooter Wilde. The redheaded cop, Harvey, might be the one who got the deeds done, but the orders came down the line from Shooter.

Ginny got up again. 'I'll rest when we've found Juliet.'

He liked that tone in her voice, when she wasn't gonna be told what to do. He liked the fire in her, the way it flared up from time to time, as if someone had thrown petrol on the flames.

'I'm gonna have to talk to Heartbreak again,' he told her. 'We can't move on carrot-head or Shooter at the moment. They're mixed up in something together, and you've already been warned off twice. If we can prove the drugs connection, how Juliet fits into it, we might stand a chance. You're gonna have to be patient.'

He could see she'd like to scream. She wanted to know what had happened to her friend, and she wanted to know now. Her frustration was almost tangible. 'Jesus,' she said. 'I want a drink.'

'Getting pissed won't help.'

'Screw you, Stone.'

He wanted her to lie on the bed, to rest, to get her self well again. She'd been in the hospital earlier in the week. Drinking wasn't gonna help.

He got her coat from the back of the door, handed it to her. 'We'll go to the Botanic,' he said, feeling like Nero with a blowtorch.

28

THE OLD LAG'S SURVIVAL MANUAL

Heartbreak was waiting for him outside the house he'd been born in at the top of Newland Avenue. The old guy still lived upstairs. The ground floor he'd let out to various enterprises over the years. It had been a fish and chip shop, a pet shop, a chemist, a bike shop and a dress shop for outsize ladies. Now it was a café proudly called the British Breakfast Café, and was doing a great trade in glistening eggs, crunchy bacon, sausages, black pudding, fried bread, mushrooms, beans, tomatoes and tea brewed to the consistency of molasses. Heartbreak led him to a table by the window. He brushed away a porthole of condensation so they could see the road, the women doing their shopping with toddlers being dragged along in a haze of exhaust fumes.

'Two breakfasts,' Heartbreak said to the young kid who came to the table, a waiter in blue jeans. He wore a T-shirt that could once have been white and a red peaked cap with a logo on the front that was drowned by polyunsaturates.

'Two breakfasts,' he yelled through to the kitchen, and a disembodied voice repeated the order and set up an echo that seemed to go on for ever. The amplified voice of Emmylou Harris burst from the speakers above the counter, promising she'd be someone's *San Antone Rose.*

'What can I do you for?' Heartbreak asked.

'The red-haired guy, the one mixed up with Shooter, he's the one warned Ginny off.'

'Yeah?'

'So it stands to reason Shooter'll know what happened to Ginny's friend. Juliet.'

'Yeah?'

'So, d'you know anything?'

'Why would I?'

'You work for Shooter, Heartbreak. You've seen him with the red-haired guy, even knew he was a cop. D'you know the girl? Have you seen her?'

'I've seen the photo what's on the poster. That's all.' He reclaimed a part of the window that had misted over, looked out at the world. 'Nice-looking girl.'

The young kid with the T-shirt brought a dinner plate of buttered Wonderloaf slices, and placed it in the middle of the table.

'I need help here, Heartbreak,' Stone said. 'We can't go to the bottles and stoppers. This girl could be in real trouble, she might be dead. We need to know. You could find out.'

Heartbreak took a couple of slices of bread and put them together. He bit into them and chewed. Stone watched his wiry throat contracting as the bread went down. His face was deeply furrowed and there was a vacant plot behind his eyes, gave him the look of someone under the shadow of eternity.

Heartbreak said: 'Reason I'm still here is because I don't ask no questions. I'm not a fuckin' hero.'

'Don't tell me about Shooter. I don't want you in no bother. I thought you might know something, you might've seen the girl, or heard something on the grapevine. I've just asked you the question, and you've told me you don't know nothing. That's cool. That's all I wanted to establish, here. You don't know nothing. That's great. It would've been good if you'd known something, like if they were holding her, and if they were, where they were. Or if she'd ended up with concrete boots in the Humber. At least we'd've had something to go on then. I mean, we wouldn't've been able to do anything about it, but at least we'd've known. But we don't – know, that is – because you don't ask questions and you're not a fucking hero. Well, that's great. Thanks for the breakfast, when it comes. At least I'm not gonna starve to death.'

The T-shirt kid put a plate down in front of each of them. The plates were piled high with protein swimming in hot fat. 'You want some more bread?' the kid asked. 'For mopping?'

'We'll let you know,' said Heartbreak.

The old guy sawed off a slice of sausage and plunged it into the yolk of the egg. He held it over the plate with his fork until it stopped dripping, then consigned it to his mouth. He took a swallow of tea and creased up his face. The face was ambiguous, could've signified enjoyment, or pain. 'Trouble with you, Stone. Your mouth is so wide it gets in the way of your ears.'

'I'm agreeing with you, here,' Stone said. 'You don't ask questions, that's cool . . .'

'Why don't you listen instead of mouthing off? That's what I'm trying to tell you.'

Stone put up his hands. 'OK, go on. I'm all ears.'

'When you work for a guy like Shooter, long as I have, and you've still got all your faculties, not too many scars, there's a reason for it. The main reason is you haven't been asking too many questions. Because you can't help noticing that all the guys who used to be around, asking questions and giving it mouth, just aren't around any more. And you know why? Because Shooter's sent 'em up to the angels. If you want to live longer than those guys did, you've got to act different. First, you don't ever want it to look like you represent any kind of threat to him. You're useful, but you're not ambitious. You don't get up his nose. The trick you've got to learn is not to get too visible. So you stay quiet, and you stay out of sight.'

'You should write a book about it,' said Stone through a mouthful of bacon and Wonderloaf. '*The Old Lag's Survival Manual*, or one of them Do-It-Yourself books, *How to Work for a Nutter and Stay Invisible.*'

Heartbreak shook his head. He made a sandwich with bacon, beans and egg. He put his head down towards the plate to save dropping beans on the table. With his mouth full he looked over the table at Stone and raised his eyebrows.

'It was a joke,' Stone said. 'I'm listening.'

Heartbreak finished chewing the food in his mouth, washed it down with a mouthful of tea. 'So am I,' he said. 'That's what I've been trying to tell you.'

'Listening?'

'If I start asking questions, Shooter'll smell a rat. I won't get any answers, and I'll end up out of a job, you could come visit me in casualty. So, it won't work, asking questions. But what will work is keeping me ears open. If I hear anything, I'll let you know.'

'But you haven't, up to now, heard anything?'

'No,' Heartbreak said. 'How could I? I haven't been listening.'

29

PORRIDGE

Stone took some time on his way back to the flat, turned into Pearson park and found a quiet bench.

Some con had used the word porridge to describe what being in the joint was like. Porridge was being confined in time and space, abandoned to the existence of things and events which take place in spite of you. An external and detached world which is ordered and therefore to some extent reliable. It is always there and always a stranger to you. You can reach out and touch it, but never be touched by it. You can take it, and it will not resist, but it will never give itself to you. It is a world of objects. Even the other people you meet in a prison are objects. They are not human beings, they are screws and cons and they are not there for you. The prison and the objects it contains and the events that occur within its walls are common to everyone inside, but they cannot meet each other there. The prison is solid, its substance sustains you; but if you die in there, you will never have really lived.

And all the time you were there, you fantasized about the time you would be set free. That time of freedom took on mythic proportions; you would be given wings. Like Ginny's bird of freedom, her drawing of the swallow on the wing, with its forked tail, its red throat, and deep blue back. It would be as if you were freed from the material world, the constraints of your physical body. The whole universe would suddenly be there for you to explore.

But it wasn't like that when you came out. Once you were put behind those bars you were damned. The dreams of freedom were part of the punishment. The whole long count of the days, one after the other, each one the same as the last; it was all an illusion. Because when the last day came and they set you free, you found that you couldn't leave your cell behind. You had to take it with you. You were bound to it for eternity. You couldn't forget it, and the things you can't forget live inside you and fester like a boil.

Porridge. That was the truth.

Porridge.

It was unpalatable. The poets in there would look for another metaphor, something more prosaic but less confining than porridge. 'The asshole of the world,' they'd say. 'We're in the asshole of the world.' Or, 'C Wing is like a long dark vagina. There's always tension here, and from time to time it works itself up into a shrieking orgasm.' And those things were true too. Everything they said was true, or part of the truth. But the whole truth was porridge.

Before he'd gone to prison Stone had been somebody. He'd not been anybody important, just another man finding his way in the world. Oh, he'd thought he was big back then, somebody who was gonna be somebody. A wheel.

And then he'd killed a man. He'd attacked a man and killed him. Stone had wondered about that one, short incident for years and years and years. He'd had time to think about it. He'd thought about the man who had died, wondered if he should write to the man's relatives, his wife, his mother. He hadn't written, though, those people didn't want to hear from him. Those people didn't want to think about him. They wanted to rebuild their own lives.

But somebody. That's who Stone had been. And during the time he'd been banged away he'd lost whoever that somebody was. That somebody had disappeared.

Like Juliet.

Like Robert Johnson.

And Hammett.

Vanished.

And yet something of them was still around, an essence, an echo. Robert Johnson was everywhere, his voice, his guitar, his style, there was something of him in every black voice and most of the white ones. And Hammett was around as well, everywhere that writers or film makers were working with alienation or the crippling effects of the political state. Whenever the cynical and disillusioned were standing defiant in the face of adversity, old Hammett was there at their shoulder, giving them whatever was necessary to carry on.

Robert Johnson and Hammett were dead men. The images they had left behind were lodged in a mythic America, an America closer to consciousness than to geography or politics. They were no longer a blues singer and a writer, but had metamorphosed into a force, a state of mind, a collective consciousness for those who had ears to hear and eyes to see.

When Stone Lewis walked out of the gates of the prison and into the pub, and the guy behind the bar asked him what he wanted, he didn't know. He stood there and shook his head. He didn't know what he should drink, the drink that fit his image, because his image hadn't followed him through the gate. It was still serving time.

30

A SAD-LOOKING GINGER CAKE

Four people replied to the posters, said they'd seen Juliet, or thought they had. Ginny went to see all of them, but didn't turn up any new leads. One guy was clearly off his trolley and tried to sell her a second-hand fountain pen without a nib, said he'd invented it himself. There were two old-age pensioners who were lonely and replied to everything they saw. They didn't invite her into the house, though; they'd never met anyone Vietnamese before. The fourth was a young man with acne who'd lived near Juliet and followed her when she took John for a walk. He had obviously been infatuated with her, and was just as obviously harmless. 'If you need help looking for her,' he said, 'I don't have a job at the moment.'

Stone had gone out this morning with another load of odds and ends for a charity shop. If he carried on giving things away at this rate, the flat would be empty in a few weeks. 'I'm getting rid of dross,' he'd said, when she asked him about it. 'There's new stuff coming in all the time. It's not possible to get rid of everything.'

Ginny had been reading Simone de Beauvoir's *Le Deuxième Sexe* in the original French, and had left it by the side of the bed. It wasn't there any longer, though, and she couldn't find it anywhere else in the flat. Odds on it was in a plastic bag down at the Age Concern shop.

*

While Stone was at work, Aunt Nell arrived in the Lump and took Ginny for a ride along Anlaby Road. 'Just in case,' she said. 'You read that homeless paper, sometimes people just lose it and wander off. Don't know where they are, don't know *who* they are.'

Ginny thought Sherab was a bad driver, but being in the Lump with Aunt Nell was like being on a fairground. The woman was so tiny; her eyes only reached the top of the steering wheel. When she put it in gear and moved off, the vehicle began a slow bucking dance. Not violent movements, the bucking had a kind of grace to it. You didn't feel it was out of control, and if there were no other users on the road, or if you were in the middle of a field, you might have enjoyed it. Felt like being on a huge animal, an elephant, say, which had been in full flight and suddenly stepped on a broken bottle.

After bucking along for a couple of hundred metres, the Lump would hit a smooth patch, and then the only problem would be speed. Nell outstripped everything else on the road, left them standing. Bats out of Hell would pull up in the gutter and wonder what'd rushed past. But as soon as she had to slow down or stop for whatever reason, the bucking would start again. There didn't seem to be any way that Aunt Nell could avoid it.

They didn't see Juliet and ended up back at Nell's house for coffee. Heartbreak and Sally met them at the gate, and when Nell parked, Heartbreak stepped forward and stroked the Lump as if it was a horse. When she got out, Ginny gave the car the once over, and was amazed to find not one scratch on the paintwork. The bumpers, the lights, back and front, were all immaculate. Must be the angels designated to look after Methodists were on full-time alert.

'Is it ready?' Nell asked Heartbreak.

'Course it is.'

'Heartbreak's made a cake,' Nell said to Ginny, leading them round to the back garden.

'You two go dancing, don't you?' said Ginny.

'Yeah,' said Nell. 'You should get Stone to bring you along. Dancing is wonderful training for girls; it's the first way you learn to guess what a man is going to do before he does it.'

They sat around the garden table. White plastic with matching chairs. Nell poured coffee into cups and Heartbreak cut huge slices from a sad-looking ginger cake. The inside of it was still damp. Everybody Oo'd and Ah'd as they received their slice.

'It's like a celebration,' said Ginny. 'Is it somebody's birthday?'

'Kind of,' said Aunt Nell. 'What we've decided, all of us – me and Sally and Heartbreak – we're gonna help you find your friend. Shooter Wilde's been a thorn in the side of this family for a long time now and we've put up with everything he's thrown at us. But we're not gonna do it any more. We're gonna make a stand this time. So, cheers, my love.' Nell picked up her coffee and took a sip. 'Whatever happened to Juliet, we're all gonna pull together till we find out what it is.'

Heartbreak picked up his cup and said, 'Cheers.'

Sally had her mouth full of uncooked ginger-cake mixture from Tesco's, but that didn't stop her. She lifted her cup and nodded towards Ginny. 'Cheers, darlin'.'

A wasp landed on the table, among the crumbs of the cake. Had a quick sniff and decided there was better fare elsewhere.

Ginny's eyes filled with tears. The last time she was overcome with emotion like that was when a touring English choir had sung *Jerusalem* in an old church hall in downtown LA. And she wasn't even a patriot.

31

BLACKHEADS

Shooter Wilde lived in an old house on Cottingham Road. It had been built by a former Lord Mayor and public benefactor, a man of impeccable taste who had spent the last twenty years of his life planning and planting the extensive gardens, which had been featured in *Homes and Gardens* and *Yorkshire Life*. Shooter had fallen in love with the place as soon as he saw it. It was the biggest house on the market at the time, and was planted in an exclusive part of town, a reservation for old money.

The gardens extended to around five acres and were surrounded by high stone walls, quarried and dressed locally. An inner hedge of briar and holly, with arches and porticoes at regular intervals, separated the cultivated garden from a wilderness of scrub around the periphery. Shooter had had the original gardens modified, and most of the free land was now planted with fruit trees. He'd put a pool in next to the house, and had a triple-glazed and heated glass-house built around it. There was an extensive chicken run, because Shooter was partial to organic eggs, and a dog pen to contain the three black Alsatians and two snarling Dobermanns that were kept as guard dogs.

The house was largely as it had been built. Shooter had had the original casement windows taken out and replaced with huge picture windows. The architect had advised against this move on aesthetic grounds, but Shooter got his way, and the architect didn't refuse the cheque. Central heating had been installed, and several of the smaller rooms on the ground floor had had walls knocked out, and been incorporated into an open-plan design. A large extension to the back of the house contained a full-size snooker table and a bar. The door to this extension was subtly signed MEN ONLY.

The nerve centre of a computerized intruder alarm system, designed by the security consultants who looked after the al-Fayed family, had a room to itself off the main hall.

Stone walked up the pebbled drive to the front door and pressed the bell. There was a spy-hole in the door, and after a moment or two he felt himself being observed. He smiled into the aperture, tried to make himself look as inoffensive as possible. The guy who opened the door was familiar. Stone had seen him before, but couldn't put a name to the face. He was a minder or a butler, Stone couldn't decide which. The spray of blackheads on his cheeks, nose, chin and forehead and the abundance of grease in his hair were not conclusive proof of either. There was a swelling under the left side of his jacket, which could have been a shoulder holster or a tumour. Stone checked the guy's complexion again, but could find no evidence that he was on chemotherapy. Far off, somewhere in the bowels of the house, Luciano Pavarotti was singing *O sole mio*.

'Yeah?' the guy said. 'You want somefink?'

Not a butler, then.

'Shooter in?' Stone asked.

'Not less he's expecting you. Who wants him?'

'Tell him Stone Lewis.'

'You ring in,' the guy said. 'Make an appointment.' He shut the door.

Stone rang the bell again. He was aware of the eye at the spy-hole, and stood with his finger on the bell for a full minute. But the door didn't open.

Stone backed off and wandered into the grounds behind the house. No one challenged him, which was strange. He'd expected someone to stop him before he got this far. The main object of the exercise was simply to get in Shooter's face. Push him to make his move.

There was a raised brick pond with circular concrete stepping stones and lily pads. It was stocked with some fairly hefty long-finned koi and highlighted by a copper fountain in the shape of a telephone, the spray emanating from the mouthpiece. Behind glass and plastic fences there were a couple of terraces with hanging containers and portable tubs. He stopped to inspect an oriental summer-house, discovered that its roof consisted of lead-coloured glass fibre. There was also a reproduction Victorian conservatory and a free-standing gazebo with a shingle roof and Celtic crosses cut into its corner posts.

Shooter was sitting on an ornate wrought-iron chair on an old-fashioned-looking terrace. Above him was a roof of criss-crossed white plastic strips, intertwined with figs, camellias and evergreen jasmine. The terrace was paved with red quarry tiles, and all was still apart from the whisper of wind in the lattice. He was peeling an apple with a small sheath-knife, but when he looked up and saw Stone he missed the apple and pared a section of skin off his thumb. His eyes widened for a moment, then he regained his composure. He sucked his thumb.

'I'm thinking of opening it up to the public,' Shooter said. 'But there's still some people wouldn't be welcome.' His trousers alone were a sin. They were designer plaid, and he wore them with white trainers and a wapontak. There was a movement in the foliage to his right, and Stone made out the shadow of one of his soldiers. There would be others. If Stone tried anything, he'd be stopped well before he could reach Shooter.

175

Stone controlled his voice. 'I'm looking for someone, and the word is you know where she is.'

A thin smile spread itself over Shooter's face. 'She? You tried Missing Persons? They usually run off with a bigger dick.' He laughed loudly at that, must've been the best joke he'd heard all day. 'Tell you what,' he said, getting into it now, 'she might've found somebody with hair on his head, or somebody didn't have fuckin' ink all over his face.'

Stone let it all go past. One day he'd kill Shooter, and then all this stuff, everything that had gone between them in the past would be avenged. For now he needed to help Ginny. That was also why he was here. Shooter could play his stupid games, Stone would ride it until he'd got the information he needed. He'd play the snake, watch the way of Shooter's world until it was time to strike.

'I've got a picture,' he said, fishing inside his pocket. He held out a copy of Juliet's photograph. Shooter didn't move from his seat, waited for Stone to step forward. The older man took the photograph and looked at it, shaking his head.

'Girlfriend?' he asked, his eyes still on the print. There was a shift in his tone, a hint of weariness, as though the accumulation of battles had suddenly caught up with him.

'No,' said Stone. 'Friend of a friend. You know her?'

Shooter handed the photograph back. 'Never seen her before,' he said. 'Somebody say different?'

'There's a cop works for you. Redhead called Harvey. Been using her as a mule.'

'Ask him, then,' said Shooter. 'You know cops as well as I do. Law to themselves. Do what the fuck they like. Finger in everybody's pie. Up your ass if you don't watch them.'

Stone watched him. If you didn't know that Shooter lied every time he opened his mouth, you wouldn't be sure. If you were on a jury, sitting there listening to the man, there'd be no way you'd think he was hiding something.

There was conviction there, behind his words, sincerity, even naïvety. You'd be convinced the man wouldn't have the gall to lie consistently. He seemed far too transparent.

'Thing is,' Stone said, 'the cop doesn't wanna talk to us. I thought he might be different with you.'

Shooter smiled thinly. 'I owe you something?'

Stone didn't reply. He fingered the teardrop tattoo under his right eye.

Shooter shook his head. 'You think I owe you one for that?'

'You don't owe me. I'm asking a favour. There's a cop in my face.'

Shooter got to his feet. 'I'll show you the dogs,' he said. 'See what you could've come up against if I wasn't cool.'

Stone followed him through the fruit trees to the dog pen. The Alsatians and Dobermanns were feral, slavering beasts. Had there been no wire fence to keep them at bay, they would not have distinguished between Stone and Shooter. Both men were meat on the hoof.

'Pretty, eh?' said Shooter.

'They look half-starved. Can you control them?'

'Their handler can. We call him Cap'n Hook. Guy's only got one hand. The dogs think if they wait long enough, they'll get that as well.'

'What about the cop?' Stone asked as they walked back towards the house, leaving the snarling dogs behind.

'I'll ask him. Do you the favour for old times' sake. Nobody can say Shooter holds a grudge.' He slapped Stone on the back. 'If you want more work, let me know. Can always use a driver, or muscle that can follow orders. You can follow orders?'

Stone shook his head. 'I don't know,' he said. 'I'll get back to you. I need to sort this thing out with the girl. When that's behind me, I'll let you know.'

'I'm not offering you the world, here,' Shooter said.

'You'll always be the bottom of the pile. But we don't wanna live in the past.'

'No, and it's a thrilling prospect. I'm gonna have to give it a lot of thought.'

Shooter faltered in his step, trying to work out if Stone was stupid or not. Then he grinned. 'Take your time,' he said. 'It's a big decision.'

'But you'll ask the cop?'

'About the girl? Yeah. I said I'd do it.'

When they got to the house a girl still in her teens came out of the patio. Armani slacks and a short-sleeved embroidered blouse. She had a cocktail in each hand, something with cherries, and she handed one to Shooter, kept the other to herself.

'Aren't you going to introduce me to your friend?' she said.

'He's not a friend,' said Shooter. 'Name's Lewis. Stone Lewis.'

'I'm Cuddles,' said the girl, extending her hand. She giggled. 'It's not my real name.'

Stone shook her hand. It was small and cold. She had full red lips, long legs and boobs the size of silicone.

Pinned to the blouse, just below the collar, was a ladybird brooch. It was a very red ladybird, six spots on its back. Only one centimetre long, but the parts perfectly proportioned.

Stone had seen something like it before, he recognized the style.

Shooter put his arm around Cuddles and pulled her towards him. She moved in to his body willingly, and Stone left them locked together like young lovers.

Stone was reminded of a time he had almost forgotten, when Shooter had been his mother's lover. He had been the same with Sally, until she crossed him. And then he had shown her no mercy.

32

THE HUSBAND

Ginny wore a red skirt which splashed against her thighs as she walked. Sherab had sent a telemessage asking her to meet him at Paragon station. He was flying from LA to London, then travelling up to Hull by train. He would expect Ginny to return with him, to continue the task of rebuilding their marriage. But she wouldn't go. She had a job to do, an obligation to fulfil.

He was standing by the magazine stall, looking strangely small and lost. He had a video camera over his shoulder and a brown leather rucksack at his feet. When she approached him he picked up the rucksack and stepped forward to embrace her, holding her close to him, shaking his head from side to side. He held her at arms length. 'Jesus,' he said. 'I thought you weren't going to turn up and I'd never see you again.' Relief impregnated every word, it whistled in his breath and was painted on his face.

Ginny realized she'd walked into a trap. She'd have to play the concerned and obedient wife, or be branded with the responsibility for all Sherab's insecurities and shattered expectations. He was in love with her, or with what he perceived her to be, but she had no love to return to him. There had been a time, early in their relationship, when she had thought love, had said love, when marriage had seemed like an extension of love. But *l'amour vient de l'aveuglement*, love comes from blindness. Now she could only think of the chains of her marriage, and love had little or nothing to do with it. Her marriage was but a souvenir of love.

He watched her face, and his own features were like a mirror as they collapsed into disappointment.

'You shouldn't've come,' she told him. 'I'm not going home until I've finished here.'

'But I thought . . .'

'I know what you thought, Sherab. You thought if you turned up in person I'd drop everything and come back to LA with you. But it's not going to be like that.'

'Why, Ginny? I need you at home. I can't think or sleep while you're away. I can't work. I'm worried to death all the time.'

In the station café Sherab looked over the table at her with adoring eyes. 'I miss everything about you,' he said. 'Your temper, your impetuosity. Jesus, hon, I'm stuck in the house in LA, wondering what you're doing, if I'm ever going to see you again. It's torture.' He reached around the table and placed his hand on her thigh. She lifted it off and put it on the table, covered it with her own.

'Nice skirt,' he said. 'Red always suits you. Looks sexy.'

'Sherab,' she said. 'I came here to look for Juliet, but now everything's been thrown up in the air. I'm not sure what I think any more, about you, about us. I wish you hadn't come. I don't mean it isn't good to see you, but I need to spend some time away from you. To be by myself, be with people I don't have a history with. I can't think clearly when I'm with you. The world looks as if it's coated in mud.'

'Thanks a heap, hon.' He shook his head. 'I've always been dynamite with women.'

Ginny smiled and squeezed his hand. 'I wanted to put all my cards on the table. It must be better if we're straight with each other. I can't know who *we* are before I know who *I* am. And I'm gonna have to take the time.'

'That's what's so scary about it, hon. As soon as you see how great you are, the first thing you're gonna do is unload me. You'll find someone who's an asset.'

Ginny cast her eyes down to the table.

'Hey,' he said. 'You've already found somebody. That's what this's about. Who is it?'

'There's nobody.'

'Yea, yeah. I wasn't born yesterday, and I just got off a jet, not a turnip truck. What're you giving me here, all this crap about cards on the table, being straight with each other? This's me, here, and I'm getting the run-around.'

'There's a guy, but it's not like you think.'

'Stroll on. There's a guy and my wife doesn't want to talk about it, she wants to deny that the guy exists, and now she tells me it's not like I think. It couldn't be worse than I think. If there's a guy, how can it be better than I think? What're you doing buying new skirts for a guy, walking round showing off your legs? Who is this guy?'

'Someone's been helping me look for Juliet. He's called Stone.'

'You and someone called Stone swapping spit? You getting stiffed by someone called Stone? Gimme the details, hon.'

'Nothing like that. I had an accident and he looked after me.'

'What accident?'

'Someone attacked me. I was unconscious. Stone took me in. He's been good to me.'

'You're living with the guy?'

'In his flat, yes. We don't sleep together.'

'Why?'

Ginny shook her head.

'You live with the guy in his flat. Why don't you sleep with him?'

She glared at him across the table.

'Why, hon?'

'Because he hasn't got around to it yet. Because I've been ill.'

'But not because you don't want to? Not because you're racked with guilt thinking about me living on the Pacific coast on canned beans?'

'No.'

'While you're parading your fucking cooz in front of some English guy.'

Ginny picked up the remains of her coffee and threw it across the table. Sherab took it full in the face. As the liquid hit him he got to his feet and pushed the chair over backwards. Everyone in the place looked at him. He stood and dripped, his hands out in front of him.

'Aw, what was that for?' He stooped to inspect his video camera, wiped some streaks of coffee off it.

'Being a full-time prick,' Ginny told him.

The café manageress came over to them. 'Would you please leave?' she said. 'Before I call the police.'

Ginny walked towards the door.

'You could've killed me,' Sherab shouted, collecting his bag and camera. 'You could've scalded me.'

'With cold coffee?'

'You didn't know that. You didn't know it was cold.'

Ginny turned in the doorway. 'If it'd been hot,' she said, 'I wouldn't've wasted it.'

They sat on a bench in Queen's Gardens, half a metre between them. 'I can't get on a plane and go home without you,' Sherab said. 'I'd be a failure. What'd I tell our friends?'

'The truth. Tell them I'm here looking for Juliet. When I find her I'll come home. I've got nowhere else to go.'

'Don't do me any favours, hon.'

'Sherab, I'll come back home. I can't tell you we're gonna make it, that we're gonna grow old together, because I don't

182

know if that's gonna happen. How I feel at the moment, we won't even make it through the summer. But when I've found Juliet, I'll come back to LA, try to sort things out. That's a promise.'

'You won't change your mind and shack up with this Stone character?'

'If I do, I'll still come back to LA to tell you.'

'Christ, hon, you've only known him a couple of days. You're already living in his flat, the guy could be a criminal. He could be dangerous.'

Ginny laughed.

'You don't know about men, hon. I don't want to see you get hurt. The guy'll be expecting something. Some kind of pay-off. Guys like that, they don't do things for nothing.'

'Don't patronize me, Sherab.'

'I'm not. Just giving you a bit of advice. I don't want the guy to talk you out of your pants.'

She smiled and moved closer. 'You're a fountain of wisdom, Sherab.' She wanted to reassure him so he'd go catch a plane back to LA. She didn't want to see him like this. Fate had written him a tragic part, and he was playing it in tights. There was only a possible future for them if he maintained some dignity.

'Just remember the guy's brains are in his prick,' he said. 'Remember that one thing and you'll probably be all right. And don't wear that skirt around him. Get yourself some baggy jeans, something from a thrift shop. They have those here?'

'Yeah. They have them.'

'Get some old rags. Sacking would be good, so you look like a bag lady. Then you'll be safe.' He wiped a tear away from his cheek. Sucked in all the available oxygen he could find. Turned to look at her, shaking his head and pursing his lips. His voice cracked when he spoke again. 'I'll go home, then.'

Ginny said, '*Forsan et haec olim meminisse iuvabit.*'

'Is that English? I was only taught to speak the American language.'

'Virgil,' she said. '*Maybe one day we shall be glad to remember even these things.*'

'Now who's being patronizing?'

'*Touché.*' She smiled deferentially.

'Can I get a couple of shots of you?' he said. 'With that statue in the background.' He reached for the video camera.

She shook her head. 'It's time to go. You'll miss the plane.'

'You gonna walk me back to the station?'

When he walked through the barrier towards his train, he said, 'You know where to reach me.'

Ginny lifted her hand in a half-hearted wave. She said, 'Don't sit by the phone.'

When she got back to the flat, Beige was waiting for her. She was sitting on the bottom step with Darren between her legs. Beige was talking in a high-pitched voice and the child was laughing with his whole body.

'What happened to you?' she asked Ginny. 'You look like you lost a tenner and found fifty pence.'

'Not quite as bad as that,' Ginny said. 'Sherab, my husband, turned up.'

'From *America*?'

'Yeah. Just turned up at the station. He's impulsive.'

'So where is he now?'

'I sent him back home.'

'To *America*?'

Ginny smiled. 'Americans can *do* Europe in a few days, got it down to a fine art, he'll probably get a video out of it. Show it at his high-school reunion.' She held her arms out to Darren, and he came to her, letting himself be swept up in the air. She held him close, inhaling the aroma of lavender soap and post-toddler sweat in which he was constantly swaddled.

Beige reached up and smoothed Ginny's skirt above her knee. 'Nice bit of red stuff,' she said. 'Where'd you find it?'

'It was something my mother had. Doesn't fit her any more.'

'You wearing it for Sherab or Stone?'

Ginny looked down at her sharply, and Beige flinched but returned the look without smiling.

'I'm wearing it for myself,' Ginny said.

'I don't think so.'

Ginny had to choose which way to go. Her first impulse was to lose it, tell Beige to go sit on a tap. But she smiled instead. 'You think it's over the top?'

Beige got to her feet. She shook her head. 'It'll do the job,' she said.

'Why'd you come?' Ginny asked her when they got inside.

'I heard from Vince Gurney, Juliet's ex. He's got John.'

'Her child? How come?'

'Juliet dropped him off the day before she disappeared. She was gonna leave him there for two days, but she never showed to collect him. He's still there, with his father.'

Ginny sat on the arm of the couch, let herself slide off it on to one of the cushions. She watched Darren crawl under the table and sit on one of its supports. He seemed far off, as if he was at the wrong end of a telescope. Beige came towards her and placed a cool hand on her forehead.

'Are you all right?' she mouthed. Ginny nodded.

Beige was wearing a denim jacket with a silk maroon vest under it. When she leaned forward the neck of the vest dipped and exposed a purple nipple. It flashed past in a moment, joined that store of images that one might have conjured from fancy or reality. You can never be quite sure.

When her head cleared Ginny asked, 'What did he say? Did Juliet tell him where she was going?'

'They'd been planning it for some time,' Beige said. 'Vince had wanted John to stay with him, but Juliet had never been keen. Then she rang him out of the blue. "Can I bring John over?" She said she needed a break, that she'd collect him in a couple of days. And that was it.'

'What's he gonna do with the child?'

'He's the father. He hopes Juliet's gonna turn up. That's why he rang me, see if I knew where she was. But if she doesn't turn up, he'll keep John with him. Bring him up as best he can, like I do with Darren.'

'So we haven't made much progress. We still don't know what happened to Juliet.'

'No, but we're only looking for *her* now. At least we know the kid's OK.'

Ginny reached for the arm of the couch, thought about getting back on her feet, but decided to stay where she was. She was glad Juliet's son had been found, and that he was all right. But she feared more for Juliet now. It was as if her friend had sensed danger and done everything possible to find a safe place for the child. Then she had walked alone into whatever it was that threatened her.

33

THE BUTCHER

Stone got off his mattress early and used the bathroom. When he'd finished in there he put the water on for coffee and watched Ginny stagger across the room in her blue satin dressing-gown. She smiled as she went through the bathroom door, her eyes still puffy from sleep. He heard her peeing as he put cereal bowls on the table, opened up a wrapped cylinder of Weetabix. She flushed the lavatory as he went to the door for the milk. He eyed the picture of the swallow on the wall, the forked tail, the incredible blue of its back. Made him shake his head in wonder. He got a pair of clean mugs and set them next to the cereal bowls. He spooned coffee into a cafetière and damped the grounds with hot water. That was the one vow he'd kept to a hundred per cent since leaving the joint. No more instant coffee. Never again. Ginny was humming a tune through her toothbrush, a sentimental song, something from Mary Coughlan.

Stone picked up a fork from the table and put it in the rubbish bin. It had been bugging him for days. The metal was corroded and pitted and no matter how you washed or polished it, the thing put you off eating. He found the tape of *The Smiths* that was stretched and made Morrissey sound like he was stuck in vibrato. Put that in the rubbish as well.

When she came out of the bathroom, tying the belt of her dressing-gown, the infusion of ground coffee was getting to his olfactory nerves and the first stirrings of an erection backed him up against the table. She'd brushed her hair and left it loose, so it framed her pale face. Her eyes opened wide when she saw he'd set the table, and she turned towards him and said something.

Stone didn't hear her. He took her by the shoulders and brought his lips down on hers. She tasted of Extra Mint fluoride toothpaste, and for a moment she fluttered like a bird, her whole body trembling. He wrapped his arms around her and pulled her close to him, absorbing the shock waves that quivered beneath the surface of her skin.

She didn't struggle, but neither did she respond. While still holding her tightly, Stone moved his head back and looked at her eyes. They were coal-black and glaring, and her lips were knitted together in a sullen moue. Stone relaxed his grip of her, and while still holding her around the waist with his right hand, he brought up his left and gently pulled her head against his chest. Her breathing slowed and returned to normal.

She sighed, and when he looked down at her again, she reached up and pulled his face down to hers. He felt her tongue flicker against his lips, and without thinking he scooped her up into his arms and moved towards the bed. He placed her on the sheet. The dressing gown had come partially open and one breast looked cautiously out at the world. Stone moved his fingers briefly over the nipple, and Ginny sucked in air through her teeth. Her right leg jerked involuntarily, and the open skirt of the dressing-gown revealed a pair of white cotton pants. Stone's hand moved down her body, and she reached for it and brought it back to her lips. 'It's not going to work,' she said.

'Why?'

'I'm not ready. The D and C. I'm too sore. Bruised.'

'Jesus.'

'It takes time.'

They laid together, touching each other with fingers and

lips. Stone got up on one elbow and looked into her eyes for almost a minute. He shook his head and eased himself back by her side.

Ginny raised herself and stared at *his* face. She brushed hair away from her eyes.

'What're you thinking?' he asked.

'Wondering what you'll look like when all the tattoos've gone.'

'What'll I look like when all the tattoos've gone?'

'*Schön*,' she said. 'Good-looking. Heart-throb handsome.' She leaned over and kissed his eyes. He wanted to reach out and touch every part of her at once, but her otherness paralysed him. She was contrary to everything in his world, alien and glamorous and extravagant, and he wished he had more words to help him define her essence. All the adjectives he knew felt angular and inadequate. They limited her, robbed her of stature and freedom, whereas the words he desired would fit her like a well-made dress. They would cling to her in a mutually loving embrace.

'What're you thinking?' she asked.

'About words,' he said. He tried to explain. 'Hammett would know what I mean.'

'Anyone would know,' she said. 'When you get close to someone, words become more important.'

'Yeah,' he said. He thought of *Taoism*, which was a good-sounding word, and of *celandine*. And there was another word he'd always liked, but it was evading him. Ginny shifted her weight and moved her body in close to his. Her hand caressed his face, moved down to his chest, and he felt her finger and thumb loosen the button on his jeans. When she moved her hand inside the waistband, the words he'd been trying to harvest rose up like a flock of birds and filled the sky.

Stone was dreaming about words. In the dream he'd mix

them up, saying *transpire* when he meant *transcend*. He told a lion-tamer that Moses climbed all the way up Mount Cyanide to get the Ten Commandments. Stone couldn't work out what was wrong with that, but he knew something was, and it struck him as terribly funny. He laughed until tears rolled down his cheeks.

A lion, which had been sitting on a metal stool, roared and leapt at him, and he raised his arms to ward it off. The beast was enormous and he went over backwards with the weight of it, ready to fight until the last, but resigned to the fact of his death. It was Ginny's scream which woke him, the weight of her body as she landed on top of him, the recognition of the blue satin stuff of her dressing-gown. Her elbow dug into his throat and he shifted on the bed to let her slide down beside him.

She was talking rapidly, her voice high and shrill, dragging him up out of sleep. She repeated his name over and over again, and he felt her tug his arm and when he opened his eyes he could see fear in her face.

Stone was up on his knees in a moment, but the sight that met his eyes pinned him to the spot.

There were two men in the room.

Shooter's doorman was one of them. His cheeks, nose, chin and forehead wreathed in blackheads, his hair lathered in grease. The swelling under the left side of his jacket was ominously present, but his hands were empty fists. The other man was a foot taller, with a vacant stare. He had a fence post for a neck, huge boots with no laces, and he carried a sledgehammer, cradling it in his arms like a bereaved father. To stop him, you'd have to ring the zoo, get a keeper to come out with a stun gun and a net.

Blackheads said, 'This is my associate.' He indicated the big guy. 'We call him the butcher.' The butcher did something with his face that could have been the prototype for a smile. He looked at his boots momentarily, then glanced behind him, towards the entrance hall. His attention span had the shelf life of a pancake. And the guy wasn't acting, he was a natural.

'Ass-o-ci-ate,' Stone said. 'Four syllables, that's really pushing the language. And you didn't even stumble.'

'What?'

'Stum-ble. It's like when you make a slip.'

Ginny was trembling on the bed beside him. Stone slid his arm under her shoulders and held her close. He'd discounted any ideas of fighting these guys with his bare hands and no trousers on. Some things look better just passing through. 'You want something?' he said, pushing the part of his voice that was shaking way down inside him. It didn't seem like the best script in the world, but he wasn't pitching it to the BBC for a pilot.

The one with the blackheads sneered, curling a corner of his top lip like he'd been watching old *noir* movies. 'Message from Shooter,' he said. 'He don't wanna see you no more, hear your name. And there's no redheaded cop.' He hesitated, seemed to go over the message again in his mind, checking to see if he'd left anything out. 'Got it?' he asked.

'Yeah.'

'And the Chinky skirt should go home, save her having another accident.' He turned to go, and the one carrying the sledgehammer followed him to the door.

'Was there anything about the missing girl?' Stone asked. 'Shooter was gonna let me know about the girl. Juliet.'

Blackheads came back into the room. 'Yeah,' he said. 'Shooter don't know nothing about no girl. And keep your face out of his business or you're brown bread.'

'You should get somebody to write it down,' Stone said. 'When messages get as long as that, I wouldn't trust your memory. You sure there wasn't something else?'

The guy thought it through. 'That's it,' he said. 'All of it.'

They left the door open when they went.

'What happened?' Stone said. 'How'd they get in?'

'Knocked on the door,' said Ginny. 'You were sleeping, so I opened it. The big one picked me up and threw me on top of you. I didn't stand a chance, I felt like a rag doll when he got hold of me.'

'I should've been awake,' he said. He felt guilty and wanted to spend the rest of his life making it up to her.

Ginny couldn't stop touching him. Not that Stone minded, it was simply that he couldn't help noticing. *Minded?* He loved it. The whole surface area of his body had become sensitized to her. It was as if his skin had developed consciousness, forged new links with his cerebral cortex, so that he was aware when she was near without the aid of sight or smell or hearing. He could feel when she was about to enter the room, and he knew when she was going to leave it. She couldn't have been freer, more distinct from his own image of himself, but at the same time she betrayed her every intention with regard to him.

He found himself searching her face, her hands, her legs, exploring and discovering tiny blemishes and enhancements, nuances of genetic code, which he filed away in his mind like a squirrel preparing for winter. As if he was trying to learn her off by heart.

It made him laugh, the way he was with her, the way she was with him. Because it was extraordinary and unthinkable and real, and it might not last for ever. He found he could be funny, crack jokes and make her laugh, although he couldn't understand where the humour, the jokes, came from. He'd never heard them before. Because he hadn't laughed, not really laughed, for more than a dozen years. He told himself he'd been storing it up, saving it for this girl who he'd never imagined, who was unimaginable. Perhaps that was true, or maybe she'd handed the humour to him, unconsciously, a gift which she'd carried with her unknowingly through her life.

They speculated together, reinventing magic and music and myth, and defining and articulating the terms under which they would live their lives. Stone realized that he was envisaging a future which did not involve the killing of Shooter Wilde and his own death or incarceration. That he was beginning to envisage a future which involved living.

They were sitting around the table at Aunt Nell's house. The table was covered with a new ultramarine cloth in Irish linen. Nell had put a large blue and white teapot on the table with matching milk jug and sugar bowl. Sally brought five blue mugs over from the cupboard and handed them out, while Nell arranged an assortment of digestive and ginger biscuits. Heartbreak was supposed to be there as well, but he hadn't showed.

Sally scraped her chair back and sat down heavily. She began to cry silently. Covered her face with her hands and let out a long stream of breath like a snake. 'They've cut my phone off,' she said.

'Not the end of the world,' said Nell practically. 'We can go round there and get it reconnected.'

'It'll cost a fortune,' Sally said, still covering her face. 'Why'd they have to do that?'

'Did you pay the bill?' Stone asked.

'No, I didn't pay the bill. I was ill when the bill came, then I forgot. I was going to pay it last week, but I was ill again.'

'She's been in bed the last three days,' Nell said. 'Crying and carrying on. Not eating, drinking herself stupid.'

'Depressed,' Sally said.

'Depressing, more like.'

'It's a medical condition,' Sally said.

'Christ, Mother,' said Stone.

Sally took her hands away from her face and looked at them, tears cascading down her cheeks. 'Everyone's against me.'

'Where's the violin?' said Nell.

Sally opened her mouth. 'Wah.'

Stone stifled a laugh while it was still in the womb and felt for Ginny's hand under the table. But when Sally rushed from the room, Ginny followed her.

'Leave them to it,' Nell said. 'I've had her up to here the last few days. She never answered the phone before they cut it off. She's had the door locked and refused to open it. When I'm in my room upstairs I can hear her crying through the wall.'

'Is she having a breakdown?' Stone asked.

Nell shook her head. 'Sometimes I wish she would. Get the thing out of her system. But she seems to teeter on the edge for ever. Trouble is, it's true, what she says. Nothing does work for her. She bought a sofa-bed a couple of weeks ago, and it collapsed after three days. So she got another one, just the same. Cheap. It'll fall apart on her, and confirm everything she's always known. Men, furniture, diet, whatever she's into, she only really goes for the things that have flaws in them. If anything substantial comes along, she's not interested. It's almost as if she's afraid of things that might last, things that might offer some kind of security.'

'I can understand that,' said Stone.

Nell laughed. 'Yeah. So can I. But it drags you down.'

'She's a weight, my mother. No doubt about it.' Stone could remember being a boy, when he had to tell Sally he loved her every time he saw her. Whenever he slipped and forgot to tell her, she'd go into a sulk. In the end he stopped loving her. He couldn't keep it up. He didn't tell her, that would have been cruel. But he couldn't find the warmth for her that should have lived within him. Only duty, which, like love, was for ever, but which was a heavier burden.

Heartbreak came up the path with his hot-footed gait, tapped on the door and stuck his head around it. 'It's me,' he called, so nobody would get a shock when he arrived in the kitchen. 'Five mugs and only two of you,' he said. 'Three with me. Tea smells good, though. Got a new table cloth, Nell?'

She smiled at him. Stone thought she'd begun to look younger as soon as they heard Heartbreak's footsteps on the path. 'My new Irish linen table cloth? It was a present from an admirer.'

'Very nice,' said Heartbreak fingering the hem of the cloth. 'Must've set him back a few bob.'

'No,' said Nell. 'Fell off the back of a lorry.'

'Still.' He touched her shoulder. 'I'd've paid for it if I'd had to. Can't help it if I'm lucky.'

Nell poured tea into a mug and handed it to him. 'Where's the other ladies?' he said. 'Or is this the full gathering?'

'Let's start,' said Stone. 'They're busy.' He drained his mug and nudged it towards Aunt Nell for a refill. He told them about the visit of Shooter's men at his flat, and the message Shooter had sent. 'So we're warned off,' he said. 'No two ways about it, but we still don't know what happened to Ginny's friend.'

Heartbreak shook his head. 'Down at the house they're all talking about your visit to Shooter's. He nearly shit himself when you walked on to that terrace. Nobody's allowed in there when Shooter's there. Even Cuddles has to wait till he comes out.'

'You hear anything about the girl?' asked Stone.

'I heard something about Ginny, how she got dumped on your doorstep. It was the cop, Harvey. He was supposed to work her over, frighten her off so she'd go back to the

States. The guy thought he'd be doing Shooter a favour if he dumped her on you. Was gonna arrange to have a beat copper find her in your doorway, so you'd be packed off back to the slammer. And it was Danny Boy who stopped him doing it. Realized that if he implicated you, you'd spill everything you knew about Shooter to the Old Bill.'

Stone licked his lips. 'So Danny Boy's not totally stupid?'

'Hell, no,' said Heartbreak. 'When it comes to looking after Shooter, he takes the job seriously. Most of the others fuck up from time to time, but Danny Boy acts like Shooter's ass is a perfume factory.'

'What about Juliet?' said Stone. 'You hear anything about her?'

Heartbreak shook his head. 'What I heard, I'm not sure you wanna hear it.'

'Just spill it, Heartbreak. That's what we're here for.'

'You see the dogs while you was there?'

Stone nodded. 'Wild animals.'

'They say Cap'n Hook fed them somebody Shooter got rid of. Couple of the lads saw them tearing up what looked like a thigh bone.' Stone caught Aunt Nell's eye. Neither of them spoke, just stared at each other.

'Is it true?' Stone asked.

'I'm telling you what I heard,' said Heartbreak.

'I wouldn't put it past him,' said Nell. 'He's capable of anything.'

'Would be a foolproof way of getting rid of the body,' said Stone. 'I don't suppose there's much left when those buggers've finished with it.'

Ginny appeared in the doorway. 'Sally wants to be alone,' she said.

'The guy who told me about the thigh bone,' Heartbreak said. 'He said there was some women's clothes in the shed next to the freezers.'

'Where do they keep them?' Stone asked. 'The freezers?'

'There's an outhouse, back of the house. I could draw you a map. But it might be locked. And it's not safe to go round there again. Specially you, Stone. Maybe I could take a peek, myself. I'd have to wait till there was no one around.'

'Let's think about it,' said Stone. 'But we'll have to move fast, if the clothes belong to you-know-who, they'll get rid of them as soon as they realize.'

'What?' said Ginny. 'What d'you mean, a thigh bone? What's so important about the clothes, what they're feeding to the dogs?'

Stone looked at her without speaking. He didn't know how to say it. When her voice came it was small and far-away, like a whisper in a dream. 'Juliet?'

She took a week to fall down.

She slid along the frame of the door as if it was lathered with butter. Her legs splayed out in front of her. She was conscious all the time it was happening. Conscious and legless.

34

DOG MEAT

Nell had been looking after Sally for most of her life. Her elder sister had been born with a fatal flaw, a weakness that wreaked havoc within her. It ran in the family, like arthritis and glaucoma. The family tree was hung with blind, cooped-up ancestors with claws and alternative visions of reality. Their maternal grandmother, Ellen Annie, had inherited the weakness and spent the last twenty-eight years of her life in bed. Both of their uncles had had it. Uncle Ben started crying when he was forty-two and didn't stop until he died in the psychiatric hospital up on the hill when he was sixty. His brother, Uncle Mac, developed an hysteric illness that left him paralysed for most of his life. Mac was paraded before a procession of specialists over a thirty-year period, but none of them found anything physically wrong with him. They chipped away at him, taking his tonsils, a kidney, all of his teeth, his prostate, several nerve clusters, his gonads and his foreskin. Didn't cure him, just eliminated a few items from further enquiry.

Nell's and Sally's mother had not been afflicted, though, and, as far as she was aware, Nell herself had escaped the malady. The indications were that it was giving Stone a miss, too. Perhaps it had sated its desire for revenge within this particular family, and would now move on to persecute another lineage. Nell hoped so. She hoped it would find its rightful place in some well-heeled upper-middle-class household. It seemed like an affliction designed for people of rank.

Heartbreak took her to the Rock'n'Roll Club on Tuesday night, jiving to the records of Buddy Holly and Little Anthony and some people she'd actually met in her earlier incarnation as rock'n'roll promoter. Martha Reeves, Gene Chandler, Ritchie Valens and Roy Orbison. Nell had wanted to meet Elvis Presley, but his constitution had taken over before she got anywhere near him.

Heartbreak's feet weren't a total liability on the dance floor, he moved them two beats to the bar. He still had strength in his shoulders, and his centre of rhythm was way up there as well, so he could twirl Nell about like the boys used to do in the old days. Felt like they were flying as long as she didn't look down.

Heartbreak had all the gear, a sky-blue drape jacket with a black velvet collar, black drainpipes and crêpe-soled shoes. He had a shirt with a ruffle down the front and a bootlace tie. The women queued up to dance with him, waiting to catch his eye. A raised hand across the room, a nod, and he would be up and at it, his shoulders and feet pumping away to the beat. When he was younger, he told Nell, he used to carry a bicycle chain in his pocket, in case anyone wanted to argue. But these days they could argue all they wanted, he didn't care any more. And since he'd stopped worrying about trouble coming his way, trouble seemed to stay on the other side of the street.

'Like this business with Stone and Shooter and the missing girl,' he said. They'd got a couple of high stools at the bar, and Heartbreak had ordered them a pint of orange squash each to replace the liquid they'd sweated out. 'I say I'll help Stone, so I go looking for trouble, and what happens? What happens is I find it. That's how it works. If I'd told Stone I didn't want to know, I wouldn't've found no trouble. I'd never've heard about the dogs being fed human meat, and I'd've been ignorant and safe. As it is now, I know too much, and if Shooter finds out, I'll end up like a can of Chappie. Marrowbone fuckin' jelly.'

'You saying you want out, Heartbreak?'

'No, Nell, I'm just explaining to myself how I got into this thing. We're in it together, right? Whatever happens? But a guy can wish himself not to end up as dog meat. Or you, or Stone, or any of us. How'm I gonna live if it's you, Nell? I wake up at night and you're not around any more and I know you've been shredded by one of Shooter's mastiffs?'

She thought about it for a moment. 'Have you got a gun?' she asked.

Heartbreak shook his head. 'I have got a gun, yes, but it's older than Methuselah. Last time I looked at it, about 1988, the trigger'd seized up.'

'It wouldn't frighten a dog, then?'

He laughed. 'What would frighten a dog? Only thing'd frighten a dog is another dog. A dog twice as big as the one you want to frighten. That gun of mine? I once walked into an off-licence with it, and the guy behind the counter laughed. "I'll've drunk myself dead before you kill me with that thing," he said.'

'Couldn't you fix it?' she asked. 'Have somebody mend it?'

'Nell, I couldn't have somebody mend it, because it isn't legal. And, yes, I might be able to oil it and get the trigger moving again, and the other bits that don't work too well. It would take some time, but that wouldn't be a problem. Trouble is, somebody, you or me, or preferably somebody else, somebody with only half a mind, would have to load it up and stand with it in his hand and shoot it. And the fuckin' thing is liable to implode, explode, whatever, and take the hand and the arm, maybe even part of the head of the guy who was holding it.'

Nell thought about that a moment. 'So, you haven't got a gun?'

'No, that's what I'm saying. I haven't got a gun.'

'Heartbreak, if you'd said you didn't have a gun to start with, we could've avoided all this.'

'What's to avoid, Nell? This's a night out. It's conversation. I'm enjoying myself, here.'

Nell supped about a third of a pint of orange squash. She licked her lips. Shook her head from side to side.

'What is it?' Heartbreak asked. 'Sometimes you disappear, so I can't reach you. It's like you're off on safari somewhere.'

'Stone and Ginny,' she said. 'They're gonna keep looking until they find some answers. Dealing with Shooter, Shooter and his dogs, because that's what it comes down to. What chance do they stand? What're the odds, here, Heartbreak, fifty-fifty?'

Heartbreak pushed his lips out, brought up both his palms as if he was turning into a pair of scales. 'Something like that,' he said. 'Not good odds. Maybe sixty-forty. Either way, I wouldn't wanna bet on it.'

'What I want to do,' Nell said, 'is reduce the odds in their favour. How do we go about doing that?'

'If it was a horse race, you'd nobble the opposition. Put Shooter's eyes out, say, or poison the dogs.'

'We can't do that,' she said impatiently. 'Look, Shooter's got enemies, right?'

'Sure, plenty of 'em.'

'So, why don't they blow him away?'

'They would if they got the chance. But Shooter, he's canny. He looks after himself. Always has a minder somewhere around.'

'Why can't we do that?'

'Blow Shooter away? You must be joking.'

'No, why can't we be minders for Stone and Ginny?

Watch their backs. Keep out of their hair, they don't even have to know about it. But when they go anywhere near Shooter or his organization, they've got three minders.'

'Three?' said Heartbreak, looking around.

'Me and you, and Sally.'

'Yeah, Sally as well.' Heartbreak finished off his orange squash in one go. He looked at his reflection in the mirror behind the bar and shook his head from side to side. 'Shooter gets to hear about this, he'll piss his pants. He'll shake to fuckin' death.'

'Me and Sally've been minding Stone all his life. We know how to do it. You wanna help out, that's up to you.'

'Oh, I wanna be there,' Heartbreak said. 'Done some professional minding in my time. Long way back, but the *experience* is there. Gotta count for something.'

The DJ put Norman Greenbaum's *Spirit in the Sky* on the turntable, and Heartbreak took Nell's hand. 'You dancin'?' he asked.

She slid off the stool and followed him on to the dance floor. 'Nineteen-seventy,' she said. 'Where were you when you first heard it?'

'Banged away for something or other. Can't remember.'

'How about the odds now?' she asked. 'With three minders, one of them an ex-professional, they must've come down.'

'Oh, yeah, sure,' said Heartbreak, taking her through the opening steps of the dance.

'But it's still not anything I'd wanna bet on.'

35

HUMBER FOG

'There's no reason for you to come,' Stone said. He had that I'm-a-man-and-that's-the-last-word-on-the-subject look on his face. He was standing in the kitchen with his legs apart, rooted to the position he'd taken, and nothing short of artillery was going to shift him.

Ginny shrugged. 'I'm coming, Stone.'

'She's dead, Ginny.'

'This is the night that either makes me or foredoes me quite.'

'What's that? Shakespeare? Jesus, Ginny, you know what kind of people we're dealing with here.'

'OK, but I'm coming with you. You might have an argument to settle with Shooter Wilde. Your whole family may want to get even with him. But Juliet was my friend, and if that bastard killed her, then I want to be there when you confront him. I want to watch him squirm, and if at all possible I want to get close enough to give him a good kick in what you euphemistically call his Henry Hall's.'

'Dream on,' Stone said. 'You'll never get that close to Shooter. The best we can hope for is that there's still some of Juliet's clothes left in that shed. That'd be evidence. With that we could put him away.'

Ginny looked out of the window at the heaps of rubbish in the long garden. The sky was the colour of a flophouse sheet. A thin mist had hung over the city all morning, and it gave a ghostly, eerie appearance to reality. The mist

occasionally coalesced in clumps and she imagined something more solid moved on the periphery of her vision.
Juliet, maybe? Or one of Shooter's thugs?

Ginny sat at the table. She opened Juliet's letters and
began skimming them. She couldn't think about Juliet
dying like that, couldn't begin to dismember her in her
mind. Stone could think what he wanted; there was no way
she was going to be left out of the action now. Whenever
Stone made his move, she'd be only a step or two behind.

As she read her friend's familiar hand, she was vaguely
aware of Stone picking up a book and moving over to the
couch. It was Sunday and it felt like Sunday is supposed to
feel. Nothing to do and nowhere to go, put your feet up and
get stuck into a book, read some letters. Let time drift by.
Dream of vengeance.

She couldn't think of Juliet as dead. Although she'd
accepted it was unlikely her friend was still alive, whenever
she thought of her, she thought in the present tense. It
seemed inconceivable that the person who described the
events in the letters, the events of her life, had ended up
being torn apart by a bunch of wild dogs. It didn't make
sense. It had no pattern or reason to it. The last few days of
Juliet's life, even the last months, may well have been
directed towards her death, but there was nothing in
Ginny's *experience* of Juliet that pointed towards such a
meaningless and violent end.

In a way Juliet's death was random and chaotic, like
someone killed in a road accident on the way home from
work. She didn't ask for it, or deserve it. She happened to
be in the wrong place at the wrong time. She made one
wrong decision, and wrapped up in that decision was
everything that followed. If Juliet had told Harvey, the
redheaded cop, to get lost when he'd propositioned her,
she'd probably never have heard any more from him. He'd
have had nothing to gain by busting her on a trumped-up

charge, and he wouldn't have wanted to draw attention to himself.

But Juliet was worried about losing her child. She'd lost him once before, and only got him back after months, years of anguish. So her decision to go to work for Harvey was already built into the equation. Her past had robbed her of choice. She didn't know that, no one did. It was only in retrospect or with the benefit of a god's-eye-view that it became apparent.

Ginny turned to Stone, who was skimming Hammett's biography on the couch. 'I had a sister,' she said. 'Did I tell you that?'

He shook his head.

'Catherine died when she was sixteen. Leukaemia. She was fit in August, and she died the day before Christmas Eve. She was two years older than me.' She glanced back at Juliet's letters, and picked one up off the table. 'This was the last letter I ever had from Juliet. She was fine when she wrote it, then a couple of days later she was probably dead. What am I supposed to do with things like this? How'm I supposed to make sense of them?'

Stone got to his feet but she waved him away. 'No, I don't want comforting. I want to know where the sense is in someone being there one minute, and then when you turn around, they've gone for ever. Juliet was coming to LA, she was coming to see me, coming to stay. That's what she says here. Her plans. I miss her.

'And Catherine. She was adopted, like me. Born in Poland and never spoke a word of the language all her life. We used to sit on the step outside the house and smoke cigarettes. Mother wouldn't have us smoking in the house. We'd light up and talk, first thing in the morning, after breakfast, before we went to school. And we'd be there again, in the evening. It was a small step, a slab of concrete, so we'd sit close together, and there'd only be Catherine and me, and no room for anyone else. Everyone else in the world was inside or alone somewhere, but we were together on that step. After she died I couldn't sit there again. I tried a couple of times, going outside by myself with a cigarette, and there was so much room on the step it became a steppe. Vast, achingly lonely, the wind whistling round and lashing my face, my legs. It wasn't like that when Catherine was alive. It was a quiet, peaceful place then.'

She returned to Juliet's letter. She didn't expect Stone to say anything. She'd only wanted to tell him something about herself, about how she was feeling. There was a line in Ibsen's *Ghosts*, she'd thought about it twice lately: *It's not that they actually live on in us; they are simply lodged there, and we cannot get rid of them.*

Stone brought his book over to the table. He sat opposite her. 'I'd like to meet you,' he said. He opened the book and read from it: ' "325 Bel Air Road, Hollywood." That's where Hammett lived. It's a huge place, and he lived there with a couple of black men, Jones and Winston, who were lovers. When this is all over, when I've finished getting rid of the tattoos, and got enough money together, I'm gonna get on a plane and come visit you. And that's where I'd like to meet. Outside that house. Maybe we can get inside, knock on the door and ask whoever lives there.'

'You're a dreamer,' she said.

'Yeah, but I'm not the only one.'

He leaned over the table and kissed her, giving birth to a rash of goose pimples on her neck and shoulders.

He said, 'When I go to Shooter's place, I'm going alone.'

She gave him a quarter-inch smile. 'Great body,' she said, running her fingers over his biceps. 'Pity about the brain.'

Nell's face was flushed when Stone and Ginny found her in her sitting room. She was standing by the sideboard wearing a full-length hippy skirt that must have witnessed hallucinogens, and a black silk blouse with the top three buttons unfastened.

Heartbreak was sitting on the couch on the other side of the room. He had one shoe on and the other one was down by the side of the couch, just out of his view. The room was charged with electricity, Ginny thought, little flashes of static exploding everywhere you looked.

Stone didn't notice a thing. He walked over to the side of the couch and picked up Heartbreak's shoe. 'What's this?'

'Yeah, I was looking for that,' Heartbreak said, taking it from him and slipping it on his foot. He laughed. 'Like a scene from Cinderella.'

'Eh?' Stone wasn't at his sharpest today, another good reason for not letting him go to Shooter's house by himself.

Nell's flush had faded a little. She moved a couple of steps over to her left so she could see herself in the mirror, fastened another button on her blouse. 'Didn't expect you quite so soon,' she said. She looked at Stone, avoided Ginny's eyes.

'We've decided to have a look in Shooter's shed,' Stone said. 'Thought we'd go over there tonight.'

'We?' said Heartbreak. 'Who's we?'

'Me and Ginny.'

Heartbreak shook his head.

'Something wrong with that?' asked Stone.

'Wouldn't you be better off by yourself?'

'Ginny wants to come.'

'I'm going with him,' Ginny said. 'We've already had the argument.'

'OK,' said Heartbreak. He held his hands out. 'Whatever you want. It's your lives.'

Nell said, 'It's a good idea. They can watch each other's backs.' She looked out of the window. 'This mist'll help.'

'I didn't say anything,' Heartbreak protested. 'I made a suggestion, if other people think differently, that's OK by me. Jesus, everything you do, somebody's calling you sexist.'

'Who called you sexist?' Nell wanted to know.

'Nobody said it, it's just there, like an implication.'

'If nobody said it, then nobody meant it. If you feel it's in the air, then it's your own conscience saying it.'

'Let's drop it,' he said.

'It's up to you. You started it.'

Heartbreak opened his mouth, but closed it again. He went away somewhere in his mind. Ginny couldn't tell if the place he went to was a place he could be a winner or a loser. But it was somewhere different, a more ordered and settled world.

Nell went into the kitchen and Ginny followed her. 'Sorry,' Ginny said. 'We shouldn't've barged in on you like that.'

'Don't worry. No damage done. Stone's never had to knock on my door. I wouldn't want him to.' She busied herself with the teapot, got a tray for the mugs.

Ginny took milk from the fridge, found a sugar bowl and teaspoons. 'Heartbreak seemed to get more trouble than he asked for.'

Nell smiled. 'He'll get over it. Heartbreak's made more mistakes with women than Henry VIII. It never stops him coming back for more.'

'I wanted to explain about tonight,' Ginny said. 'It's important that I go with Stone.'

'You don't have to explain to me,' Nell said. 'I'd be the same. In fact I've been the same all my life. If it's important, you don't leave it to someone else. Men always want to do the jobs that'll give them status, power. As women we have to cream some of that off, or they'll get so big for their boots we won't be able to love 'em.'

Ginny laughed. 'Is that post-feminism?'

'Call it what you like, love. When you're as small as I am,

you have to be able to think or the world'll trample all over you.'

'I never think about you as being small,' Ginny said.

'Don't underestimate size,' Nell warned her. 'It's important. High heels would never've been invented if some jerk hadn't kissed a woman on the forehead.' She collected the tray and marched through to the sitting room. Ginny followed.

Nell got the cards out and they played Hearts into the early evening. Heartbreak won most hands, and gradually came back into the space of the living. By the third pot of tea, he was smiling to himself and chewing his cud. Ginny noticed that Nell gave him a smile with a future in it from time to time.

The mist that had pervaded the town all day began to thicken into soup. The Humber bubbled away, cooking algae and a mixture of aquatic cryptogams up into a roke that rolled off the river and enveloped the city and the surrounding countryside.

An hour before dusk they listened to the latest k.d. lang CD, which Sally's lorry driver was playing loudly next door, most probably to drown the sound of Sally's screams. Nell said, while she and Ginny were waiting for the fourth kettle to boil, that Sally always screamed herself to orgasm. 'Either that, or it's to let me know she's still getting it.'

Twenty minutes after k.d. lang had quietened down, the lorry outside was driven slowly along the street, and a little later Sally appeared in Nell's sitting room with a large box of Terry's chocolates. 'Treats for everyone,' she said. 'But not for me. I'm weight-watching.' Ginny thought she looked ten years younger than the last time she'd seen her.

'Will he be all right in this weather, your boyfriend?' Nell asked, looking out of the window. Heartbreak got up from the table and walked over to join her. Ginny stood between them and wondered what had happened to the view. The fog outside the room was so thick, milky and white, it was like marshmallow pressing itself up against the windows.

36

DANNY BOY

Both dressed in black, Ginny and Stone left the house and walked slowly in the direction of Shooter's place. Heartbreak had explained exactly how to get to the outhouse that contained the clothes.

'This is a one-step trip,' Stone said. 'We find the outhouse and have a look-see. Whatever we find, that's it. We get out of there as soon as we can.'

'If we find ... remains?' Ginny said.

'We go to the old Bill. You go down the police station, and I'll go to the press. We have to make sure the redheaded cop, Harvey, doesn't stymie us. If he hears about it first, Shooter'll've cleaned up before the cops arrive.'

'And if we don't. find anything?'

'We get out of there and think again, Ginny.'

'What about the ladybird brooch? You said Shooter's girlfriend was wearing it. She could only've got it off Juliet, and I know Juliet wouldn't've given it to her.'

'It doesn't prove anything. She'll've got it from Shooter, and he'll say he found it somewhere. Just because her brooch turns up doesn't prove that Juliet's dead, let alone been murdered.'

They went around the back of the estate, along an overgrown path that had once been a railway line. The stone wall that surrounded the gardens varied in height, and when they found a stretch that wasn't too high, Stone made a step with his hands and hoisted Ginny up. She sat astride the top and gave Stone her hand, gripped the wall with her knees long enough for him to clamber up beside her. His face was set in a mask of determination.

They dropped down into an area of trees and shrubs, and Stone placed a hand on her shoulder and stood in silence for a minute. When his voice came it was a barely audible whisper. 'Stick close. If I stop, you stop and go into a crouch. And don't speak. If you see anything, anyone, tap me on the shoulder and point.'

She nodded. Pocahontas, she hear white chief. Him heap big man.

They headed towards the rear of the house, following a circular course, through belts of self-sown sycamore and wild blackberry that booby-trapped the scrub grass with long swarming pullulations. The mist swirled around them like huge sheets of butter muslin.

A dog barked far over to their right, and another replied with two quick yelps, a sound that could have been caused by the pain of a kick or a trap, or the excitement of a new scent on the wind. Stone stopped and whispered into her ear. 'They're not loose. The pen's over there.' He turned back and stepped over a rotting tree trunk, beginning the descent into the cultivated gardens of the estate.

The site had originally been a chalk quarry, and Ginny stumbled after Stone and let her mind wander off into geological time. This place had been laid down around 140 million years ago, and what was now calcite had originally been the shells of microscopic marine organisms and unicellular coccoliths. From what she'd seen and heard about Shooter Wilde, he had surrounded himself with the remains of the life forms and intellectual talents to which he was a true heir.

They turned around a huge Spanish chestnut tree and came to what Ginny thought was a greenhouse, but which turned out to be a glazed swimming pool. There were halogen lights burning inside the structure, which showed off the green-blue hue of the water, but barely penetrated the fog outside. There was a poolside table and chairs, and someone, Shooter or one of his thugs, had left a red silk dressing gown in a heap on the tiles, just one sleeve sucking at the surface of the pool.

Stone kept close to the building and followed it around, skirting another new extension which Ginny guessed was the games room with the MEN ONLY notice on the door. They were now in a cobble-stoned courtyard, with the games room behind and a range of former stables in front of them. Stone stopped and leaned against a wall, pulling Ginny in close beside him. He nodded towards the stable block. 'The clothes're in the end stable,' he said. 'You sure you're ready for this?'

She squeezed his hand and nodded. She wasn't at all sure that she was ready to open a door and discover Juliet's clothes, maybe bloodstains, or a butchered carcass, but this was no time to back out.

'Come on,' he said, striding out over the courtyard. Ginny followed, hanging on to his hand.

She heard a door opening behind them, and glanced back through the swirling mist. She tightened her grip on Stone's hand and jerked back to slow him down. He already had his hand on the door to the outhouse when Shooter Wilde came around the corner of the building with a smile on his face and a shotgun in his arms. Stone half-turned, looking for a way out of there, and Ginny followed his gaze behind her, to where the stooge with blackheads and greasy hair was standing with a machete dangling from his right hand. He brought the weapon up to waist height and supported its weight with his other hand as he slowly shook his head from side to side, like some paternal schoolteacher who'd discovered them smoking in the bogs.

'Yeah,' Shooter said. 'This is Danny Boy. We call him

that because he's a singer. Never got a recording contract, though, because he prefers chopping people up. That right, Danny?'

Danny Boy nodded his head. He looked at Ginny and let a thin sliver of saliva run down his chin.

'Brought the girlfriend this time,' Shooter said, eyeing Ginny. 'Bit of oriental snatch. You should've let us know you was coming, I'd've got Cuddles to bake a cake.' Blackheads, or Danny Boy, whatever he was called, laughed at that, a high-pitched sound, like a goose on a lake at night. It was an overdone laugh, could only've come from someone who was looking for a surgeon to sew his lips to his boss's ass.

Ginny's heart pounded faster as she tried to take everything in. Shooter's shotgun was similar to one Sherab kept in the bedroom at home. A three-shot pump-action twelve-bore magnum. It was a Beretta with a walnut stock. Sherab said it was the best balanced shotgun he'd ever handled.

Stone launched himself at Shooter, sending the Beretta skittering over the cobble-stones. Shooter fell back against the door of the freezer room, Stone's hands at his throat. Shooter went down on his knees, and Stone got a purchase on the bigger man's neck and slammed him up against the door, once, twice, and then again. Shooter had an idiotic smile on his face while this was happening, as though he was happy that someone was making such a fuss of him. His hands came up to try to break Stone's grip, and his eyes bulged as his face turned purple.

Danny Boy made a move to help his boss, and Ginny turned to bar his path. The man's eyes were cold slits beneath his larded hair, reflecting no inner being, no consciousness. The gaze was vacant, like that of a terrestrial arthropod. He brought up his machete, and she knew he would use it on her without compunction. There would be no cogitation on the matter; he was not the type to ruminate on the vicissitudes of right and wrong. He was already raising the weapon, and when he brought it down it would be with the intention of splitting her skull.

Ginny backed off. She said, 'Stone,' to draw his attention to the danger. Stone clung to Shooter's neck and lashed out with his feet behind him, trying to keep Blackheads at bay. But Shooter wasn't beaten either, and he wriggled free of Stone's grasp, and both of them, Shooter and Stone, got each other in a semi-head-lock. Without the intervention of Danny Boy the fight could have gone either way, Shooter was red with exertion, and Stone, though the smaller of the two, was physically aroused, like a hound with the scent of blood in his nostrils.

Danny Boy swung the machete at Stone's head. He used the flat of the blade, mindful of his boss's safety, as the two heads were close together. But it was a long swing, double-handed, from behind his right shoulder. The impact of head and blade sounded like a coconut being cracked on concrete. Stone shot out of Shooter's grasp, bounced off the wall of the stable and crumpled up on the cobble-stones.

Ginny went to kneel beside him. A long split had appeared on the top of his head, from just above his right temple travelling diagonally over to behind his left ear. Blood oozed from it easily, like lava from a lazy volcano. His eyes were closed, he had nothing to say, and his breath came in short bursts as though it was under the control of someone who knew the theory but had never actually seen a lung before.

She turned on Danny Boy. 'Bastard,' she said. Letting it rip out of her, feeling the edges of the word scrape against her throat. 'Fucking bastard.'

Danny Boy and Shooter looked at each other. Then they began to laugh. Shooter walked over to retrieve his shotgun, he picked it up still laughing, and came back to stand over Stone.

'What's so funny?' Ginny shouted. 'Look at the state of him. He needs a doctor.'

Stone opened his eyes and groaned. He tried to sit up, but fell back into the dirt again.

Shooter threw back his head and laughed. His thick pink tongue throbbing away behind his teeth. 'Jesus Christ, darling,' he said. 'You're either green or lame, I don't know which.' There was no humour in his laughter, he was not amused, it was more as if he'd heard a cue, which meant he had to turn it on. Either that or some deeply buried insecurity beyond the scope of his consciousness was being stimulated. He turned back to Danny Boy, shaking his head, and the two of them threw their heads in the air and hooted like some huge species of exotic bird.

Ginny made Stone sit with his head between his knees for some time before she let him back on his feet. Danny Boy, reluctantly, brought a towel from the swimming pool, and she managed to staunch the flow of blood from the cut on Stone's head.

Shooter and his page had long since stopped laughing and were becoming irritable with Ginny's ministrations. Danny Boy kept walking round her. He'd stand off to one side and bend his knees, bringing his face level with hers, and he'd look her in the face, his eyes flicking from left to right, up and down, taking in every feature, deliberately letting his gaze drop to her breasts. He went down on one knee and wiped a thin line of spittle away from his chin.

Ginny looked up at Shooter. 'Has he been fed?' she asked.

'OK, we walk,' Shooter said. 'That way.' He waved the Beretta towards the heart of the garden. They went around a trellis which was hung with honeysuckle and through the paved terrace with the roof of plastic strips. They were ushered across a small clearing which was home to a sawhorse and a chopping block. On one side were the stripped trunks of felled trees, and on the other stacks of logs, sorted according to size. There was a two-handed bow saw hanging from the branch of a young flowering cherry, and a long-handled axe casually leaning against its red bole.

The dogs stormed the wire surround of their pen as soon as Ginny and Stone turned the corner that brought them into view. They were difficult to count at first, because they were all over each other, snapping and snarling and dripping saliva, like a many-legged, multi-headed – and toothed – monster, a tangle of muscle and psychotic aggression.

They were ravenous, and there were five of them, three black Alsatians and two Dobermanns. Their eyes were wild, wolfish, and the sound of their howling and baying rooted Ginny to the spot. Stone stumbled up alongside her, and she heard him say, 'Jesus,' but Jesus, if he'd ever been there, was off on another errand. Shooter put the muzzle of the gun in the small of her back and pushed her forward. Danny Boy, taking a lead from his boss, slapped the back of Stone's thighs with the flat of the machete blade.

They stopped about a metre away from the wire and stood in silence. The dogs went into a cacophony of movement and sound, throwing themselves at the barricade that hemmed them in, getting their legs lodged in the apertures of the woven fencing and tearing their forelegs and the skin on their bellies as they slid backwards, yelping and snapping, into the pack.

Ginny turned to Stone and he raised his eyebrows, pursed his lips and shook his head from side to side. She wanted more than that. Irrationally, she wanted him to forget the injury to his head, the fact that their captors had weapons. She wanted Stone to be transformed into a super-hero, to raise himself out of the ashes of their predicament and sweep her away to freedom and security. But you can't have both, she told herself. Freedom and security are mutually exclusive. You have to choose one or the other.

Shooter's face held a broad smile, which Ginny tried to read. There was pride there, for his dogs, ultimately, she felt, for himself; and there was a sadistic edge to the smile, something that thinned his lips and pushed his teeth forward. She wouldn't have been surprised if Shooter had joined the dogs in their barking or if he had suddenly grabbed her and sunk his teeth into her flesh.

Security, she told herself. If I can choose, I'll take the security. Fuck freedom.

When the dogs tired and calmed a little, Shooter stepped forward and kicked at the fence, renewing their vigour and determination and setting off the howling, scrambling frenzy once again.

When he'd had enough and the dogs had been reduced to feral archetypes, Ginny and Stone were marched back through the garden to an empty loose box. Before he locked them inside, Shooter jerked his head back in the direction of the dog-pen. 'Wanted you to see that,' he said. 'Makes you think what it must've been like in Rome. The amphitheatre? Those slaves they fed to the animals? Poor buggers didn't stand a chance.'

He slammed the doors, and they heard him tell Danny Boy to take the car. 'Get Cap'n Hook and Harvey, and you'd better bring the butcher as well. Looks like we're gonna need him.'

'I'll take the Shôgun,' Danny Boy said. 'Keys in the ignition?'

'No. In the house. I'll get them.'

They heard Shooter's footsteps walking away, then the silhouette of Danny Boy's head appeared in the bars of the upper door to the loose box. Ginny couldn't see his eyes, and was glad of it. His gorgon stare was robbed of some of its power. 'Don't get too comfortable in there,' he said. 'Shooter'll keep you company. And when I get back, there's gonna be some fun.'

When he'd gone, Ginny felt around for Stone in the darkness. 'I'm here, he said, reaching for her hand.

'Are you all right?' she asked. 'Has the bleeding stopped?'

'I'm OK, don't worry.'

37

LURCHING ALONG IN THE LUMP

Nell waited while Sally, behind her, and Heartbreak in the passenger seat next to her, had both fastened their seatbelts. 'All set?' she asked.

Heartbreak fumbled around for a couple more seconds. 'Yeah, go for it,' he said.

She turned the key in the ignition and the engine of the Lump roared into action. She pushed down on the clutch and eased into first gear, letting the pedal out slowly and easily while pumping away on the accelerator. The vehicle whinnied and went up on its hind legs like a stallion, before lurching away from the curb and galloping off into the muddy night.

'Whoa,' said Heartbreak.

'Ha ha,' laughed Sally, who'd had a couple of drinks before she came out.

'Something funny?' asked Nell.

'No, I was thinking about Parliament.'

Nell didn't reply. She concentrated on the driving. The mist swirled around them as they gobbled up the road.

Heartbreak half-turned to Sally. He winked and said, 'If it wasn't for the government, we'd have nothing left to laugh at.' Sally did a little chuckle at that. Nell nodded inwardly, glad to hear her sister in good spirits. That might be important, because when Sally was feeling good, Nell couldn't think of anyone she'd rather have beside her in a crisis.

They'd given Stone and Ginny a good ten-minute start, but now they were on the road, Nell wanted to get to Shooter's house as soon as possible. Not that they'd go inside. At least she didn't think they'd go inside. They didn't have a plan, except to be in the general area in case they were needed.

'How long d'you think we should wait?' she asked.

'Give 'em half an hour,' said Heartbreak. 'If they're still inside then, something'll've gone wrong.'

'So what're we gonna do? Ram the gates?'

Sally said, 'Whatever we *have* to do. We just go in there and raise hell.'

'They'll be OK,' Heartbreak said. 'Stone'll be careful, extra careful while Ginny's with him.'

'I know that,' Sally said, her voice coming from the back of the car, almost as if she was speaking to herself. 'But Shooter's a wily bastard.'

Nell wrestled with the Shôgun, actually got it to run smoothly for the best part of a mile, all wheels on the tarmac, while they travelled along Cottingham Road. But when they turned into the private road leading to Shooter's estate, the thing started bucking again. It was as if it recognized they were entering hostile territory, and would only go closer if it was forced.

She brought it to a standstill at the side of the road, left the engine running and listened to it fluttering and injecting itself with small revs, though her foot was nowhere near the pedal.

'Trouble,' said Heartbreak, and Nell thought he meant the engine, until she saw the diamond-black Scorpio Granada pull alongside her. 'It's Harvey,' he said. 'The cop.'

Nell switched off her engine as she watched the man's head and shoulders appear over the roof of his car. He was shrouded in mist, but his carrot-coloured hair was like a beacon, brighter than the torch he carried in his left hand.

He walked round the rear of the Scorpio, and came up to Nell's door. She watched him approach through her outside mirror, and wound down the window while she adjusted her smile.

'Spot check,' he said. 'Is this your car?'

Nell said it was.

He shone the beam of his torch through the Shôgun, letting it linger on Heartbreak's face for a moment, then he transferred it to Sally in the back.

'Not in my *eyes*, lovey,' she said, turning up the corners of her mouth in a sardonic smile.

The redhead brought the beam of the torch back to Heartbreak. 'Don't I know you?' he asked with his thin voice.

Heartbreak shrugged. 'Maybe. I've been around.'

The cop gave him a long stare and shook his head. Nell couldn't tell if he recognized Heartbreak or not. Heartbreak wasn't a high-profile player in Shooter's organization. He did errands and worked around the garden, and this wasn't a cop who swapped jokes with subordinates. He turned his attention back to Nell. 'What's the registration number of the vehicle?'

She told him, taking in the tobacco smoke in his clothes and his musky body odour.

He switched off the torch. 'You are parked in a private road. What's your business?'

He had a bony face with a ridged forehead, and his eyes had translucent webbing at the corners, giving him a curiously reptilian look. This was accentuated by a small tick under his left eye.

'The engine was racing,' Nell said. 'I was gonna have a look at it.'

'Take it to a garage, or whatever you have to do, but get it off this road.'

'I'll move it as soon as I can,' Nell told him. 'Might have to call the AA.'

'You move it now, lady. I told the Chinese bint to stay out of this one, and we know you're connected with her. So, move along. Fast.'

'What if it doesn't start?'

He grinned at her and the webbing at the corners of his eyes swelled infinitesimally, then shrank back again. 'Your friends'll push you.'

'Move it, Nell,' Heartbreak said.

She wound up the window and turned the key in the ignition. The engine roared back into life. She moved into gear and the Shôgun leapt forward. She let it run and leap along the road for a hundred metres, then did a three-point turn and came to a halt facing back towards the Scorpio. The mist swirled around the road, shrouding the view, so she couldn't be sure if she could see the Scorpio or if she only imagined she could.

'Supercilious bastard,' she said.

'Don't let him get to you,' Sally said. 'Leave the car on the main road. We can walk back down here if necessary.'

Nell revved the engine two, three, four times, listening to the cylinders screaming, as if in sympathy with her own frustration and anger. She gunned the Lump forward, feeling its excitement as it responded to the weight of her foot on the accelerator. As the car hurtled along the tarmac the distant shape of the Scorpio Granada came into clearer focus. Harvey was leaning against the bonnet, shaking his head from side to side. Nell recalled a scene in a movie, she couldn't remember what it was called, when one car, travelling at speed, passed so close to another that it shaved off the outside mirror and door handles.

'Let's give Mr Self-Important a fright,' she said.

Heartbreak put his hands forward to brace himself against the madness of the night.

Nell fixed her sights directly on the front of the Scorpio, experiencing all the emotions and passions of a kamikaze pilot about to explode on the flight deck of an aircraft carrier. As the Lump picked up speed, bucking and screaming with rage and indignation, the section of mist surrounding the Scorpio lifted. It was as if whoever was in charge of the weather wanted to make absolutely sure that Nell didn't miss her target.

Harvey, leaning against the front of his vehicle, looked long and hard at the Shôgun tearing up the tarmac in his direction. If its present trajectory were held, it would seem that his destiny was heading for a turning point. Goodbye corrupt cop; hello fresh sandwich filling. He stopped shaking his head from side to side. Suddenly didn't look so proud.

As she watched panic take hold of the cop, Nell felt a smile invade her face. It began as a feeling of warmth around her lips, her mouth, and quickly spread itself into the tiny wrinkles around her eyes. It brought some colour to her cheeks and neck.

She flicked on the main beam and Harvey's arms fell away to his sides. He was trapped in the light like a rabbit, unable to move to either side. In each of his eyes was a reflection of the Shôgun bearing down on him. Two avenging angels. If the right one don't get you, the left one will.

Nell was as cool as fresh cotton sheets. Thirty feet from impact she nudged the wheel fractionally to the left, touched the brake pedal lightly, and gave the beast its head, knowing that she would trim the Scorpio's wing mirror, send it skittering down the road.

At the same moment, Harvey was released from his paralysis and had to choose which way to go. If he'd moved to his left, or if he'd stayed put, welded to the front of his vehicle, the most he would have been faced with was a couple of small bills, one to replace his mirror, and another to dry-clean his trousers. As it was, he decided to go to his right, into the path of the Lump, and the costs suddenly escalated out of control.

'No!' Nell screamed when she saw him move into the road. She tried to miss him, wrenching the steering wheel hard over to the left, at the same time pushing hard on the brake. The Lump screeched with rage, pawed the road in front of it for an instant, then adopted a loose and pendulous, loping motion, which took it flopping along the road with the broken body of the redheaded cop coupled to the radiator grille.

When it finally came to a halt, Nell, Heartbreak and Sally tumbled out on to the road. Nell's heart was pounding irregularly, her breath coming in sharp bursts. She could hear tiny cries coming through the night, and she thought Harvey was whimpering in pain and fear, but realized that she was making those sounds herself.

Heartbreak was kneeling by Harvey's body. After a moment or two he got to his feet, shaking his head. 'He's done for,' he said. 'Just been handed his wings.'

38

DRIFTWOOD FROM THE PAST

Stone pulled Ginny towards him and gave her what felt like
a pickaxe handle. She explored it in the darkness and he
heard her catch her breath as she recognized what it was.

'A spade?'

'Might come in handy,' Stone said. 'If we start digging
now, we could be out of here by Christmas.'

'He's terrifying, the guy with the blackheads,' Ginny said.
'He paralyses me.'

There was a movement outside, and Shooter's head
appeared in the bars to the loose box. 'Danny Boy?' he said.
'That's a real pity, because I told him he could have you for
a couple of hours when he gets back. He's dribbling at the
thought of it. He's big on doomed women. Wanted the
other one real bad, that friend of yours.'

'Juliet?'

'Yeah, that was it. We thought it was a joke at first. But
that was her real name. She didn't have no Romeo, though.'
Shooter laughed at that one. 'Not like you, girl, she didn't
have no night of passion to look forward to. Just a ginger
cop with shaky hands.'

'Back off, Shooter,' Stone said. 'Do what you've got to
do, but spare us all the mouth.'

'I could never resist a captive audience,' Shooter said.
'Besides, I think your girlfriend here would like to know
what happened to her friend.'

Stone fingered the handle of the spade, which he'd leaned

226

up against the wall behind him. He felt Ginny's cool hand touch his, a gentle pressure, encouraging him to let Shooter talk.

'She got too greedy, that was the problem. We expect people to filch a little, feed their own dragon. It's costed into the price. But this Juliet was taking more than her fair share. Like she was running her own business. Customers complained, and when customers get upset, we start losing their business. They move over to the Jamokes or the Paki dealers, and then we've lost them for ever. Never get them back.'

'So you killed her,' Stone said.

'Not me,' said Shooter. 'Never laid a hand on her. We've got this new policy in the firm. More democratic. The one who does the hiring does the firing. So, as that little girl was hired and run by our rozzer friend, Harvey, we gave him the job of clearing up his own mess. He wasn't keen at first, tried every which way to get out of it, but by the time he was through with her, I think he was beginning to enjoy himself.'

'Did you really feed her to the dogs?' Ginny asked. Her voice was small, as if she was shrinking away in the darkness.

Stone put his arm around her, held her close to him, hoping there would still be something left when Shooter had finished with his revelations.

'Yeah, the dogs really appreciated her. An economic decision. Cut down on the meat bill for one thing. But a body is a problem to get rid of. If you bury it, there's always someone'll come along and dig it up. You put it in the river, and it don't matter what you weigh it down with, it's sure to wash up sooner or later. And when these bodies turn up, the local boys in blue get agitated, start asking questions. When the relatives come up with reward money, you just know somebody's gonna be tempted. So all in all, the dogs is the best bet. They don't leave any clues. The whole thing is reduced to dog shit in a few hours. It's neat.'

'Neat?' Stone wondered what the odds were of throwing the spade and hitting the guy between the eyes. He had a flash vision of Shooter wearing the spade in his forehead, standing there a moment while the realization hit him that he was dead. It wouldn't work, though. He touched the handle of the spade, promising himself that the next time he made a move, there wouldn't be any odds at all. He would be absolutely certain.

'OK,' Shooter said. 'You don't like it. I can understand that. But you've got to agree it was a neat solution. And it taught Harvey a lesson he won't forget. He had to scalp her after he'd strangled her, save the dogs choking themselves on hair. And we let him feed them the first course. He learned a valuable lesson. He came to me later and said he'd be more careful in future. And I think he will, too. He'll use people who can be trusted. Is that neat or is it neat?'

'It's barbaric,' Stone said.

'Big word for a convicted killer. But you always were full of shit.'

'Is that what you've got planned for us?' Ginny said.

'Yeah, more or less,' Shooter told her. 'You're dog meat.' He laughed. 'Don't know how they'll take to *you*, though. They never had Chinese before.' His laugh again, a forced cackling with little humour behind it. More of an excuse to make a noise. 'Fucking chop suey dog food.'

Stone ran for him, his arms outstretched, reaching for Shooter's throat. But the man stepped back, out of reach.

'I've got a good one for you as well,' Shooter said. 'About the time you served for Gingell's murder? This's gonna kill you, but you didn't do it. Oh, you gave him a good going over, must've had shit on your boots when you'd finished with him. But he wasn't dead. When I found him he was still breathing. And it struck me that if I gave him one more big boot in the head, it would be like you and your family were paying back part of what you owed me.'

'I don't believe it,' Stone said. 'You're shooting the shit, living up to your name.'

'They call it irony, these days,' Shooter said. 'When something like that happens. Gingell was still alive, I'm telling you. I kicked him in the head so hard it broke his neck. I did the crime and you did the time.'

'You think it's true?' Ginny asked, when Shooter had gone.

'I don't know.' Stone had lived with the belief that he had killed Gingell for years. He couldn't give it up from one moment to the next. His identity was inextricably bound in with the knowledge that he had taken someone's life.

When Shooter had cut his mother's face, Stone had wanted to kill him. He'd gone round to the place where Shooter lived then, not this estate, but a block of flats on Coltman Street. Gingell was Shooter's minder at the time, and he'd refused to let Stone through. It was a steaming day, and Gingell was wet, wearing Bermuda shorts and a hunting knife on a cord round his waist. He must have been out in the garden because Stone could remember hearing water running and thinking it was a hose-pipe.

'Get out of the way,' Stone told him. 'I don't have a beef with you, but I'm gonna have a go at Shooter.'

Gingell had grinned. 'You gotta get past me first,' he said, and he took the knife out of its sheath. It was a big knife with a serrated edge and a bone handle. The blade must've been ten inches long.

Stone was possessed that day. He passed a dummy and then smashed a hard right into Gingell's nose. He saw the knife go clattering off along the floor, and watched as Gingell went down on his hands and knees and tried to go after it. Stone stamped on Gingell's hand and kicked him in the face.

There was a point when he still knew it was Gingell he was kicking, but then he lost sight of Gingell, and was taking his revenge on Shooter. The body on the floor in the Bermuda shorts ceased to be the minder and became instead the man himself.

It was only later, when he'd spent his strength, that Stone looked down and recognized what he'd done. Gingell's body was inert, his face a bloody pulp, his breath coming in ruptured spasms, because a rib had punctured a lung.

Stone tumbled out of the building and ran up the street looking for help. But when a doctor finally arrived at the house there was no life left in Gingell's body.

Stone thought it was all down to him. He had always thought that he'd kicked the man to death. But now Shooter had added a new dimension to the story.

Did it make any difference?

He shook his head. He couldn't decide. He'd taken Gingell to within an inch of his life. If Shooter hadn't finished him off, the guy would probably have died anyway, or maybe he'd've carried on living with brain damage or some form of paralysis.

Technically, he supposed, the murder was down to Shooter, but Stone had come to think of himself as a killer, and he knew he'd always carry the guilt for Gingell's death. As he sat in the darkness of the loose box, his arm around the trembling body of Ginny, he prayed that before the day was over, he could add the death of Shooter Wilde to his score.

39

DOUBLE VISION

It wasn't easy to lift him. Sally and Nell took his shoulders and arms, and pushed, while Heartbreak backed into the Shôgun carrying his legs.

'I'm gonna have nightmares about this,' Nell said. 'Probably for the rest of my life.'

'Why?' asked Sally. 'If you'd bowled over an old-age pensioner or some young mother with a baby, I could understand it. I'd probably have a couple of nightmares myself. But this guy isn't worth it. I wouldn't lose an afternoon nap over him.'

'The guy was flawed, anyway,' Heartbreak said. 'He ran under your wheels. He was due to buy it. If you hadn't caught him there, he'd've gone through a red light or drunk poison. OD'd on his own dope. And look how quick he died. Didn't feel no pain. Didn't struggle. It was humanitarian. Saint Peter was waiting for him in the street.'

Nell closed the door on Heartbreak and the corpse and walked round to the driver's door. She got in and sat behind the wheel. Sally climbed in beside her. 'What now?'

Heartbreak got out of the car and came round to her window. 'I drive,' he said.

'You don't trust me? I'm not gonna hit anyone else. It was an accident.'

Heartbreak shook his head. 'Wait here,' he said. He walked back to where Harvey's Scorpio Granada was parked, and retrieved the keys from the ignition, making sure he didn't leave prints on the car. He locked the doors and walked back to the women in the Shôgun. 'OK, Sally,' he said, handing her the keys to the Scorpio. 'You get in the back with our dead friend, and put the keys in his jacket pocket. What I want is for you to make room back there so you can get your head down below the level of the window. The cop can sit up.'

'Seems ass about tit to me,' she said. 'Wouldn't it be better if we laid him down and I got to watch the scenery?'

'Just do it,' he said. Sally shrugged and got in the back. Nell was sure her sister was going to argue some more, but she didn't say a word, just set about arranging Harvey's body. There was a hint of authority in Heartbreak's voice that had not been evident in recent years. She caught his eye, and he nodded at her as if to confirm that he was taking over, that he also recognized that this was his moment. He looked taller, like someone had packed fertilizer in his boots.

Nell settled herself on the floor next to Sally and waited until Heartbreak adjusted the position of the driving seat. 'OK back there?' he asked.

Nell and Sally both said they were. Harvey wasn't talking to anyone; since he'd died, he'd gone into a sulk. Couldn't seem to accept that it was all his own fault.

Heartbreak started the engine and eased the Shôgun forward. It didn't lurch in any way, even when he changed up into second gear. Simply moved along the road like a normal car, all four wheels in contact with the ground. It struck Nell momentarily that he might be a better driver than her, but then she remembered that this was a good night for him. The Lump would do whatever he wanted, and come morning Heartbreak would probably be in line for canonization.

He drove slowly up to Shooter's house, got out of the car and opened the gate, then he drove through into the pebbled driveway and got out of the car again, went back and closed the gate. 'Keep your heads down,' he said between his teeth as he guided the vehicle along the drive, round the rear of the house and the swimming pool, and parked it at the entrance to a cobbled yard which fronted a stable block. 'Get ready to move the body,' he said, as he hopped out of the car. He opened the end door of the stable block, which contained three large chest freezers. 'OK,' he said. 'Start humping.'

They managed to get the body out of the Lump without too much difficulty, but they had to leave it on the concrete floor of the room while they transhipped frozen hunks of shrink-wrapped meat from one freezer to another so as to make enough room. When they'd finished they laid the body of Harvey on a bed of frozen vegetables and Black Forest gateau, and closed the lid of the freezer down on him. Sally lifted it again and quickly arranged the corpse's hands in the pious funeral-parlour position over his chest. Nell caught her sister's eye and gave her a nod of approval, but Heartbreak didn't want to hang around for any niceties.

'You can send him a wreath later,' he said. 'Now, I want out of here. While we're still young, eh?'

He reversed the Shôgun back down the drive. Swung the wheel over so that the rear wheels cut a gouge out of the lawn, then drove slowly up to the gate. He got out and opened the gate, then came back to the Shôgun and hit the accelerator so hard that the thing leapt forward like a shot out of a gun. When Nell raised her head above the level of the seat, they were already out of the private approach road and belting along Cottingham Road. Heartbreak had a thin line of sweat on his top lip and he hadn't started smiling yet.

Cuddles poured him a cognac in a large balloon with a vermilion stem, and Shooter sat on his white leather sofa, the barrel of the shotgun sticking up between his splayed legs like a dildo. The surveillance monitor in the corner of the room thumbed through different sites in and around the house, and as he sipped his cognac he let his eyes flick between the images on the screen and Cuddles sitting in the middle of a thick-pile rug painting her toe nails purple. She'd been in the sauna and she was pink and white, wrapped in a cherry-red towelling bathrobe. Her silver-blonde hair, still wet, hanging loose and uncombed around her shoulders, sent an occasional trickle of water and perspiration into the gully between her implanted breasts. Silicon Valley, she called it. She'd let the bathrobe ride high on her thighs, exposing a new pair of silk appliquéd, French knickers.

'What's going on out there?' she asked, looking up at him.

'Couple'a prowlers. We've got 'em covered.'

She turned her attention back to her toes. Shooter watched her work. She was a miniaturist, her whole being intent on the accuracy of each short brush-stroke. For a moment Shooter couldn't understand why he screwed other women, and wondered if he should give monogamy a try. He knew it wouldn't happen, because he'd fuck a frog if it didn't jump, but it was interesting to speculate. Shooter thought about lots of things, that was the way his mind worked.

Cuddles was an enigma, he concluded. She was a video hermit, and he didn't like that, was always threatening to get rid of the VCR. But on the other hand, she was the kind of girl who, if you gave her a whip, could make a living out of the dominance trade. And Shooter thought he probably did like that.

A movement on the surveillance monitor caught his attention. The Shôgun was back, and Heartbreak was getting out of the driver's seat and opening the gate. Looked like Harvey in the back. He watched as Heartbreak drove the car out of range of the gate camera.

Something didn't quite fit, because he'd expected Harvey to come in his own car, the diamond-black Granada. And he hadn't noticed Danny Boy or the butcher in the Shôgun. Still, that was life, *c'est la fucking vie*, if you were surrounded by idiots, there was no use expecting them to get things right first time. Or the second or third time, come to that. It was like a disease they passed on to each other, an epidemic. One of them had come in with an idiot germ, and now it was running riot through the whole firm. There was only Cuddles and him who were unaffected. And he wasn't entirely convinced about her. Sit her in front of a video and she was a goner.

Shooter poured himself another glass of cognac, put some fire inside him while he waited for them to come up. He worked hard for his money, might as well enjoy the perks. No good being the commanding officer if it didn't improve your standard of living. All that responsibility, twenty-four hours a day, no holidays.

Cuddles was finished with her nail varnish now, and was lying on her back with her legs in the air wriggling her toes. 'I'm coming for you later,' he told her.

She looked at him, her toes curled up. She giggled. 'I'm completely at your mercy,' she said.

Ain't that the truth. But mercy was about compassion, and Shooter had neglected to cultivate his. He'd concentrated on severity. When you're the captain of the ship, you have to be in complete control, and everyone has to know that you're the one. You have to be cruel to be kind. And love hurts, it has to hurt or it gets boring and dies. All those sayings mean something, they're ancient wisdom carried down through the generations. Something the old people knew in their blood and wanted to pass on to us so we didn't turn into wuzzies.

That was Shooter's philosophy. And tonight, when work was over, he'd be giving Cuddles some philosophical instruction.

Cuddles sat up on the rug as if she'd read his mind. 'Not too heavy, Shooter.'

'You enjoyed it last time.'

'I did not. I'm telling you, I don't want it. Christ, I could hardly walk for a week.'

He sipped his cognac. 'I got carried away. It won't be like that.'

'Jesus, I hope not.' She got to her feet. 'Thought I might go in the garden.'

'I'm letting the dogs out in a minute. It'll be dangerous out there.'

She turned to him. 'Jesus, Shooter. I like it when you're gentle.'

He worked up a smile that was bankrupt before it was born. 'I look after you, don't I?'

'I'm not just going to take it,' she said. 'I'll fight back.'

'That's what I like to hear.'

The Shôgun was back at the entrance again. Shooter watched Heartbreak open the gate and get back behind the steering wheel. Then the car leapt forward like it was in a Formula One race. Shooter shook his head. It was always the same, if you want a job doing you have to do it yourself.

He put his glass down and stood over Cuddles for around half a minute, giving her the look. 'Be ready,' he said eventually. Then he backed out of the door, pinning her to the spot with his eyes. In the joint there'd been this guy called himself a lepidopterist, could only pin butterflies down. Because he loved them.

40

A SPANISH CHESTNUT

Ginny had something in her eye. Stone took her by the hand and led her to the door of the loose box. He found a fleck of straw above the dark pupil, and lured it from the glassy surface of her eye with the cuff of his shirt. Her eye make-up had smudged, the mascara staining a tiny salt brook that ran free for half an inch and then parched on the high ground of her cheek.

Stone took the spade and pushed it through the bars. By grasping the wooden handle he could get enough leverage to hack away at the sneck of the door. Ginny smiled grimly when he turned to look at her. He couldn't read her all the time. He thought she was worrying that Shooter would return before they got out of there, but he couldn't be sure. When he looked at her he realized she could be thinking about the dogs, or the death of her friend, even her husband.

When he stopped to rest she asked, 'Shall I have a try?'

He shook his head and went back to work. She didn't have the height, she'd have to stretch too far out, and maybe drop the spade. It had been Stone's idea to come here, now it was his responsibility to get them out.

As he chopped away, he remembered the Mad-Fucking-Talking-Shop. Toby, an old friend, had formed the organization way back, before Stone had gone to prison. Toby had just left his wife, not for another woman, but because he'd realized that she'd dominated his life for so long, and that if

237

he didn't do something about it, she'd carry on for ever. The Mad-Fucking-Talking-Shop was an exclusive organization, Toby and Stone were the only members, except occasionally there was a neighbour of Toby's who used to come along. A woman in a mauve duffle-coat who swung one arm like she was at a military tattoo. Stone couldn't remember her name.

They just talked. It was a reaction against thirty-something wankers who played obscure music and gazed at computer-generated postcards, trying to decipher what's hidden in them. Shallow bastards.

After a while the organization withered away.

Stone took another bash at the sneck and watched it come away from the door and fall to the ground. He dropped the spade and withdrew his aching arm. He turned towards Ginny as he touched the door with his index finger and pushed it open. 'Coming?'

They were like Adam and Eve, he thought, as they emerged from the broken door of the loose box into the swirling mist of the fecund garden. He retrieved the spade. Ginny took his free hand and he led her back the way they had come, past the brightly lit swimming pool with the red silk dressing gown still swirling its empty arm in the water. It seemed an age since they had passed this way before.

When they turned, by the old Spanish chestnut, into the narrow path that would take them up towards the walled perimeter of the estate, Stone stopped. He drew Ginny up beside him, but kept his eyes fixed on the path ahead. 'Don't move,' he said. 'Listen, and do exactly what I say.'

He felt her stiffen beside him as she saw the Dobermann blocking the path about fifteen metres ahead. The dog bared its teeth and tossed its head. The beast took a step forward, then stopped again, as uncertain, at least for the moment, as an English spring.

'I'm gonna make a step with my hands,' Stone said. 'And you're going up the tree.'

'What about you?'

'I'm coming too.'

He clasped his hands together and lowered them so she could put her foot there, then he hoisted her up and watched her scramble into the crook of the lower boughs. He sensed, rather than saw, the Dobermann begin his run.

'Quickly,' Ginny said, hysteria taking her tone into a higher octave. Stone reached up and grabbed her hand, kicking his feet against the deeply fissured grey bark of the trunk in an effort to evade the snapping jaws of the Dobermann.

For a moment it seemed as though he would make it, that the two of them would be higher than the frenzied dog could reach. But when those jaws snapped together around his ankle, Stone let out a howl of pain that ripped his vocal cords. His grip on Ginny's hand slipped, and there was a moment when they were connected only by the hooks of their fingers. The crushing jaws of the dog shook him free of the tree. Suddenly he was on his back on the patchy earth, and the dog was dragging him around like fresh road-kill.

A sixth sense took over, and Stone struggled back on to his feet. The Dobermann kept up an incessant growling in the back of its throat, and it didn't loosen its hold on Stone's ankle for a second. He swung the spade at the animal's head, but the dog saw it coming and side-stepped, letting the ankle go and taking hold of the wrist that wielded the spade.

The spade flew from Stone's grasp. He watched it do a somersault in the air before it landed in a patch of bramble thorns. Ginny screamed, 'I'll get it.'

'No.' Stone heard the word come from his mouth in a series of modulated tones. It was a command that paralysed her where she stood in the tree. The dog had transferred its hold back to his ankle now, and the pain was costing him his consciousness. The mist had spread to the inside of his head, and the tree and the dog and Ginny came together suddenly in a spiral.

As he fell he watched the ground coming to meet him, knowing that he was going to land on his face, but deciding not to worry about it. Voices from his childhood chanted something about the queen, and he couldn't work out if they meant her or Freddie Mercury. *These are the days of our lives.*

Ginny couldn't jump from the tree. The lowest bough, on which she was standing, was still too high for that. If she jumped, she would break a leg, but if she *climbed* down the Dobermann would sink its teeth into her before she reached the spade.

She was shaking from head to foot, rooted to her perch in the tree by fear and hysteria. The Dobermann had blood on its teeth, Stone's blood, and Stone's leg, down by the ankle, was running red.

The dog left Stone for a moment and howled as it sprang up the trunk of the tree towards Ginny. She screamed down at it, horrified that it was able to get so far up the tree. If she'd been a few inches lower, it would have reached her. She felt its breath on her legs and saw far down into its mouth, the lewd pink flesh of its gums against the porcelain white of those red-rimmed teeth. This was no guard dog; it was an animal that had been fundamentally and consistently mistreated, a canine psychopath with as much compassion as dental caries.

Ginny closed her eyes, gritted her teeth and made a huge effort to bring her breathing under control. She gripped the upright branches of the tree. When she opened her eyes her knuckles and fingers were white and bloodless. Her breath was still not rhythmical, but she had stopped screaming, and quiet had fallen over the scene. The Dobermann was standing over the fallen body of Stone, its ears cocked and the hackles along the ridge of its back vibrating nervously.

Somewhere behind the tree, over by the house, a dog barked, and another replied from deep in the cultivated part of the garden. The Dobermann trotted away from Stone a few paces, cocked its ear again, then came back and worried Stone's already broken ankle. Ginny jumped and shuffled in the tree to distract the dog's attention, and when it looked up at her, she deliberately lowered her leg to within striking distance. The Dobermann came for her quickly – for its size it had a remarkable turn of speed – and she only narrowly missed getting caught in its jaws.

It fell back down the trunk of the tree and came again, this time leaping even higher. Ginny stepped back and heard an involuntary cry escape from her lips. She looked around for a higher perch, thinking that the dog might have more reserves, or that its madness would fling it up there into the tree with her.

But it didn't leap again. Suddenly its attention was focused on the black Alsatian with the wild eyes that had skidded on to the path. The two of them circled around Stone, keeping their distance, but watching each other intensely. The Dobermann restarted its low growl, and the Alsatian snarled and bared its teeth and pawed at the ground from time to time. Each animal in its way was trying to force the other to back down.

The Dobermann regarded the inert body of Stone as its own preserve, and was not prepared to give it up without a fight. The Alsatian wasn't interested in any philosophy of personal property. As far as it was concerned, the world was a jungle where only the fittest survived.

They observed the rituals, though. There was that period

of silent communication which experienced hunters talk about. An inactive battle which precedes the battle proper, an encounter which seems to involve only the eyes, but which really engages the wills of the two opponents. A struggle beyond the physical.

This period passed quickly.

Suddenly the black Alsatian leapt forward, it grabbed at Stone's arm and pulled back savagely, ripping the cloth of his sleeve. The Dobermann was on it immediately, snapping at its face, its neck, and finally its flanks as it turned away. The Alsatian retreated a few steps, then renewed its attack. It made a bid for Stone's hand, which, had it been successful, could easily have removed his fingers. But the Dobermann was steadfast in defence and took a bite from its opponent's ear, sending it whimpering away to the foot of the tree.

The Alsatian shook its head, sending a spray of black blood in a wide arc over the head of the Dobermann. It pawed its injured ear, looking as if it wanted to draw the wounded part down so that it could lick it clean. Then it yelped impetuously at the Dobermann, as if it was blaming it for not fighting fair. But Stone's guardian had won the skirmish and was now intent on consolidating its position. It took hold of the bloodied ankle once more and set about dragging the body away from the tree and into the undergrowth.

Ginny felt something break inside her. She suddenly had no fear. As she watched the body of Stone being dragged away from her, she lost all sense of personal safety and steeled herself to leap down from the tree. The spade was several metres away, almost hidden by a thick growth of thorns, but she could see the light reflecting from its blade. With luck she would not break a leg when she jumped, and she'd have time to get the weapon, and lay about both dogs before they had time to overpower her.

Stone still had a chance. And his chance was her.

She took a breath and gripped tightly with both hands as she worked out exactly where she would land. She came to earth a couple of metres in front of the black Alsatian and let the impetus of her leap take her over into a roll that brought her up against the bramble bushes. She tore at the thorny branches with both hands, only glancing behind her briefly to see the Alsatian get to its feet and begin its approach, looking like its personal angel had just delivered a free meal. Ginny recovered the spade and turned, holding the weapon in both hands.

'Don't move,' said a tinny, amplified voice. She looked up, trying to work out where the sound came from. Then there was a sharp crack, which could only have been the report of a rifle, and the black Alsatian slumped forward where it stood.

The Dobermann released Stone's ankle at the sound. And as Ginny turned her attention towards it there was another crack, and the dog turned its head slowly to look at the bright red dart that had entered its flank. But before it could turn its head far enough round, it too was slumping forward into a heap.

'Stay where you are,' said the tinny voice. 'This is a police warning. There are other animals around, and we have reason to believe they may be dangerous.'

But Ginny took no notice. She dropped the spade and scrambled over to Stone. His ankle was in a mess, his wrist was badly torn, and he was bleeding from a deep head wound. She felt for a pulse and placed her head on his chest to listen for a heartbeat.

Heartbreak appeared at her side, and when she looked up and past him she saw Sally and Aunt Nell. The two women were white and clinging to each other, flanked on either side by armed policemen.

'Is he all right?' said Heartbreak.

Ginny nodded. 'He's unconscious, but he's breathing. We need an ambulance.'

IV
AMERICA

41

LETTERS FROM STONE

Dear Ginny,

Thanks for your letter. It was good to hear from you, though you sound as though you're having a tough time. Sherab seems to be taking it all very hard.

I can understand why you feel responsible for him, and I can see how he is exploiting your feelings. I don't suppose there is much point in me telling you not to let him get away with it. The emotional blackmail, I mean. You have to grieve for whatever it was that you had, the bit that has died and left him feeling alone and you feeling guilty.

But I'm not a philosopher.

I'll tell you the good news, maybe take your mind off your immediate problems. Shooter Wilde has been charged with the murder of Harvey, and it looks as though he's going to do some time at the pleasure of her majesty. From my point of view there's a wonderful irony about the fact that he didn't do the evil deed, and that it was all down to Aunt Nell's driving. Hammett would've loved it, he'd've written a book about it.

But – and you'll like this – Shooter has also been charged with the murder of Juliet Gurney. The forensic scientists collected the topsoil from the dog pen in Shooter's garden, and they've come up with flakes of human bone. In itself that's only circumstantial evidence, but they've also managed to do some DNA tests with John, Juliet's son, and they can prove that the remains they got from the dog pen were once Juliet.

I don't suppose you'll ever forget Danny Boy, the guy with the blackheads. He's been charged with conspiracy to commit murder, kidnapping (that's us), and accessory to murder. The general consensus seems to be that he'll never come out of the slammer. But Cap'n Hook, the guy who was in charge of the dogs, and the butcher who carved up your friend and was on his way to do the same honours for us, seems to have disappeared.

Cuddles wasn't charged with anything. She came to see me the other night and handed over the ladybird brooch. I won't send it through the post, because it might get damaged, but I wanted to tell you that I've got it, and when we meet, I'll give it to you.

She said that Shooter was kind to her, gentle most of the time. He lost it from time to time and gave her a black eye. One time he kicked her when she was on the floor. But mostly he took care of her. She said, 'There were bad times with Shooter, but most of the time he adored me.'

I know what she means. I remember when he and Sally were an item, in the early days before they went sour on each other. Shooter was like a father to me then. He'd have done anything for me.

But there is another part of him that is a monster, and it is that part that we had to contain.

I wonder if there is a monster in everyone. I know there is one in me.

Cuddles reminds me of my mother when she was younger. They both fell for Shooter, as did lots of other women with world-weary eyes. Aunt Nell says it's because they are looking for someone to take on responsibility for them. What do you think?

So you think my expectations about America are naïve. I do know that the rich guys run the world for their own benefit, and the rest of us can go squat. I read newspapers, books, I've seen the Scorsese films. But what *you* seem to have missed is that it is not America that I'm looking for. I'm coming to LA soon, maybe take in New York as well. But then I want to go visit as many cities as I can, in Europe as well, everywhere. When I was banged away, I had a continuing fantasy, a dream that I was at large in a huge metropolis, and that the whole penal system of the world was looking for me. But I was a step ahead of them all the time. I was in Chicago or Vienna or Capetown or Moscow. I was in Jerusalem or Lhasa or Buenos Aires or Stockholm.

I was no longer confined to the broken ruins that Thatcher left behind. Do you understand what I'm saying? The city is the imagination of the age in concrete form. It is the only place we can be free.

My ankle is still bad. I'm seeing the physio every other day now, and even though she tells me I'll always need a stick to walk any distance, I tell her she's full of shit, and I'm gonna beat this thing.

Love
Stone

Dear Ginny,

Yes, I'm still having the laser treatment. The bullet-hole tattoos on my temples have gone. We're still working on the others. But I've decided to keep the teardrop.

Eve Caldwell, my boss at System.ini has given me an extra day's work every week, and she's going on a trip to the Middle East, so I'll be working full-time while she's away. Heartbreak will help out. He doesn't know shit about computers, but he can brew a wild cup of coffee. Only trouble is he does some terrible farts. Seems completely unconscious about them. He'll be walking over to a customer's table with a tray of drinks, and suddenly drop this huge raspberry. Nothing at all delicate about it. None of your small explosions behind the legs. I should be so lucky.

I suppose we'll manage. They are usually benign, but every so often he does one with a punch. This afternoon he emptied the café in five seconds flat. Not just the customers, *I* was out there too, and Heartbreak. 'I didn't want to die in there alone,' he said.

We sat outside for fifteen minutes, didn't even go in to answer the phone. I wanted to ring the fire brigade but Heartbreak said it'd clear on its own eventually. I hope he's right.

When Eve gets back from her trip, I'll've earned enough to get myself over there to your part of the world, and by that time you should have sorted yourself and Sherab out. Whaddaya think? I don't want to be greedy; I'll just take whatever's going.

I don't have a photograph of you, you know. That's not a request. I've got a picture in my head. Well, it's more like a video actually. Starts with the night I found you in the porch, you all white and wan, and me wondering what I was doing washing spew out of your hair. Then it goes on with you growing stronger and more substantial, getting more real in my imagination until you fill the whole screen of my world, a flickering image or reflection of Virginia Rebecca Bradshaw. The Chinese girl who turned out to be from Vietnam, and wears too much make-up and who crept inside my consciousness and got lodged there. So don't send me no snapshots.

Beige sends her love. She looks washed out and weary every time I see her. I gave her your address so you can expect to hear from her. She calls in the café from time to time, wanting to talk about Juliet and what happened to her. It's as if she can't believe it, as if the reality of it all is beyond her comprehension. She accepts it when we talk, nods and looks sad and then goes back into the world with

Darren. But a few days later she's back again and needs to talk it through some more. She says, 'Juliet was looking for happiness. Why'd they have to kill her?' I don't know what to say to that. It's true, she was only looking for happiness. All you can say about it is that she got in the way of something heavy. It happened to be Harvey, or Shooter, or whoever it was that killed her, but it could just as well have been a truck. It can happen to anybody or anything, sometimes life ends abruptly and with our limited consciousness we can't understand why it happened. When you're close up to the action, it looks like a tragedy, but with an historical or distant perspective the people involved seem like specks, inconsequential. They roll over and die so that something else can happen, so that someone else can take their place. They've done their job. We don't know what happens to them. Religious people tell us that they go on to better things. I dunno. I never met Juliet, only read her letters, but when I think about her life, I want to believe she's in a better place.

I'll post this letter now and start another one when I get back.

Lots of love
Stone

Dear Ginny,

Thanks for the letter. It made me think. Especially what you said about how you make up stories about yourself, or embroider the truth to make yourself more interesting. I do that as well, probably everyone does to some degree. Guys in prison are masters at inventing maverick pasts. But I'll come back to that in a minute.

I've been thinking about moving. Somewhere a bit lighter, a flat in one of those big houses in Pearson Park would be nice. It's OK here, once you get inside, and there's so much about the place that reminds me of you, so I haven't made my mind up yet. But I went to look at a place in the park, and it would be great to walk out and feel grass under my feet rather than that wasteland of Spring Bank. Also, I don't have many possessions any more. After I came out of the hospital I had a purge and threw away most of the stuff I'd accumulated. I think about replacing things from time to time, but there isn't much I want. Nothing in the world, except maybe a Vietnamese refugee.

There's birds in the park.

I went to see Sally on Sunday. I felt guilty and wanted to spend some time with her, see if we could retrieve anything of our relationship. Mother and son. We watched television most of the day, because there was nothing to talk about. And she has it on all the time anyway, even when she's playing CDs. And while I was watching the telly she went in the kitchen and fried eggs and tomatoes, and mixed up some Bisto in the tomato gravy. And she cooked chips and fried bread, and asked if I was hungry, and I knew if I said no she'd give me it on a big plate, and if I said yes she'd open a can of beans as well.

I realize it's her way of telling me she loves me. It's not her fault that she's inadequate, or that she thinks she's inadequate. I would like to be more generous with her, but ever since I was small she's been able to get up my nose, and now it's become a way of life, the way we are with each other. If I'm objective about it, and I can be if I make myself step back, then I can understand that she experienced her childhood as a trial, and all the rest is a consequence of that. But when I'm up close, I get irritated.

I stuck the day out. Ate all the fried food and smiled my way through the afternoon. I kissed her before I left, a peck on the cheek, and she squeezed my arms, up near the biceps. But we both know it was hopeless. She probably breathed as much of a sigh of relief as I did when it was all over.

When I think about it, some people are like deep wells of crystal-clear water, and the effort needed to bring it up is worthwhile. With Sally, when I put in the effort, I believe I'm going to find that crystal-clear water, but I get something muddy. After a while I forget about it, or I chastise myself for not making the right effort, and I begin to believe the crystal-clear water is there again. And I go knock on her door, give it another go.

Sorry to use you as a confessional. Being brought up as a Methodist has left great areas of wasteland in my soul. Do Buddhists go to confession?

Something else. Working with computers all day at System.ini gets the old brain cells working. You know how when you erase the information on a disk, the information doesn't actually go away? It's still there on the disk just like it was before, only the index is erased so that the computer can't find it. Well, thinking about that got me thinking about what is truth and what is make-believe, what is truth and what is fiction.

Because when you erase the info (even though you don't), it does give you the opportunity to put something else in its place. To over-write it. And it struck me that that's what we do when we elaborate on the things that have happened to us, when we invent stories about ourselves, about our pasts. We are reinventing ourselves.

Apart from the fun we get out of it, it makes us more interesting, and it makes us more accessible. Because the truth isn't accessible (like on the erased disk), and we need stories to help us feel our way towards it. When we turn ourselves into fictions, we achieve the imaginative power to interpret our truths.

When I was in the slammer, I made up new stories every day. There was a part of me that understood that if I kept on inventing new stories, then one day I'd actually hit on the truth.

Hammett was trying to do that as well. He was born on a tobacco farm called Hopewell and Aim in St Mary's County in 1894. The Hammetts were farmers and the Dashiells sailors. He went to work with the Pinkerton National Detective Agency when he got to be a man. And then when he was a famous writer he sometimes ended up throwing knives, forks and spoons across a restaurant. He couldn't cope with all the info on his disk, had to over-write it every day. Or maybe he needed a low-level format?

Love

Stone

Dear Ginny,

Strange question, that. What happened to the dogs? It never occurred to me. I asked the police, and they had to be put down. The possibilities for dogs in our culture is that they work or become pets, and unfortunately for Shooter's animals, they were never going to fit into either of those slots. Now Shooter's gone, there's not a lot of call in Hull for dogs that are addicted to human flesh.

A group of people who were victims of Shooter have got together to get me a pardon from the Home Secretary. I wouldn't have bothered. I've done the time, and I'm not gonna forget I've done the time. I don't even regret it in some ways. It was an experience. It made me grow in unexpected ways, forced me to become the man I am, the man I feel comfortable with.

If it happens, though, if the Home Secretary calls round one day and says, 'Here's your pardon, son,' I won't throw it back in his face. I reckon anything you can get out of the government must be a bonus. They don't give that much away.

Aunt Nell's affair with Heartbreak seems to be going as strong as ever. They're down at the Rock'n'Roll Club two or three nights a week. I expect he'll move in with her sooner or later. The potential problem was Sally, because Nell and Sally go together like steak and kidney, but Heartbreak seems to manage the two of them. Never hear him complain. In fact, if anything, he looks younger on it. Didn't someone say: *You're as old as the woman you feel*?

Your picture of the swallow is still up on the wall. It's the first thing I see when I come back to the flat, and it reminds me of the past and in a strange way it reminds me of the future.

When you walked out of the hospital that day to catch your plane, I really thought I'd never see you again. It was almost as bad as being back in prison, cut off from life. Condemned to an existence of half-light and scary dreams.

It's better now. I'll actually see you at 325 Bel Air Road, Hollywood. I'll be the guy who limps, in case you don't remember what I look like.

I've got two months holiday. I've changed all my savings into dollars. There's a whole lot of things I want to see over there in the US of A, and when I've finished seeing them, I want to have a go at Europe. You might want to come with me?

Don't give me your answer on the first day. Think about it and tell me towards the end. Who knows, after a month together we might never want to see each other again.

Love

Stone

42

LAX

She used a small packet of tissues and a good dollop of cold cream to remove her make-up. She washed her face with warm water and soap and patted it dry with a paper towel. She stood in front of the mirror for a long time, looking at her reflection, wondering if she could face the world like that. Hamlet to Ophelia: *God hath given you one face and you make yourselves another.*

Eventually she put on some eyeliner and mascara. She closed her bag and headed for the door. Then she turned around and went back to the mirror. She outlined her lips carefully, with a pencil, then brushed on a pale peach lipstick. It looked and felt better.

She went out on to the concourse and checked which gate Stone would arrive at. Only another five minutes.

She turned around and went back to the women's room. She added a covering of gold lipstick over the peach, and blended black and gold eyeshadow to her eyelids. She found a reddish blusher and layered it from her cheekbones up to her temples and over her brows.

She was wearing a knee-length black leather coat with a fitted waist. Beneath the coat she had a black and white striped cotton T-shirt and a black and white skirt. Her bag was scotch plaid and her shoes were sling-backs with tiny flowers on them, à la Versace.

In the bottom of her bag was a pair of long dangly

earrings and a plaited chain, both in gold. She put them on and nodded at her reflection. Looked like a million dollars.

Stone came through the gate carrying a thin black cane with a silver knob. He stopped a few feet from her and took her in. Apart from the teardrop there were no tattoos on his face, which was crinkled in a smile. He had started to grow his hair again, and it had fallen over his forehead in a fringe. He wore tight black jeans and a black silk shirt with a black and white tie that matched Ginny's skirt. His light leather jacket hung loosely from his shoulders. His shoes were fastened with a buckle.

Ginny moved towards him.

As she kissed him she noticed something on his neck and pulled down the collar of his shirt to get a better look. It was new, had never been there before. A tattoo of a swallow on the wing with a forked tail, red throat, and a deep blue back.